PRAISE FOR THE NOVELS OF MARY BALOGH

WEB OF LOVE

"A beautiful tale of how grief and guilt can lead to love."
—*Library Journal*

SIMPLY MAGIC

"Absorbing and appealing. This is an unusually subtle approach in a romance, and it works to great effect."
—*Publishers Weekly*

"Balogh continues her superb Simply romance . . . with another exquisitely crafted Regency historical that brilliantly blends deliciously clever writing, subtly nuanced characters, and simmering sensuality into a simply sublime romance." —*Booklist*

SIMPLY UNFORGETTABLE

"When an author has created a series as beloved to readers as Balogh's Bedwyn saga, it is hard to believe that she can surpass the delights with the first installment in a new quartet. But Balogh has done just that." —*Booklist*

"A memorable cast . . . refresh[es] a classic Regency plot with humor, wit, and the sizzling romantic chemistry that one expects from Balogh. Well written and emotionally complex." —*Library Journal*

SIMPLY LOVE

"One of the things that make Ms. Balogh's books so memorable is the emotion she pours into her stories. The writing is superb, with realistic dialogue, sexual tension, and a wonderful heart-wrenching story. *Simply Love* is a book to savor, and to read again. It is a Perfect 10. Romance doesn't get any better than this."
—*Romance Reviews Today*

"With more than her usual panache, Balogh returns to Regency England for a satisfying adult love story."
—*Publishers Weekly*

SLIGHTLY DANGEROUS

"*Slightly Dangerous* is the culmination of Balogh's wonderfully entertaining Bedwyn series. . . . Balogh, famous for her believable characters and finely crafted Regency-era settings, forges a relationship that leaps off the page and into the hearts of her readers." —*Booklist*

"With this series, Balogh has created a wonderfully romantic world of Regency culture and society. Readers will miss the honorable Bedwyns and their mates; ending the series with Wulfric's story is icing on the cake. Highly recommended." —*Library Journal*

SLIGHTLY SINFUL

"Smart, playful, and deliciously satisfying . . . Balogh once again delivers a clean, sprightly tale rich in both plot and character. . . . With its irrepressible characters and deft plotting, this polished romance is an ideal summer read." —*Publishers Weekly* (starred review)

SLIGHTLY TEMPTED

"Once again, Balogh has penned an entrancing, unconventional yarn that should expand her following."
—*Publishers Weekly*

"Balogh is a gifted writer. . . . *Slightly Tempted* invites reflection, a fine quality in romance, and Morgan and Gervase are memorable characters." —*Contra Costa Times*

SLIGHTLY SCANDALOUS

"With its impeccable plotting and memorable characters, Balogh's book raises the bar for Regency romances."
—*Publishers Weekly* (starred review)

"The sexual tension fairly crackles between this pair of beautifully matched protagonists. . . . This delightful and exceptionally well-done title nicely demonstrates [Balogh's] matchless style." —*Library Journal*

"This third book in the Bedwyn series is . . . highly enjoyable as part of the series or on its own merits."
—*Old Book Barn Gazette*

SLIGHTLY WICKED

"Sympathetic characters and scalding sexual tension make the second installment in [the Slightly series] a truly engrossing read. . . . Balogh's sure-footed story possesses an abundance of character and class."
—*Publishers Weekly*

SLIGHTLY MARRIED

"[A Perfect 10] . . . *Slightly Married* is a masterpiece! Mary Balogh has an unparalleled gift for creating complex, compelling characters who come alive on the pages."
—*Romance Reviews Today*

A SUMMER TO REMEMBER

"Balogh outdoes herself with this romantic romp, crafting a truly seamless plot and peopling it with well-rounded, winning characters." —*Publishers Weekly*

"The most sensuous romance of the year." —*Booklist*

"This one will rise to the top." —*Library Journal*

"Filled with vivid descriptions, sharp dialogue, and fantastic characters, this passionate, adventurous tale will remain memorable for readers who love an entertaining read." —*Rendezvous*

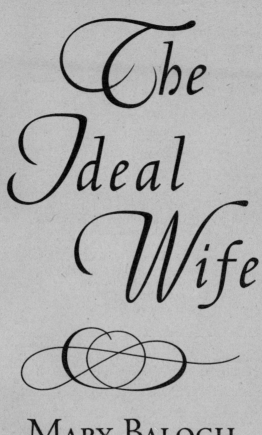

The Ideal Wife

MARY BALOGH

A DELL BOOK

THE IDEAL WIFE
A Dell Book

PUBLISHING HISTORY
Signet mass market edition published August 1991
Dell mass market edition / July 2008

Published by Bantam Dell
A Division of Random House, Inc.
New York, New York

This is a work of fiction. Names, characters, places, and incidents either
are the product of the author's imagination or are used fictitiously. Any
resemblance to actual persons, living or dead, events, or locales is
entirely coincidental.

Dell is a registered trademark of Random House, Inc., and the colophon
is a trademark of Random House, Inc.

ISBN: 978-0-440-24462-2

Printed in the United States of America
Published simultaneously in Canada

www.bantamdell.com

OPM 10 9 8 7 6 5 4 3 2 1

The
Ideal
Wife

1

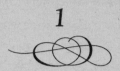

"IF YOU COULD SET BEFORE ME THE PLAIN-est, dullest, most ordinary female in London," Miles Ripley, Earl of Severn, said, "or in England, for that matter, I would make her an offer without further ado."

Sir Gerald Stapleton laughed and drained off the final mouthful of brandy left in his glass.

"It would be better to be like me, Miles," he said, "and just tell the world in no uncertain terms that you will remain a bachelor as long as you please, and that that will be for a lifetime, thank you kindly."

The earl sighed and hooked one leg over the arm of the chair on which he sat. "There speaks a mere baronet," he said. "A man without a care in the world. I was one myself until fifteen months ago, Ger. And I used to complain about lack of funds and consequence. I was living in heaven and did not realize it."

His friend hauled himself to his feet with an effort

and crossed the crowded and rather untidy bachelor room that he rented close to St. James's Street to the brandy decanter. His neckcloth had already been abandoned, and his shirt was unbuttoned at the throat. It was late at night, the two men having left White's a few hours before.

"If that was heaven, you could be living now in a far greater paradise," he said. "You have inherited an earl's title and the three estates to go with it. You have more money than a whole army of princes should decently possess. You are thirty years old—in the very prime of life. And of course you still have those looks, which have been throwing females into the flutters and the vapors for the past ten years or so."

"You have forgotten my most important possession," Lord Severn said gloomily. His brandy was still untouched in a glass at his side. "My mother and my sisters. They are going to be here within the week, Ger, all three of them, and I am going to be leg-shackled within the month. I can hear the chains rattling already."

"Nonsense," Sir Gerald said. "All you have to do is say no. You are the head of your family, aren't you? The man of the family?"

"Ah," the earl said. "There speaks a man with no female relatives. Things are not nearly as simple as that, Ger. They worshipped and coddled me all through my growing years, especially after my father died when I was twelve. They have worshipped and loved me through my adulthood. And now they are preparing to show me the ultimate sign of their love. They are going to give me away to another female."

Sir Gerald yawned and sipped on his fresh glass of brandy. "You have to stand up to them, old chap," he said. "Listen to the advice of someone all of one month your senior. You have to make clear to them that they cannot have your life in exchange for their love. You can't get married, Miles. What is she like, anyway?"

"Frances?" The earl thought for a moment. "Exquisitely lovely, actually. All blond ringlets and wide blue eyes and pouting rosebud lips. Has her father and her brothers and all their manservants and the village vicar eating out of her hand. She is eighteen years old and about to descend on London to be the belle of the Season and carry off the man of most impressive rank and fortune available—me, as it turns out."

His friend grimaced. "Let's run off to America," he said, "to seek our fortunes. But of course, you already have a fortune. Don't do it, Miles."

"A man does not know how weak he is until confronted by a parcel of determined and well-meaning female relations, I swear," Lord Severn said. "Am I a weakling, Ger? Am I a doormat? I spent a month at Galloway's before coming here two months ago—I went with my mother and Connie. The Galloways have always been particular friends of my mother's. And I found myself lifting Frances up and down from saddles and in and out of carriages—she could never seem to use the steps—and carrying her gloves and her psalter in and out of church, and plucking posies of buttercups and daisies for her to bury her pretty nose in, and doing so many other things that I cringe at the very memory. They are going to have me married to her before the Season is out. And there is not a mortal thing I can do about it."

"I think we had better run off to America, fortune or no fortune," his friend said, downing the remaining contents of his glass and getting to his feet again.

"I could feel the noose tightening almost as soon as I had set foot in Galloway's house," the earl said. "It was glaringly obvious why I had been invited there and why Mama had brought me there. It's amazing I escaped at the end of the month without being trapped into some declaration. But now my mother insists in her letter that there was a tacit understanding and that she can scarce wait for it to be made official. *Tacit*, Ger! What does the word mean, pray?"

"Galloway and the girl are coming soon too?" Sir Gerald asked.

"They are all going to be here within the week," Lord Severn said. "And I have the feeling that they are all going to act as if Frances and I have that tacit understanding, whatever it means. I know what it means, actually. It means that we are going to be planning a wedding at St. George's before the month is out, and I am going to be done for."

"Shall I find out what ships are in dock?" Sir Gerald asked.

"The trouble is," the earl said, "that I will feel honorbound. I hate honor, Ger. It always means having to do something one does not wish to do, usually something painful as well as unpleasant. I won't even have to open my mouth to be trapped. I have less than a week of freedom left."

"I still think you ought just to say a firm no," his friend said. "As soon as your mama sets foot in your house, Miles, just say to her straight out, 'I am not marrying Frances.' Nothing could be simpler."

"The very simplest thing would be to marry someone else," the earl said. "Run off with her or marry her by special license before my mother even gets here. That's what I ought to do."

"How did you describe her?" Sir Gerald chuckled. "Plain? Dull? Very ordinary? Is that what you said? Why not a beauty while you are at it, Miles?"

"Because beautiful women are invariably vain," Lord Severn said, "and think that men were created to fetch and carry for them. No, Ger, my ideal woman is someone who would be nice and quiet, who would be content to live somewhere in the country and be visited once or twice a year. Someone who would produce an heir with the minimum of fuss. Someone who would make all the matchmaking mamas, including my own, fold up their tents and go home. Someone who would quickly fade into the background of my life. Someone I could forget was there. Does that not sound like bliss?"

"Better still to have no one even in the background," Sir Gerald said.

"That seems not to be an option." The Earl of Severn got to his feet. "I should be going. It must be fiendishly late. I had better go to Jenny and enjoy myself while I still can."

Sir Gerald frowned. "You don't mean you are going to give up Jenny when you marry Frances?" he said. "Miles! You are the envy of the whole membership of White's and probably that of the other clubs too. There aren't many who could afford her, and not many even of those that she would cast a second look at."

"Let's not talk any more tonight about my marrying Frances," the earl said, picking up his hat and cane from a chair by the door. "Perhaps I will meet that woman of my dreams within the next week, Ger. Perhaps I will be saved yet."

"It's all very well to talk," his friend said, yawning

loudly and stretching. "But you wouldn't marry such a creature, Miles. Admit it."

"Oh, wouldn't I?" Lord Severn said. "A nice, quiet, demure female, Ger? She sounds far preferable to what I am facing. Good night."

"Give Jenny my love," Sir Gerald said.

IT HAD BEEN VERY LATE when the earl arrived at the house where he kept his mistress. And Jenny, having been woken from sleep, had been warm and amorous and had kept him busy until dawn was already lighting her bedchamber. He had slept until well into the morning.

This was the part of having a mistress that he always liked least, he thought as his steps took him finally onto Grosvenor Square and to the door of the house he had inherited with his title more than a year before. He hated walking home in crumpled evening clothes, feeling tired and lethargic, Jenny's heavy perfume teasing his nostrils from his own clothes and skin.

He looked forward to having a hot and soapy bath and a brisk ride in the park. But no, it was too late to ride in the park at more than a walk. He would go to Jackson's boxing saloon. Perhaps he would find someone worth sparring with, someone to put energy back into his muscles.

He handed his hat and cane to his butler when he entered the house and directed that hot water be sent up to his dressing room without delay. But his steps were halted as he turned to the staircase.

"There is a lady in the yellow salon waiting to speak with you, my lord," the butler said, his voice stiff and disapproving.

The earl frowned. "Did you not tell her that I was from home?" he asked.

His butler bowed. "She expressed her intention of waiting for your return, my lord," he said. "She says she is your cousin. Miss Abigail Gardiner."

Lord Severn continued to frown. It was possible. In the two months since he had been in London, having completed his year of mourning for the old earl, who was a second cousin of his father's, and whom he had not known, he had met numerous relatives—almost all of them poor, almost all of them with favors to ask. Dealing with them was one of the burdens of his new position that he had not expected.

He hesitated. Should he merely instruct Watson to pay the woman off? But no. She would doubtless be back again the next week, palm extended. He must speak with her himself, make clear that whatever gift he gave her would be for that one occasion only, that her claim to kinship did not make him responsible for supporting her for life. He sighed.

"If she is prepared to wait," he said, "then wait she must. I will speak with her after my bath, Watson."

He turned without further ado and ran up the stairs to his room. He was still feeling depressed after his mother's letter of the day before and after his evening with Gerald. And he was tired after his night with Jenny. Miss Abigail Gardiner would leave the house if she were wise, and not risk facing his morose mood.

He frowned in thought. Gardiner. Were there relatives of that name? If there were, he had never met any of them. But doubtless the woman would be armed with a family tree to prove his obligation to give her charity.

Almost an hour passed before he was back downstairs, nodding to his butler to open the doors into the yellow salon. If earldoms and all they brought with them could be hurled into the ocean and drowned, he thought grimly, he would row to the deepest part of it he could find and tie granite rocks about his before tipping it overboard.

Miss Abigail Gardiner, he saw at a glance, was younger than he had expected. From her name he had expected a thin and elderly and sharp-nosed spinster. This woman was no older than five-and-twenty. She was dressed decently but plainly in brown. There was a faint hint of shabbiness about her clothes. Certainly they had not been made by a fashionable modiste.

She was a very ordinary-looking young lady, her brown hair smooth beneath her bonnet and almost the same color as it, her features quite unremarkable. She had no maid or female companion with her.

She was standing quietly in the middle of the room, her hands folded in front of her. He wondered if she had stood there the whole time or if she had sat on one of the chairs for a while.

She looked remarkably, he thought—and the thought afforded him the first amusement he had felt for more than twenty-four hours—like the ideal woman he had described to Gerald the evening before. Except that the ideal did not look quite as appealing when it was standing before him in real flesh and blood.

He set one hand behind his back and raised his quizzing glass to his eye with the other. He favored the woman with the look he had acquired in the past two months as the one best suited to dealing with would-be dependents and hangers-on.

She curtsied to him but did not, as several of her predecessors had done, continue to bob up and down like a cork.

"Miss Gardiner," he said. "What may I do for you, ma'am?"

•   •   •

"YOU MUST DRESS PLAINLY," Laura Seymour said. "Not shabbily, of course, but not too prettily either, Abby."

Abigail Gardiner chuckled. "That should not be difficult," she said. "The only clothes I possess that might be described as pretty are at least ten years out-of-date. Will my brown do, do you think?"

"Admirably," her friend said. "And, Abby, remember what we decided last night. You must act demurely. You really must. I cannot emphasize it enough. He will not be impressed if you are bold."

Abigail grimaced. "Bobbing curtsies and directing my gaze at the toes of his boots and not speaking until I am spoken to and all that?" she said. "Must I really, Laura? Can I not be merely myself?"

"One curtsy," Laura said. "And I think you may look him in the eye, Abby, provided you do not stare at him boldly as if daring him to gaze back without being the first to drop his eyes."

"As I did with Mr. Gill the day before yesterday," Abigail said, and both young ladies exploded into smothered mirth.

"His face, Abby, when you spoke to him as you did in the schoolroom!" Laura held her nose in an attempt to contain her laughter.

"Sir!" Abigail allowed her bosom to swell, placed her hands on her hips, and glared coldly at an imaginary Mr. Gill at the other side of her small bedchamber on the second floor of that gentleman's town house. "Your behavior is quite, quite intolerable." She sucked in her cheeks in an effort not to laugh and ruin the reenactment of the scene that had taken place in the schoolroom two days before when she had entered the room in order to save her governess friend from molestation, the children not being in there at the time.

" 'If I see you one more time p-p-pinching Miss Seymour's b-b-bottom . . .' " Laura rolled backward onto the bed and gave up her attempt to imitate the cold accents of her friend.

Abigail doubled over where she stood. Both gave in to gales of laughter and soon had tears running down their cheeks.

Abigail took a deep breath and straightened up. "Then I shall p-p—"

They both howled with laughter.

"Pinch yours, sir." Abigail clutched at her stomach. "Oh, it hurts," she wailed. "I had no idea what words were going to come out of my mouth, Laura, until I heard them for myself. Can you imagine what a delight it would be to pinch Mr. Gill's derriere?"

Her friend was laughing too hard to answer the question.

Abigail straightened up again. "It is not funny," she said at last, sobering. "It really isn't, Laura. I have been dismissed without a character and with only one week's notice—on the pretext that I have been ogling Humphrey. Humphrey! I would rather ogle a crocodile or a fish than Humphrey Gill. He has an entirely suitable name, by the way. I must say I am not brokenhearted not to be companion to Mrs. Gill any longer. Peevish, vaporish women make me so cross that I could scream, especially when one knows that they are merely trying to imitate the nobility. But still and all, to be out of work with no character, Laura. It is definitely not funny."

Laura got up off the bed and smoothed out her dress. She looked at her friend from contrite dark brown eyes. Her pretty auburn hair was in disarray. "And all on account of me," she said. "I am so sorry, Abby. But when I asked you to keep an eye on me whenever Mr. Gill was on the prowl, I had no idea that I would end up getting you dismissed. I will still go to Mrs. Gill with the truth if you will but let me."

Abigail clucked her tongue. "Absolutely not," she said. "Both of us would be out on the street instead of just me. You would not win a reprieve for me by telling all, you know. The only thing I feel sorry about is that you will be left here defenseless. You will just have to cling to the little Gills all day long, Laura, so that fond Papa can never get you alone. And you must learn to assert yourself."

"Oh, Abby." Laura clutched her hands to her bosom

and looked unhappily at her friend. "Do you think your cousin will help you? I had no idea the Earl of Severn was your cousin. He is very, very rich, so it is said."

Abigail frowned. "Actually," she said, "I think it is a gross stretching of the truth to call him a cousin, Laura. He is a relative, that is all. But then, I daresay everyone is a relative if one is diligent enough to trace one's family tree back to Adam. And I really am getting cold feet about going to see him. I hate begging. Indeed, I don't believe I can do it. I will have to think of something else."

"Oh, but what?" Laura asked.

"I could go back into Sussex if I have enough money for the stage," Abigail said, "and grovel to Vicar Grimes and persuade him to find me another post. He found me this one. But I don't believe I could stand another job quite like this. He thought highly of the Gills."

"Oh, dear," Laura said. "Perhaps he did not know them well."

"Or I could become an actress or a whore, I suppose," Abigail said.

Laura gasped and clapped one hand over her mouth. "Abby!"

"I suppose it will have to be Lord Severn," Abigail said. "There is no point in searching Boris out. He cannot help me. He is living by his wits and does not need the added burden of my problems."

"Go, then," Laura said. "Surely the earl will help you. You are not planning to ask for money, after all. But do remember to behave demurely. Oh, don't forget, Abby."

"We are back to the curtsy-bobbing and the gazing at boots, are we?" Abigail said. She positioned herself with feet firmly planted on the floor a few inches apart. She straightened her shoulders and composed her features to blandness. She sank into a deep curtsy. "Is that good enough?"

"Perhaps if you are at court being presented to the queen," Laura said.

Abigail frowned before blanking her expression again. "How about this?" she asked, curtsying a little less deeply and raising her chin.

"The curtsy is good, if a little stiff," Laura said. "The look appears rather as if you are challenging me to a duel."

They both collapsed into laughter again for a few moments.

"It is the chin," Laura said. "Make sure it does not jut, Abby."

Abigail practiced the routine a few more times until Laura approved.

"You are the head of my family, sir, and must help me, if you please," Abigail said.

Laura sighed and sat down on the edge of the bed. "Your chin is jutting again, Abby," she said. "And there is a definite martial gleam in your eye. And must you not address him as 'my lord'? And must you sound as if you are demanding help as of right, despite the 'if you please' at the end?"

"I might as well forget it," Abigail said. "I would never be a good actress, Laura, either with my cousin or on the stage. What does that leave me?"

"Sit down, Abby," Laura said. "It is going to be time for Billy and Hortense to come to the schoolroom soon for their morning lessons. Let us try to get this just right. The Earl of Severn must not be given an unfavorable impression of you."

"So I must cringe and demean myself," Abigail said. "I shall die of mortification anyway."

"No, not that," her friend said. "You must be . . ." She waved a hand in the air. "Oh . . ."

"Demure," Abigail said. "Very well, then. It shall be done. Tell me how to do it. There has never been anyone more meek and mild than I will be."

Less than half an hour later the governess had left for her morning duties in the schoolroom and Abigail was left alone to get herself ready for the visit to the Earl of Severn's house on Grosvenor Square.

She really ought not to be doing this, she thought as she set out on her way. It was quite outside her nature to grovel, and that was what she would be doing, however carefully she followed Laura's instructions. She was going to ask a stranger to help her find another position, on the very slim grounds that he was her kinsman.

They were very slim grounds. Papa had had no dealings with the earl or his close family.

And if the earl knew anything about her family, the chances were that she would find herself outside his door on her ear with great haste. It was not a reputable family. Papa had not been reputable, and there were other facts and events that would make any self-respecting nobleman's hair stand on end.

She would just have to hope that he did not know anything about the Gardiners. Or that age had tampered with his memory. If she was fortunate, he would have snowy white hair and bushy white eyebrows and a kindly smile and all she would have to do would be to say what she had rehearsed with Laura and look meek and demure and helpless. She just hoped that he would not be so doddering with age that he would be incapable of listening to her with any intelligence at all. She hoped she would not have to deal with a young and sharp-brained secretary.

She would not think of it, she thought as she

approached Grosvenor Square and tried not to notice quite how grand the houses surrounding it looked. She walked resolutely up the steps to the earl's house and lifted the brass knocker. She remembered just before the door opened to pull in her chin and soften her expression.

And, oh, Lord, she thought a few minutes later when she had forgotten herself enough to stand up to his lordship's starchy butler and inform him in so many words that she did not for a moment believe that the earl was from home, it was a grand house. The salon was clearly used only for the reception of visitors. The chairs were not arranged about the room in any pleasing or cozy design. They were set about the walls. She did not seat herself on any of them.

The wait was interminable. She wandered about the room, looking at all the paintings, afraid to sit down lest she be caught at a disadvantage if the door should open without warning. Perhaps she should have asked the butler if his lordship was expected home within the week. She began to fear that she had been forgotten about and would be remembered when a parlor maid came in to dust the next morning or the morning after that.

But finally the double doors opened and the butler, who stood between them for a moment, stepped aside to admit a tall young man. Abigail's heart slipped all the way down inside her half-boots. She was not to be admitted to his lordship's presence after all. She was going to have to deal with a secretary, who looked as stiff and frosty as any duke one would care to imagine and who had the effrontery to lift a quizzing glass to his eye and survey her through it.

Through a superhuman effort she retained the stance that Laura had approved of. If she could not impress the secretary, there were only two other possibilities—Vicar Grimes or the London job that was not being an actress.

She was forced to waste the curtsy she had practiced with such care on a man who was as much a servant as she was.

She stood quietly and looked calmly at him. And she was very aware suddenly of her lone state, a gentlewoman in the receiving salon of a gentleman's establishment with nary a chaperone on the premises.

"Miss Gardiner," the secretary said, looking at her with a disdain he did nothing to disguise. "What may I do for you, ma'am?"

2

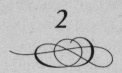

ISS ABIGAIL GARDINER LOOKED AT the earl steadily, though he guessed that it took a great effort of courage to do so.

"I wished to speak with my cousin, Lord Severn, sir," she said quietly.

She was definitely a mouse, he decided. A little brown mouse, though she was not particularly small—or particularly tall, for that matter. She was really quite nondescript, a woman it would be hard to describe one hour after she had left his sight. A woman who would fade admirably into any background.

"I am Severn, ma'am," he said, still toying with the handle of his quizzing glass, though he did not raise it to his eye again. This woman did not need to be put in her place. There was none of the boldness of manner in her that he occasionally had to contend with in other indigent relatives. "Whether I am your cousin or not, I do not have the pleasure of knowing."

Color rose in her cheeks, though she did not remove her eyes from his. They were fine gray eyes, he noticed—definitely her best feature.

"Doubtless," he said, "you did not hear of the demise of the former earl fifteen months ago. Perhaps your branch of the family was not considered close enough that anyone thought of informing you."

He felt immediately sorry for his sarcasm. It had been quite unnecessary. The woman's lips tightened for a moment, but she said nothing.

"My father was a great-grandson of the former earl's grandfather," she said, "his father being the third son of a fourth daughter."

"The former earl was my father's second cousin," he said. "And so I suppose that makes you my . . . cousin too, Miss Gardiner. What may I do for you?"

"I need your help, my lord," she said, "in a small way and for this occasion only."

He let his quizzing glass swing free from its black ribbon and clasped both hands behind his back. His eyes moved over her. She was not servile. He liked that. She held her chin up and she was able to look him in the eyes even as she begged. But she was quiet and respectful. He liked that too.

He had a sudden and unwelcome image of Frances and the inevitability of their union once she arrived in

London—unless something should happen between now and that moment to make a union impossible.

But it was a ridiculous idea, one that he had expressed the night before from the depths of his gloom but had not meant seriously, nonetheless. It was a stupid notion.

"How much?" he asked with a heavier sarcasm than he had intended.

She stared at him in incomprehension. "How much help?" she said.

"How much money, ma'am?" The earl walked a few steps farther into the room. It was time to do business and get rid of the woman before he did something unbelievably foolish, something he would regret for the rest of his life.

"Money?" she said, frowning slightly. "I have not come here to beg for money, my lord. It is for your help I have come to ask."

"Is it?" he said. He was disappointed. It would have been easier if it had been money she wanted.

"I have lost my position as lady's companion," she said, "and have no prospect of acquiring another. I wish you will provide me with some recommendation as your relative, my lord."

Lord Severn considered directing the woman to take a seat. Had she been standing ever since she entered the room? But he did not wish to prolong the interview. She was too uncannily like the ideal wife he had described to Gerald the night before.

"Is not your former employer better qualified to do that?" he asked. "I do not know you, after all, ma'am, even if there is some remote connection of blood between us."

The woman's chin lifted for a moment before she tucked it in once more. Her hands fidgeted with each other. She was clearly nervous, he thought, narrowing his eyes on her.

"I was dismissed, my lord," she said.

"I see." He watched her eyes lower to her hands and the hands grow still. "Why?"

She licked her lips. "My employer's husband has roving hands," she said.

"Ah," he said. "And your employer discovered him at it and blamed you."

She glanced quickly up into his eyes and lowered her own to his chin. She said nothing.

Yes, he thought, he could just imagine it. Miss Abigail Gardiner was young and not totally unattractive. She was impoverished and dependent upon what she could earn from genteel employment. She was quiet and unassuming—the perfect prey for a lecherous husband bored with his wife.

He felt sorry for her. She had not moved from the

spot on which she had been standing when he entered the room. She waited with quiet patience for his decision. If he gave her money, she could survive for a week or two. And then what?

But could he give her the letter she asked for? When all was said and done, he did not know the woman. He did not even know for sure that she was related to him, though he guessed that she must be. Such a matter was too easily checked for her to risk the lie. He might take a chance on her himself if he had a suitable position to offer her. But could he in all fairness recommend her to an unsuspecting stranger?

But he did have a suitable position to offer her. The thought came unbidden, causing him to frown quite unintentionally at Miss Abigail Gardiner. Was he taking leave of his senses?

She was looking directly at him, her fine gray eyes gazing steadily into his.

"Will you help me, my lord?" she asked.

In three or four days' time the peace of his bachelor existence was to be shattered and siege was to be laid to his single state. Frances was to be foisted on him.

Frances! He could see himself now down the years fetching and carrying for her, murmuring "Yes, dear" and "No, dear" a hundred times a day, listening to the envious opinions of his friends and acquaintances that he was a lucky dog to have won for himself such a beautiful and charming wife.

His voice was speaking, he became aware suddenly.

"Yes, ma'am," he was saying. "I have a position to offer you in my own home."

Her eyes widened, and for a moment she looked considerably more than ordinary. "Here?" she said. "A position?"

He listened to himself, appalled, almost as if his brain and his voice had been divorced from each other.

"Yes," he said. "I have a somewhat pressing need to fill the position of wife."

She stared at him as he stared mutely back.

"Wife," she said, the word falling like a stone into the silence between them, not a question.

His hands gripped themselves very tightly behind his back. "I need a wife, ma'am," he said. "Men in my position generally do. I would judge that you might be the kind of woman who would suit me. The position is yours if you wish for it."

He was not, he realized in some surprise as his brain caught up to his mouth, sorry that he had spoken those words. If the choice were between Frances and Miss Abigail Gardiner—and it seemed that it probably was—he would settle for Miss Gardiner without any hesitation at all. He waited anxiously for her reply.

• • •

ABIGAIL STARED AT HIM. She had been feeling acutely embarrassed and had been finding it far easier to follow Laura's advice to be demure than she had expected. Her cousin—or relative, to use a vaguer and more accurate term—was so very young and fashionable. And there she was, trapped in a room in his house, dressed in her drabbest brown, her hair in its most unbecoming coiled braid beneath her bonnet, begging a favor of him.

She would not have come if she had known that the old earl was dead, she thought. She definitely would not have. She would have taken her chances with Vicar Grimes.

Not only was this earl young and fashionable. He also had disconcertingly blue eyes, the sort of eyes that had a tendency to do strange things to one's knees.

It was not just the eyes, either. He was alarmingly handsome—tall and athletic-looking, with thick dark hair, several shades darker and several degrees glossier than her own. She felt mortified in the extreme.

And what had he just said? Under almost any other circumstances she would have thrown back her head and given in to peals of laughter. The encounter had taken a bizarre turn. Her hearing must be defective. She must be so nervous and so strained from acting out of character that she had allowed some of his words to pass her by.

"You are to be married, my lord?" she said. "You wish me to be companion to your wife? I have had some experience, though Mrs. Gill is an older lady. I believe I am capable of offering companionship to someone closer to my own age."

"I am asking *you* to be my wife, ma'am," the Earl of Severn said.

The words and the meaning were quite unmistakable.

"I have taken you by surprise," he said when she did not immediately reply. "You would like time to consider? I am afraid I cannot help you in any other way, Miss Gardiner, except to offer you a sum of money with which to keep yourself for a few weeks. I cannot recommend for employment a young woman whom I do not know."

In addition to being young and fashionable and handsome, in addition to those knee-weakening blue eyes, the man was mad. And was she to pity him or take advantage of him? Abigail wondered.

She looked at him, at the object of every woman's most secret and unrealistic dreams, and she took a mental look at herself. She was a woman who would be quite destitute in a few more days. She would not even have a roof over her head. She would be quite unable to find employment without a character from her last place of employment. And Vicar Grimes would doubtless scold and perhaps—if she was fortunate—send her to another Mrs. Gill. Or she could take to the streets.

Or she could marry the Earl of Severn.

He thought she would be just the type of woman who would suit him. Had he not just said that? What type was that? All the most dazzling beauties of the *ton* must be falling all over their dancing slippers to charm him.

She couldn't. She really could not. He thought she would suit him, poor man. And how could she marry a man she knew nothing about except that he was very, very rich?

Oh, dear good Lord. He was very rich. She thought suddenly of Bea and Clara and of another unrealistic and impossible dream—but more painful than the one about handsome men because it involved real people. And she thought of Boris and his shattered dreams.

"I shall leave you for a while," the earl said, "and send refreshments. I shall return in half an hour." He made her a half-bow and turned to leave.

"No," she said, stretching out a staying hand. For goodness' sake, she would be in a state of nervous collapse after a half an hour alone. But she could not simply accept him, could she? Without telling him a few truths and watching him scramble to rescind his offer?

It was all absurd. Totally insane. She must get out of there as soon as possible, she decided, and hurry home to share a good laugh with Laura.

Home! She had no home, or would not have in four days' time.

The earl was looking at her inquiringly from those compelling blue eyes. She wished it were possible to change his eyes, to make them more comfortable to deal with. Gray, brown, green, hazel—anything but blue. But blue they were, and they were looking at her.

"Ma'am?" he said.

"I accept," she said quickly. But it would make as much sense to take a dueling pistol and shoot herself, she thought even as she spoke. How did she know that he did not have six mistresses and three dozen children hidden away cozily in various parts of London? How did she know he would not turn out to be a wife-beater? And how did he know that she would not turn out to be quite the opposite of what he wanted in a wife—as she would? And why was he in such pressing need of a wife anyway? "But you may be sorry, my lord."

He smiled rather arctically, to reveal a dimple in his left cheek that had Abigail's heart performing a complete somersault. It was not fair. It really was not.

"I think not," he said. "I am happy with your decision, ma'am. I shall have the banns read at St. George's on Sunday and we will be married one month from now. Will that suit you?"

Several dozen questions all crowded themselves into Abigail's mind. She was going to wake up soon, she thought, and have a good giggle over the absurdity of her dream—and a good sigh over the handsomeness of its hero. In the meantime she felt rather unwilling to put a deliberate end to it, bizarre though it was.

"Yes, my lord," she said quietly.

He frowned and stared at the floor between them for a few moments. "But Sunday is six days off," he said. He looked up at her suddenly. "You are without a home, Miss Gardiner?"

"I have to leave Mr. Gill's by the end of the week, my lord," she said.

"Then I shall procure a special license," he said curtly. "We will be married . . . two days from now. Can you be ready?"

Abigail could almost feel herself floating to the surface of sleep. But she clung tenaciously to the dream. This one was too good to be given up without a fight.

"Yes, my lord," she said.

He crossed the room, passing close enough to her that she was aware of the fragrance of a musky cologne. He pulled on a bell rope beside the fireplace.

"Have my carriage sent around immediately, if you please, Watson," he said when the butler appeared almost before he had released the rope.

For her? It would be very wonderful, Abigail thought. She would be walking into the wind on the way home.

"I shall have you conveyed to your employer's," he said. "I shall come for you there tomorrow morning, ma'am, if I may. You will need some bride clothes. The morning after, I shall take you away from there to stay. In the meantime you may inform Mr. Gill that if his hands stray close to you again, he will have the glove of the Earl of Severn slapped in his face shortly after."

Abigail felt all her inner muscles tense with the effort of keeping her amusement from bursting forth into laughter. It made such a delicious mental image— the picture of the tall and athletic and handsome earl slapping an elegant glove in the face of short and fat Mr. Gill. There was something hilarious too in the idea of Mr. Gill being interested in pinching her bottom or kissing the back of her neck when there was Laura in the house.

But she sobered instantly. Should she not tell the earl something about herself? Should she not warn him?

"Yes, my lord," she said.

The earl walked beside her to the front doors of his

house a few minutes later and made her an elegant bow after descending the outside steps and handing her into his carriage. His hand was warm, well-manicured, strong.

The interior of the carriage was all dark green velvet and golden tassels and plush cushions. Abigail sank back into softness and smoothed her hands over the inexpensive brown cloth of her cloak.

Well, she thought. Well. Oh, good Lord in heaven! She did not know whether to give in to panic or to howl with laughter. Probably it would be wiser to do neither until she was safely back in her room at the Gills'.

"YOU HAVE DONE WHAT?" Sir Gerald Stapleton stopped so abruptly in the middle of the pavement that a lady and gentleman walking behind him almost collided with him. The gentleman glared at him and guided the lady safely past.

"I have offered marriage to an impoverished relative who called on me this morning," the Earl of Severn repeated. "Miss Abigail Gardiner."

"You knew her before?" his friend asked. "You discovered in her a long-lost youthful love, Miles? You are not about to tell me that she is a complete stranger, are you? You are, aren't you?"

The earl motioned his friend to resume their walk toward White's. They had met earlier, without design, at Jackson's, the earl having gone there to spar, Sir Gerald to watch. "Do you ever stop to allow a fellow to answer a question?" he asked. "Yes, she was a stranger, Ger. But she is related to me in some manner. She did explain, but the explanation was complicated, and it pertained to how she was related to the old earl."

"She must be a stunner," Sir Gerald said, frowning his disapproval. "But are you mad, Miles? You'll be sorry in a week. Can't you look all about you and see how very few satisfactory marriages there are—especially for the husbands? What is wrong with your life as it is now? You have your independence, you are master in your own house, you are free to come and go as you please, and you have Jenny. You didn't really make her an offer, did you? You merely thought that you might do so at some future date? Don't. You want the advice of a longtime friend? Don't."

"Do you remember the woman I described to you last evening?" Lord Severn asked. "The one I would marry on the spot if someone would just place her there before me?"

"Dull and ordinary?" Sir Gerald looked suspiciously at his friend.

Lord Severn nodded. "Miss Gardiner is she," he said. "I was immediately struck by the likeness, Ger. She is perfect. Not ugly, but plain. A little brown mouse. She has fine eyes, though. Quiet and disciplined and respectful without being cringing. Almost all she said to me was 'Yes, my lord' and 'No, my lord.' She has been dismissed from her employment because her employer's husband has roving hands. She had come to ask me to help her find another post."

"And you did," Sir Gerald said gloomily. "You actually asked her, Miles? She said yes, I suppose. She would have to be insane not to have done so."

"She said yes," the earl said with a smile. "I thought you would be delighted for me, Ger. I thought we would celebrate together my narrow escape from Frances."

His friend brightened. "Your mother will change your mind," he said. "And she will find some way to get you out of this mad betrothal in short order. The woman will have to be paid off. And then you must tell your mama that you are not going to marry Frances either. You have to learn to assert yourself where females are concerned, Miles."

"I will." The Earl of Severn grinned. "I will have no trouble at all with Miss Gardiner, Ger. And my mother will have no power to change my mind by the time she arrives in town. I am going to be married by special license the day after tomorrow."

Sir Gerald stopped abruptly again, removed his

high-crowned beaver, and ran a hand through his short fair curls. "Devil take it," he said. "The woman must be a witch. You are going to regret this for a lifetime, Miles. I will be saying 'I told you so' before the month is out."

"I think not," the earl said. "I think Miss Abigail Gardiner will suit me admirably. I believe she will make the ideal wife. Are you going to stand there all day admiring the scenery, Ger, or are you coming to White's?"

"The ideal wife!" Sir Gerald said scornfully, replacing his hat on his head and tapping it firmly into place. "There is no such thing, old chap. And it would be to your eternal benefit if you would realize that within the next two days."

"YOU HAVE DONE WHAT?" Laura Seymour was free of her duties in the schoolroom for the morning and had returned to her room to find Abigail pacing the floor there.

"I have agreed to marry the Earl of Severn the day after tomorrow," Abigail said, "and I don't know whether I should collapse into a quivering jelly or roll on the floor with laughter. I don't know if I am the mad one or if it is he. Or perhaps it is the both of us. We will doubtless suit admirably. You would not care to pinch me, I suppose, Laura, to prove that I really am awake? I am not at all convinced that I am."

"But you cannot marry an old man, Abby." Her friend stared at her in horror. "Oh, no, really you can't. There must be an alternative. He took one look at you—is that how it was?—saw you were young and pretty and destitute, and thought to hire himself a nursemaid at no expense. Men are quite horrid creatures. That silly Humphrey is all puffed up with conceit about being accused of being seduced by you, and has started to leer at me. Father and son both—it is too much."

She picked up her brush from the dressing table and began to pull the pins from her hair.

"I shall be sure to give him a blistering setdown before I leave here," Abigail said. "But the earl is not a doddering old man, Laura. The old earl died more than a year ago. This present one cannot be above thirty. I could have died of mortification. I mistook him for a secretary."

Laura's hands stilled and she stared at her friend in the mirror. "And he took one look at you and wanted to marry you?" she said. "An earl? And one of the richest men in England? Whatever is wrong with him?"

Abigail laughed merrily and perched on the edge of the bed. "Must there be something wrong with him?" she asked. "How flattering you are."

Laura grimaced. "I did not mean it that way, Abby," she said. "Oh, of course I did not. But there is something very peculiar in his behavior, you must confess."

"Yes, there is something wrong with him," Abigail said, sobering and frowning down at the floor. "There has to be. You should just see him, Laura. There cannot possibly be any more handsome man on this planet, and if anyone should be foolish enough to dispute that fact, she would realize her error as soon as he smiled. He has a dimple to weaken even the most firmly locked knees. And blue eyes rather like a summer sky. And yet he spoke to me for perhaps ten minutes and offered me marriage."

"The day after tomorrow," Laura added.

"The day after tomorrow." Abigail's frown deepened. "He said he thought I was the sort of woman who would suit him, Laura."

"Did he?" Laura pulled the brush slowly through her hair.

"What did he see?" Abigail said. "A woman who is plain at the best of times but made downright drab by the brown cloak and bonnet. A meek and mute creature who had scarcely two words to rub together. A weak thing who remembered not to bristle even when he had the effrontery to lift his quizzing glass to his eye. That is the sort of woman who will suit him?"

She looked up at her friend, covered her mouth with one hand, and exploded into nervous laughter.

"I ought not to have said yes," she said. "I am perpetrating a dreadful deception against him, Laura. What will happen when he discovers the truth?"

"Perhaps he is deceiving you too," Laura said. "You saw a young and handsome man and assumed that he is some god. Perhaps he is as different from what you expect as you are from what he expects."

"He is to come here tomorrow to take me shopping," Abigail said. "I suppose I should see to it that we have a long and candid talk. That will be the end of my betrothal, of course. I did not realize how seductive would be the temptation to be rich. And to be somebody. I would be able to see Bea and Clara if I married him. We would be able to be together again. And perhaps I could do something for Boris before it is too late."

"Shopping?" Laura said.

"For bride clothes," Abigail said wistfully. "Some fine muslins, perhaps. And a velvet riding habit."

"And a ball gown," Laura said. "You would surely go to balls, Abby. You would be the Countess of Severn."

"And so I would," Abigail said, startled. She got to her feet. "Do you see why I am tempted? And they are such very blue eyes, Laura. But I will probably never see him again. He was doubtless having his little joke at my expense. He must have been joking, don't you think?"

"Oh, Abby." Laura frowned and set down her brush. "Do earls joke about such matters?"

"I have no idea," Abigail said. "Do they?"

"What if he was serious?" Laura said. "Are you going to throw away such a chance for security, Abby? Why don't you continue to be his ideal woman for two days longer?"

"Would it be honest?" Abigail asked.

"But you are not a monster, Abby," Laura said. "And you would be as sweet and quiet as he seems to think you if you would just remember not to talk all the time."

Abigail laughed. "And a murderer would be as mild as the next man if he would just remember not to kill people," she said. "I don't think I could do it, Laura. Apart from the morality involved, I don't think I could do it. I almost burst a few times this morning."

"Think about it," Laura said. "Oh, Abby, I feel as excited for you as if it were me. And I would not feel nearly as bad about being responsible for having you dismissed if everything ended so splendidly for you. Think about it—two more days of being demure in exchange for a lifetime of luxury."

"I am not going to think about it," Abigail said, striding to the door and setting her hand on the knob.

"He probably will not come tomorrow anyway. I am going to concentrate my mind on devising the very best method I can think of to deflate Humphrey's conceit. No thanks are called for. You may owe me a favor."

"Oh, Abby," her friend said, laughing despite herself.

3

THE EARL OF SEVERN STEPPED FROM HIS carriage and looked up at Mr. Gill's house. The man was a cit, he guessed from the location. He was doubtless a man who thought to increase his consequence by hiring a companion for his wife. And doubtless the type who would then believe that he owned the companion and was free to use her as he would.

He hoped that Miss Gardiner had passed on his message to the man.

He stood on the pavement as his footman raised the brass knocker on the door, and concentrated on looking nonchalant. He was feeling anything but. Indeed, if the truth were to be admitted, there were butterflies dancing inside him.

He had had a day and a sleepless night in which to brood on his hasty offer of the morning before. And he had been foolish enough to spend all the afternoon and part of the evening with Gerald, who had pointed out all the possible disasters that could result from such a match, and some of the impossible ones too. And then he had gone to Jenny's and ended up spending the whole night with her when he had found her every bit as amorous as she had been the night before.

And Jenny was to be exchanged for Miss Abigail Gardiner! Unfortunately, he would not be able to reconcile it with his conscience to have both a wife and a mistress. Yet Jenny was by far the most satisfactory mistress he had ever kept.

He wished, as the door opened and a uniformed maid bobbed a curtsy, that it was the prospective bride he could shed rather than the mistress. But the offer had been made and accepted, and making his wish come true was no longer a possibility.

He must fortify himself with thoughts of Frances.

"Would you announce to Miss Gardiner that the Earl of Severn has arrived?" he said to the maid, walking past her into a dark and cluttered hallway.

She gawked past him to his footman and coachman and his carriage waiting on the street, turned to bob him more curtsies, and scurried away without a word.

Was she really as plain as he remembered her? the earl wondered, removing his gloves and hat. It was strange, deliberately to have chosen a plain woman as his bride. He had always dreamed, he supposed—if he had dreamed of the married state at all—of a lovely wife, someone he would enjoy looking at every day of his life.

And was she as quiet as he remembered? He hoped so. He would not be able to bear a prattler or someone who would wish to manage his life and that of everyone around her. He might as well have married Frances and made his mother and sisters happy if that was to be his fate.

On the other hand, of course, he did not want a dull and mindless creature of no character.

However, he thought as he turned to bow to the bald and smiling man who was bowing deeply to him, it was pointless at this moment in his life to try to picture the qualities he really wanted in a wife. She was already chosen. He was stuck with her.

The man, as Lord Severn suspected, was Mr. Gill. They exchanged pleasantries after his lordship had refused an invitation to step into the study for refreshments.

"Miss Gardiner is, ah, seeking employment with you, my lord?" Mr. Gill asked. "She is an ambitious young lady to have looked so high."

"Miss Gardiner," the earl said, one hand playing with the handle of his quizzing glass, "is a distant relative of mine, sir."

Mr. Gill rubbed his hands together.

She had not passed along his message, Lord Severn decided. "And my betrothed," he added.

Mr. Gill's hands stilled.

But the earl's attention was diverted. She was coming down the stairs and he turned to watch her. She was clad from head to ankles in gray. Only her black gloves and half-boots relieved the monotony.

Oh, yes, he thought in some shock, he had not been mistaken in her appearance.

Or in her character either. Her face was expressionless. Her eyes were directed at the floor between him and Mr. Gill. She curtsied when she reached the bottom of the stairs, without raising her eyes.

"Good morning, my dear," the earl said, bowing to her. "Are you ready to leave?"

"Yes, thank you, my lord," she said.

"Ah," Mr. Gill said, rubbing his hands together again. "Young love. How splendid. And how very pretty you look, Miss Gardiner."

The woman looked up, first at Mr. Gill and then at her betrothed. There was a gleam in her eye that looked remarkably like amusement, the earl thought. But it was gone in a flash before he could observe more closely.

She took the arm that he offered.

•   •   •

ABIGAIL HAD BEEN on Bond Street only once, with Mrs. Gill. But they had not stopped there, only strolled along it in order to look grand. Bond Street was somewhat above Mrs. Gill's touch.

But it was to Bond Street that the Earl of Severn took her, to the shop of a modiste who looked quite as grand as a duchess and who spoke with a French accent that had Abigail peering at her with suspicion. But the woman knew the Earl of Severn and curtsied deeply to him. And her eyes passed over Abigail's gray clothes with curiosity and some condescension.

This was where he brought his ladybirds to be clothed, Abigail thought, and Madame Savard—or Miss Bloggs, or whatever her true name was—was assuming that she was another of that breed. She fixed the woman with a severe eye. And she felt mortified beyond belief. She had not known that gentlemen ever went shopping with ladies for clothes—not right inside the shop and greeting the modiste and demanding to see fashion plates and pattern books and fabrics.

"We will need something pretty without delay, madame," he said. "Miss Gardiner is to be my bride tomorrow."

The eyes surveying her became sharper and considerably more respectful. Madame clasped her hands to her bosom and uttered some charming and sentimental words about whirlwind romances. She and Mr. Gill should get together to render a romantic duet, Abigail thought, and then wished she had not done so, as her stomach muscles tightened with suppressed amusement.

"But by tomorrow, m'lord?" Madame said, long-nailed hands fluttering. "*Non, non. Impossible!*"

"Possible," the earl said firmly, not giving the word the modiste's French intonation. "Definitely possible. Madame Girard was telling me only last week that her seamstresses can make up even the fanciest of ball gowns in three hours when necessary."

It seemed that it was, after all, possible to make a dress suitable for a bride before the next day. As for all the rest of the garments, they were to be delivered to Grosvenor Square, some within a week, some within two.

There followed two hours of bewilderment for Abigail. Fabrics and designs were chosen by his lordship and Madame just as if she were a wax figure with no voice or mind of her own.

In a meeting with Laura that morning for the planning of strategy, it had been agreed, much against Abigail's conscience, that she keep to her demure image at least until after the wedding—if there was a wedding. At the time, Abigail had been more convinced than ever that she would never set eyes on the Earl of Severn again. But now that the situation was real, it would have been difficult to keep to the plan if she had not been feeling so far beyond her depth.

Finally she was whisked to a back room—where the earl did not follow her, she was relieved to find—separated from all her clothes, except her chemise and stockings, stood up on a stool, and twirled and prodded and poked and measured for what seemed like a day and a half without stop.

She clung doggedly to her demure self, slipping only twice. She did protest to Madame once, when she was turned without being asked to do so, that she was no slab of beef and would appreciate not being treated like one. And she did remind a thin, bespectacled seamstress that she was not a pincushion and did not enjoy being punctured by pins. But she felt sorry for the latter lapse immediately after, when the girl looked up at her with anxious eyes and glanced swiftly across to Madame, who fortunately had not heard.

"Actually," Abigail said, "I moved when I should have stayed still. It was my fault. Is my arm raised high enough?"

The girl smiled quickly at her and resumed her work.

Abigail had hoped for a couple of muslins and a riding habit. Laura had hoped that a ball gown might be added to that list. In all the wild dreamings of a largely sleepless night Abigail had not expected the dizzying number and variety of garments that were judged to be the very barest of necessities for a countess. It would take her a month to wear all the garments she was to be sent, she decided, if she did nothing all day long but change clothes.

Ten ball gowns. Ten! Were there to be that many balls to attend? And would not one garment suffice for them all, or at the most two? It seemed not.

She was beginning to feel very much like Cinderella, except that Cinderella had had only one new ball gown. Certainly she had her own Prince Charming awaiting her somewhere on the premises. She had succeeded in persuading herself during the night that he could not possibly be as handsome as she remembered. It was just that she had seen a tolerably well-looking man and reacted like a besotted school-girl, she had told herself. But she had not been mistaken. Not at all. He looked quite, quite magnificent wearing a tall beaver hat and carrying a gold-tipped cane.

And she was beginning to believe in her own good fortune. Though common sense told her that she was foolish in the extreme to have agreed to spend the rest of her life as the possession of a total stranger, even if there was a vague tie of blood between them, common sense had a number of rivals. There were his eyes for one thing. But far more important than that was the knowledge that however unhappy she might prove to be, she would at least always be secure. She would never be poor again. And she would be able to reunite her family.

It was true that her conscience smote her. For apart from the fact that she was not as she had appeared to be the morning before or as she appeared to be today either, there were other facts that she should tell him, facts that even Laura did not know about. She was not respectable, and neither was her family. That was the truth of the matter.

But the temptation to remain quiet until after the wedding was proving to be just too overwhelming.

So much for her own motives. But what about his? It would be better not to ask, Laura had advised, and Abigail agreed. She would ask him after their wedding, perhaps. Or perhaps not. Perhaps she would not want to know.

Their business on Bond Street was not by any means over when she was finally dressed and back in the front parlor with his lordship again. There were shoes and fans and reticules and feathers and handkerchiefs and a whole lot of faradiddle to be added to the purchases. But finally she was taken to a confectioner's and fed a meat pie and cakes and tea. She felt half-starved.

"Why?" she could not resist asking when conversation did not flow freely between them.

"Why?" He raised his eyebrows and fixed her with those blue eyes, which she wished for her own comfort he would direct at some other patron of the shop.

"Why are you marrying me?" she asked.

He looked at her assessingly and his expression gradually softened so that he did not look nearly as haughty as he usually did.

"I'm sorry," he said. "This must all be very bewildering for you. I realize that marriage is far in excess of the kind of help you hoped for when you called on me yesterday."

He spoke to her gently, as if he were speaking to a child. He smiled, and Abigail's eyes strayed to his dimple.

"I have had my title and everything that comes with it for fifteen months," he said. "For twelve of those I was in mourning. Now it seems that it is time for me to marry. I am thirty years old and a peer of the realm. I have female relatives about to descend on me. They should be here before the week is out. They would like nothing better than to take the choosing of a bride out of my hands, and yet I feel a strange whim to make my own choice."

"And so the hasty marriage," she said. "You are

afraid that they will persuade you to change your mind if we are still unmarried when they arrive?"

He smiled again. And looking deliberately away from his dimple, she saw that he had attractive creases at the corners of his eyes. He would have wrinkles there when he was a little older. She would have to advise him to rub cream around his eyes at night—not that the wrinkles would look unattractive.

"Let me just say," he said, "that I would prefer to present them with a *fait accompli*."

"But why me?" she asked, looking meekly down at her plate. This must be the very last question, she decided. She was not supposed to ask any, but to speak only when spoken to. Was it just that she had walked into his house at the right moment? Or the wrong moment, depending on how this marriage would turn out. It certainly was not her beauty or her charm or her dowry.

"I seem to have been surrounded by and managed by female relatives from boyhood on," he said with a laugh. "I have a notion that I would like a quiet and sensible and good-natured wife, Miss Gardiner, one who will be a companion rather than a manager. I judge you to have those qualities that I am looking for. Am I wrong?"

Oh, dear good Lord! Conscience was a dreadful thing.

Abigail swallowed. And a crumb went plummeting in the wrong direction. Other customers looked around as her napkin came up over her face and she wheezed and gasped and coughed until she thought she would vomit. The Earl of Severn, she realized as she willed herself not to disgrace herself, was standing over her, patting her back.

"Are you all right, ma'am?" he asked as the coughing began to subside.

How mortifying. How positively and totally humiliating! If someone would be kind enough to kick a hole in the floor, she would gratefully drop through it.

"How mortifying!" she said weakly, lowering her napkin, knowing that her face must be scarlet if not purple with embarrassment and the exertions of dislodging the crumb and sending it off to a more legitimate resting place.

"Don't be embarrassed," he said kindly. "Would you be more comfortable if we left? Come, we will stroll along the street until you have regained your composure."

He tucked her hand through his arm as they walked, and Abigail, feeling firm muscles beneath the sleeve of his coat and smelling the same cologne he had worn the day before, was glad that they were walking side by side so that he was not looking constantly into her face.

She doubted that she had ever felt so humiliated in her life.

And the man was to be her husband the next day. The very next day! That meant that she was to have one more night in her bed at Mr. Gill's, and then a wedding night—with the man who walked beside her, drawing female glances with every step he took.

And he was marrying her because she was quiet and sensible and good-natured and because he wanted to be free of managing females.

She was very tempted to turn to him without further ado and tell him the truth. All of it, down to the last sordid little detail. Even that one detail that no one else on earth knew except her—not even Boris. She should do so. After all, she would not be able to hide everything for the rest of a lifetime, certainly not the truth about her character.

But she thought of the long journey into Sussex and a disapproving Vicar Grimes at the end of the journey. And she thought of Bea and Clara and their unhappiness with their Great-Aunt Edwina and the dreary prospects that awaited them when they grew up. And she thought of all the clothes being made up in Madame Savard's shop and of all the parcels and bandboxes lying in the earl's carriage at that very moment. And of being a countess and comfortable and secure for life.

She held her peace.

It was already well into the afternoon. His lordship had a pressing appointment, he explained, and must return her to Mr. Gill's. He was to be busy for the rest of the day. He would take her up the following morning and they would go to the church together. The gown from the modiste's should be delivered in plenty of time.

"Is there anyone you would like to accompany you tomorrow?" he asked as he was handing her out of his carriage. "To witness your marriage?"

"Yes," she said. "I have a friend here, the children's governess. Miss Seymour."

"Then I shall take you and Miss Seymour up tomorrow morning," he said, smiling at her. "You will feel more comfortable to have a friend with you."

"Yes," she said. "Thank you."

And she watched in fascination as he took her gloved hand in his and raised it to his lips. No man had ever kissed her hand before. She wondered if it was normal to feel the kiss all along her arm and right down her body and both legs to all ten toes. She found herself thinking of wedding nights again, and turned hastily to enter the house.

Gracious, she thought as Edna, the Gills' maid, opened the door for her and she saw as she stepped into the hallway both Mr. and Mrs. Gill waiting there for her, their faces wearing welcoming and identical smiles. Goodness gracious. She did not know his name. She was to marry him the next morning, and she knew him only as the Earl of Severn.

She smiled in some amusement, and the smiles on the faces of the Gills grew broader. Mrs. Gill came toward her, both hands outstretched.

THE EARL OF SEVERN really did have pressing business, business that he thought might well keep him busy for the rest of the day and part of the night too. He had to settle with Jenny and take his leave of her.

He would spend a few hours with her before breaking the news, he thought. He might as well enjoy her favors one more time before his wedding the next day.

She came hurrying across the room to him when the manservant he had hired for her showed him into her parlor. She wrapped bare arms about his neck and raised her face for his kiss. Her eyes were dreamy. Jenny could always give the impression that the money she earned as his mistress was of quite secondary consideration—that making love with him was the pinnacle of joy for her.

But then, she had been recommended to him for just that quality.

"No," he said, smiling at her and laying three fingers lightly over her lips. "I have come here to talk, Jenny."

"To talk?" Jenny was not strong on conversation. She communicated with her body.

"This has to be my last visit, I'm afraid," he told her. "I am getting married tomorrow."

"Tomorrow?" she said. "So soon?"

"Yes," he said, removing his fingers and kissing her briefly.

She sighed. "When will I see you again?" she asked.

"You won't," he said. "This is the last time, Jenny."

"But why?" She looked at him blankly. "You are taking your wife out of town?"

Jenny obviously could not conceive of the idea that a man might give up his mistress once he took a wife.

"No," he said. "I will have the house made over to your name, Jenny, and all its contents. I shall pay the servants their salaries for one year, and you too. And I have bought you an emerald necklace to wear with your favorite gown—a farewell gift." He smiled at her. "Is that fair treatment?"

She removed her arms from about his neck. "Where is it?" she asked.

She spoke again while he clasped the jewels about her neck. "Lord Northcote wants me," she said. "He offered me more than you pay, and I think he will go even higher. He wants me badly. Perhaps I will take him, though he is not near as handsome as you. This is pretty." She touched the emeralds.

"I'm glad you like it," he said.

She turned and raised her arms about his neck again. "Shall I say thank you?" she asked.

"If you wish," he said, smiling.

She took him by the hand and led him into the bed-chamber that adjoined the parlor. He had expected her to thank him in words, he thought, kissing her and sliding her dress off her shoulders. But he could not insult her by spurning her way of thanking him.

It even surprised him that he was reluctant. He had come there with the intention of spending many hours with her.

He kissed her throat as she began to undress him with expert hands.

"I am going to miss you, Jen," he said.

But strangely, he thought a long time later as she lay sleeping, her head in the crook of his arm, and he lay gazing up at the mirror over the bed, which had always made him feel a little uncomfortable, he was not feeling nearly as sad as he had expected to feel.

The arrangement with Jenny was all business to her, all sexual dalliance to him. There was no relationship, no emotional tie whatsoever.

He was about to enter into an arrangement in which there would be a relationship, a commitment, some emotional tie. And he was not feeling nearly as sick or as reluctant about it as he had earlier that morning.

He did not yet know Abigail Gardiner. But during the hours he had spent with her that day he had felt a strange and totally unexpected tenderness for her—almost as if she were a child who had been put into his keeping.

He thought of her as she had been at Madame Savard's—quiet, bewildered, acquiescing in the decisions he and the dressmaker had made between them. And he thought of her as she had been at the confectioner's—anxious, shy, wondering why he had chosen to marry her rather than give the letter of recommendation she had asked for. He thought of her terrible embarrassment when she had almost choked on her cake. He thought of her flush and look of surprise when he had kissed her hand. And he thought of her drab clothes and the cit's home in which she lived.

She was not pretty. And yet when she had removed her cloak at the modiste's, it had been to reveal a trim and pleasing figure. And when she had taken off her bonnet, he had seen that her hair was in a heavy coiled braid at the back of her head. It looked as if it must be very long. He liked long hair on women. And of course her eyes saved her face from being quite plain.

He was rather looking forward to his marriage, he

was surprised to find. He believed that he and Abigail Gardiner might deal well together. Despite Gerald's warnings, despite what his mother and the girls were bound to say when they arrived, he was not going to feel despondent. He was going to make the best of this marriage he had proposed in such haste.

He had his eyes closed. But he opened them when he felt Jenny's light and practiced hand moving over him again.

"No, Jen," he said, removing her hand from his body and kissing her lightly on the nose. "I have to go."

She pouted and looked for all the world as if she were sorry.

But he wanted to be out in the fresh air. He wanted to be home. He wanted to be in a bathtub full of hot suds, scrubbing her perfume from his skin.

He wanted to be well-rested for his wedding day—and for his wedding night.

4

O H." FOR ONCE ABIGAIL APPEARED TO have been rendered speechless. She stared at Laura Seymour, who was standing at the opposite side of her room beside the window. "Yes. Thank you, Edna."

Mrs. Gill's maid stared at her wide-eyed from the doorway, from which she had just announced the arrival of the bridegroom. "Ooh," she said, "you do look fine, Miss Gardiner."

Abigail looked speakingly at the girl and turned back to Laura. "I don't believe my feet will move," she said.

"Then we will have to persuade them to do so," her friend said, coming across the room toward her. "We can keep his lordship waiting for five minutes, Abby, because it is your wedding day and brides are allowed to be a little late. But not indefinitely, until your feet decide to unroot themselves from the floor."

"What if he has changed his mind?" Abigail said. "What if he is having regrets? What if he does not like me, even when I am dressed in all my finery?"

Laura looked at her friend's pale blue muslin dress with its high waistline and short puffed sleeves and flounced hem. And she looked at Abigail's hair, which Mrs. Gill's personal maid—lent for the grandeur of the occasion—had dressed smoothly down over her ears and coiled intricately at the back of her head.

"You look extremely pretty, Abby," she said. "No man could possibly look at you and dislike you."

"He thinks I am quiet and sensible and good-natured," Abigail said, her voice almost a wail.

"Well, on such short acquaintance," Laura said, "he is fortunate to be accurate about one of the three. He will get used to the fact that you are almost never quiet and not always sensible."

Abigail giggled nervously.

"But we agreed last night and again this morning that you would not think of such things," Laura said. "Abby, we have kept him waiting for almost ten minutes already."

"I don't think I will be able to speak one word all day," Abigail said. "How does one get one's stomach to turn the right way up when it insists on standing on its head?"

Her friend clucked her tongue and took Abigail firmly by the hand. "It is time to go," she said.

Abigail took a deep and ragged breath and allowed herself to be led from the room. Her new blue slippers must have been manufactured with lead weights in the soles, she was convinced.

The Earl of Severn was standing in the hallway at the foot of the stairs, talking with Mr. and Mrs. Gill. He had a stranger with him, a fair-haired young man of medium height and pleasing, amiable expression.

Abigail focused her attention on the stranger, though she was aware only of the earl, dressed quite gorgeously in pale blue knee breeches, a dark blue waistcoat embroidered with silver thread, and a lighter blue coat. His stockings, his elaborately tied neckcloth, and the lace that half-covered his hands were snowy white.

Prince Charming would have looked like a bulldog beside him, she thought as he took her hand and raised it to his lips and she was forced to meet his blue eyes.

The stranger was Sir Gerald Stapleton. Abigail smiled at him and curtsied and found herself wishing that he were the Earl of Severn. He looked very much less threatening than the man who was to be her husband. She presented Laura to both gentlemen, accepted Mrs. Gill's kiss on the cheek and Mr. Gill's bow, and before she had quite digested the fact that the moment of her doom had finally come, she was being led down the steps to the pavement with the earl's hand at her elbow and helped into his carriage.

Laura sat beside her, the two gentlemen opposite them, their backs to the horses. And Abigail, trying to decide whether to stay quiet or to burst into animated conversation, found herself having to concentrate on not giving in to a quite inappropriate urge to giggle.

Except, she thought, thoroughly alarmed by the possibility that she might give in to that urge, that there was nothing even remotely funny about the situation. She was a bride on her way to church to be married. Her bridegroom—a total stranger—was sitting across from her, his silk-clad knees almost touching her own.

She turned her head from its awkward sideways position and looked full at him. He was looking steadily back at her and smiled as Sir Gerald was addressing a remark about the weather to Laura. It was a smile that began with his eyes and caused those creases that would be wrinkles when he was older, and ended with his mouth, dimpling his cheek on its way.

It was the same kind, gentle look he had given her the day before, as if she were a timid child who needed reassurance.

And indeed, Abigail thought, she felt timid and

tongue-tied and breathless and weak at the knees—all completely unfamiliar sensations. She wondered when she would return to normal.

She tried to smile back and found that her mouth was trembling quite out of her control. She looked away in mortification.

"What a beautiful day it is," she said brightly before raising her eyes to note the heavy dark clouds overhead.

All three of her companions appeared to find her words irresistibly witty. They all laughed.

"It must be your wedding day, ma'am," Sir Gerald said. "Miss Seymour and I have just been agreeing that it is quite the most miserable day of the spring so far."

"My vote has to go to the beauty of the day," the Earl of Severn said. "But here we are, without any more time to argue the matter."

HIS COUNTESS WAS NOT so very plain after all, the earl thought later in the evening. She was standing beside the fireplace bidding her friend good night, while he and Gerald had moved to the door already. Gerald was to escort Miss Seymour home in his carriage.

His bride had looked rather lovely—and very shy—that morning when he had first seen her descending the stairs at Mr. Gill's house. It was amazing what a pretty, colorful dress and a more becoming coiffure had done for her appearance. And of course she had been bright-eyed and blushing.

But in the course of the day he had discovered a charm in her that he had not expected. She was talking to her friend now with a flushed and animated face. And she had conversed with Gerald with some ease all day. With him she had been shy, but that was understandable under the circumstances.

"I would have to say," Sir Gerald said now, holding out a hand to him, "that either you are blind or your bride is a changeling, Miles. She is not at all as you described her. I pictured a drab and mute creature. I hope for your sake that she does not turn out to be quite, quite different from what you expect."

"You hope no such thing, Ger," Lord Severn said. "You can scarcely wait for the moment when you can crow 'I told you so.' I think you may have to wait a long, long time."

No, she was not mute or uninteresting, the earl decided, turning his eyes on Abigail again. One event of the day more than any other had taken him by surprise and charmed him utterly.

When they had returned to Grosvenor Square after their wedding, his housekeeper had had all the servants lined up in the hall to meet his new countess. He had been vexed. He had expected her to be thoroughly frightened by the formality of the reception.

"If you smile and incline your head," he had murmured to her, "they will be quite satisfied. I will have you in the privacy of the drawing room in no time at all."

But she had smiled almost absently at him, released her hold of his arm, and walked along the line of servants, Mrs. Williams at her side making the introductions, talking with each of the servants in turn, even laughing merrily with some of them. And she had stooped down to talk with Victor, the bastard son of a former maid, who had run away with a neighboring groom and a box of silver forks when the child was barely a year old. The earl had had the story from his valet shortly after his arrival in town.

But then, the earl had remembered, she had been a servant herself until a mere hour before. She must feel as comfortable with them as she did with her own class. Of course, many women in her position would be in some haste to put their past behind them and to assume the airs suitable to the newly acquired title of countess. Abigail appeared to be an exception.

He had directed Gerald to escort Miss Seymour to the drawing room while he had waited for his bride to finish listening to an account of the scullery maid's brother's new post as tiger to Mr. Walworth.

"They will all love you forever," he had told his wife as they ascended the stairs to the drawing room.

"It is doubtful," she had said, flashing him a smile. "I kept them standing for half an hour and have made them late in completing their day's work. They doubtless wished me in Hades."

He had laughed. "Your friend calls you Abby," he had said. "May I have the same privilege?"

She had grimaced. "I think my parents must have had a grudge against me when they called me Abigail," she had said. "It is a quite dreadful name, is it not?"

"I like Abby," he had said.

"You are a skilled diplomat," she had said, laughing and turning to look at him, and sobering again.

She had spoken to him since only when she could not avoid doing so.

"Good night, my lord," Miss Seymour was saying now, curtsying low in front of him. "Thank you for inviting me to spend the day with Abby."

"It has been my pleasure, ma'am," he said, bowing and extending a hand for hers. "And I know that you have made the day very pleasurable for my wife."

My wife. He had scarcely had a chance to comprehend the reality of their new relationship. Just three days before, he had not known that Abigail existed. Now she was his wife.

And how was he to explain to his mother and the

girls when they arrived within the next few days that he had met her two days before and married her today, knowing very well that they were to arrive within the week?

A violent case of love at first sight?

He would think of his explanation when the time came.

He took Abigail on his arm to accompany their friends to the top of the staircase, and they watched them descend, raising their hands in farewell when the pair turned at the bottom before leaving the house.

The landing suddenly seemed very quiet indeed.

"I have not told you," he said, turning to her and taking both her hands in his, "how very lovely you look today, my dear. But I have thought it all day long."

"Why, what a bouncer," she said briskly. "Lovely I am not, my lord. But this dress you bought for me is very splendid."

"My name is Miles," he said. "You are not going to 'my lord' me for the next forty or fifty years, are you?"

"No," she said, flushing. "I did not even know what your name was until we were at the church this morning. I kept waking up last night with possible names running through my head."

"Did you?" he said. "I hope you approve. Unlike yours, my name cannot be shortened to a more attractive form, can it?"

She was trying to withdraw her hands from his without actually pulling at them, he could feel. Her eyes were on his neckcloth. She was clearly quite as aware as he that it was bedtime. The thought rather excited him.

"Mrs. Williams showed you your rooms earlier," he said, "and introduced you to the maid she has chosen for you. Alice, is it? She is doubtless waiting for you. Did Mrs. Williams explain that my dressing room adjoins yours? Go on up. I shall come to you in a short while. Will half an hour be long enough?"

"Yes, my lord," she told his neckcloth, and she turned and walked sedately halfway up the stairs to the upper floor before breaking into a run up the remainder of the flight.

The earl watched her go and wished there were some way to save a shy young bride from the terror of an approaching wedding night.

ABIGAIL EYED THE BED, which Alice had turned down for the night before leaving, and continued to stand at the foot, holding to one of the carved posts.

She could have been in bed and fast asleep long before—she was tired enough after two disturbed nights and a day of nervous emotion. And a great deal longer than half an hour must have passed. Though perhaps not. Time had a strange tendency to expand or contract at whim.

One thing she knew, at least. She would stand there all night rather than lie down on the bed to be caught there by him. There would be something quite demeaning and definitely terrifying about watching him come through that door from a supine position on her bed. Better to face him on her feet.

She felt rather like vomiting, if the truth were known. It was foolish, really, when she had never felt fear in her life, or never admitted to such a feeling, at least—even when Papa was at his worst. But then, she had had very little to do with men outside her own family.

Until her father's death a little more than two years before, she had had the full care of him—he had been an invalid after years of uncontrolled drinking and rioting—and of the younger children. Boris was only two years her junior, but men were such little boys. Some of them—most of them—never really grew up at all. Bea and Clara were years younger, products of their father's second marriage and left behind when his second wife ran off and left him.

Abigail had had no time for courting and no patience with the few local gentlemen who had been foolish enough to stammer out the beginnings of an admiration for her. How could she have contemplated marriage when she had lived with such a poor example of the institution? And how could she have married and left the children helpless?

And yet her father had left them all helpless ultimately. His debts, they had discovered after his death, were appallingly huge, his creditors panting like wolves at the door. By the time they had sold the house and all its furnishings and paid off the more pressing of the debts, there had been nothing left for Boris. And nothing for the girls either, of course.

Boris had taken himself off in search of his fortune. Abigail had written a bold letter with trembling hand to the girls' Great-Aunt Edwina—aunt of the second wife, no relation to her at all. And she had mentally held her breath for all of two weeks until the reply came that the girls could go and live with their great-aunt in Bath until they were old enough to seek employment.

Abigail had packed them off on their way after hugging them hard enough to break every bone in their bodies and crying over them enough salt water to drown them. And then she had gone begging to Vicar Grimes, who had found her a position with the Gills.

Mrs. Gill had frowned at the prospect of "gentlemen callers," as she had termed possible suitors. Not that there had ever been any gentleman to make those calls. None at all. There had never been the chance to meet any.

She was twenty-four years old, Abigail thought, eyeing the bed again with a lurching of the stomach and licking dry lips, and knew nothing at all about gentlemen except that their bodies and minds could disintegrate with alarming totality under the prolonged influence of liquor and other dissipations. And she knew what those bodies looked like—in their disintegrated state, anyway. She had done everything for her father for the final year of his life.

She straightened up hastily when she heard a door open nearby. She should be doing something. Reading a book? But there were none in the room. Brushing her hair? But it was in a braid.

There was a tap at the other side of her dressing room door and it opened before she could call to him to come in. She found herself stranded five feet from the foot of the bed with empty hands and a blank mind.

"Have I kept you up?" he asked, his eyes passing over her long white cotton nightgown.

He was wearing a dark blue brocaded dressing gown. She had not thought to put one on. She felt suddenly naked and had to resist the urge to lift her hands to cover her breasts.

"No," she said. "It is quite all right, my lord. I have

been busy."

If she had spent the past half-hour dreaming up the most stupid reply she could make to such a question, she thought, mortified, she could hardly have done better. Busy!

"Oh, Abby," he said, coming toward her, taking her by the shoulders and turning her, "I thought so. Your hair must be very long, is it? Your braid reaches almost to your waist."

"I mean to have it cut," she said. "Mrs. Gill's maid told me just this morning that there is no way of dressing my hair fashionably when it is so long."

"Then dress it unfashionably," he said. "It looked very becoming as it was today. May I?"

He did not wait for an answer, but unwrapped the ribbon from the end of the braid and began to unravel the hair. Abigail stood meekly and swallowed awkwardly. She was going to feel even more naked with her hair all down about her.

"Ah," he said, his hands passing through the ripples that the braiding had created, "it is quite breathtakingly lovely." He turned her to face him again, and his eyes were laughing down into hers. "You did promise this morning that you would obey me, did you not? Here is my first command, then. You must never cut your hair. Promise me?"

"I have never wished to," she said. "What if I did not

like it shorter? I could not stick it back on, could I? And it would take years to grow it back again. But I thought you would wish me to be fashionable, my lord."

"Miles," he said.

"Miles."

"And don't ever braid it at bedtime," he said. "I want to see it loose, like this."

He threaded his fingers through her hair to rest them against the back of her head. And he lowered his head and kissed the side of her neck.

"Oh, goodness," she said, her voice sounding quite unnaturally loud. "I really don't know what to do."

"You don't need to," he said, raising his head and looking down at her so that she had the sensation of swimming helplessly in the blue depths of his eyes, a mere few inches from her own. "I shall do the doing, Abby. Are you frightened?"

"No, not at all," she said, her voice blurting out the lie a moment before his mouth came down to cover hers.

It touched hers lightly, warmly. His lips were not closed, but slightly parted. She recoiled, startled, making an audible smacking sound, as if she were kissing the girls for bed. But one hand stayed behind her head while the other circled her waist, and he kissed her again, lingering on her lips, moving his own, holding her head steady as he brought her loosely against him.

Oh, dear good Lord in heaven!

He was all hard-muscled maleness.

Abigail became aware of her arms hanging loosely at her sides, one of them awkward over his. She did not know quite what she should do with them. Let them dangle? Put them about his shoulders as seemed the sensible thing to do?

"Come," he was saying, his mouth still brushing hers. "Let us lie down. I shall extinguish the candles. You will be more comfortable in the darkness."

"Yes," she said. Actually, she thought, she would be more comfortable behind six locked doors, but she did not say the words aloud. A jest seemed to be inappropriate to the moment. Besides, she doubted that she would be able to get so many words past her teeth without their rattling loudly enough to drown out the sound.

She climbed into bed and moved to the far side of it while he blew out the candles. He was not wearing his dressing gown when he joined her, just a nightshirt.

This could prove to be something of a massacre, she thought, and then clamped her teeth together hard. She had not said that aloud, had she?

"Abby," he said, one arm coming beneath her shoulders and turning her so that she was instantly aware of his nearness, of the warmth of his body. "I don't want to hurt you. I would like to spend a little time getting you ready. Shall I? Or would you like to have this over with without further delay?" The sound of his voice suggested that he was smiling.

It was all very well for him to joke, she thought. He was not almost blind with terror and embarrassment. "You are the expert," she said. "I don't feel quite capable of making decisions."

He laughed softly, and Abigail clamped her teeth together again, feeling all her neck muscles grow rigid.

Getting her ready involved some slow kissing until she began to relax and hope that perhaps he would be satisfied with that for one night. He must be quite as tired as she. But his hand was stroking over her shoulder, relaxing the muscles there, and down over her breast. And he was slowly undoing the buttons at the front of her nightgown.

And the gown was being nudged off her shoulder and down her arm and his warm hand was cupping her naked breast, stroking lightly over it. His thumb was rubbing gently at her nipple.

As his mouth moved downward to her throat and her breast, her nightgown was being lifted up her legs, which he was touching with light fingertips, and she was lifting her hips by instinct rather than design so that it could be raised to her waist. His hand stroked between her thighs, a little cooler than the flesh there, strong and firm, and very male. And he was reaching behind himself.

"I am going to put a cloth beneath you," he told her, and she shifted her hips again while he did so, and turned onto her back.

He was leaning over her, smoothing the fingers of one hand over her cheek, across her forehead.

"Just relax," he said. "If it hurts, Abby, it will be just briefly."

"Yes," she said, and wondered that a voice could shake so badly over the uttering of one word.

He was heavy on her, and his own nightshirt was up about his waist. She felt heat flare as his knees came between hers and pushed them wide on the bed and firm hands came beneath her to raise her.

And then it was happening. But there could not be enough room. There could not possibly be.

"Oh, no," she said. "Please don't."

But he kept coming and coming until he was deeply embedded in her body and the sharp pain had not grown into anything unbearable.

"It's all right," he said. "Just relax."

Just relax! Abigail was waiting to die. But it was possible after all, she thought as terror began to recede. There was indeed room. She was his wife. The wedding-night consummation was no longer in the future, but in the past. She felt an enormous relief.

"No, don't," she said when he began to withdraw. She was not ready yet to relinquish her sense of triumph.

And he listened to her. He came back into her.

"Hush," he said. "Just relax. This is what happens."

What happened lasted for several minutes and took Abigail completely by surprise. She lay still and quiet, fearing that each withdrawal would be the last, until she felt a developing rhythm and knew that the consummation was not yet complete. And she felt and heard the growing wetness of their coupling, the increased comfort as there was no longer the friction of dryness against dryness.

And an ache—an ache that was both pain and pleasure—spread upward into her womb and tautened her breasts and throbbed in her throat so that she wanted to beg and plead with him. Except that for once in her life she did not know the words. She bit down on her lip instead and concentrated her mind on the thrust of his body into hers.

He had lifted most of his weight onto his forearms. But finally he came down heavily on her again, slid his hands beneath her once more, and thrust slowly and deeply into her once, twice, and a third time, turning his head to sigh against her ear.

And he lay still on her, all the weight of his relaxed

body bearing her down into the mattress. She ached and ached for a continuation, but he lay still.

"There," he said, a couple of minutes later, lifting himself away from her, reaching down to draw the cloth up between her legs. His voice sounded gentle again, as if he talked to a child, and faintly amused. "It is over—the great terror. Did I hurt you very badly?"

"No," she said. "Not at all."

"Liar," he said. He drew her into his arms, cradling her head against his shoulder, rubbing a hand up and down one of her arms. "It will not hurt again, Abby. I promise. And you will become accustomed to the act itself. I will return to my own room in a few minutes' time and you can sleep. Does that sound good?"

"Yes, my lord," she said. "Miles. If you say so."

He kissed her on the mouth and she listened to his breathing deepen. He was sleeping.

How could he sleep after an earth-shattering experience like that? Abigail did not think she would ever sleep again.

There was a heavy throbbing between her legs. Her nightgown was still down over one shoulder and bunched up about her waist.

His arm was sheltering and comfortable. He smelled good—warm and sweaty, with that cologne smell lingering on his nightshirt.

5

IT WAS NOT FAIR OF HIM, THE EARL OF Severn thought, waking at some time during the night, to be still in his wife's bed. She was surely entitled to privacy and rest following what had been something of an ordeal of terror for her.

And he had told her that he would leave. How many hours ago had that been?

And yet, he thought, listening to her quiet breathing, feeling the silkiness of her hair over his arm and hand, smelling its clean soap fragrance, she was asleep and relaxed. Her head was still pillowed on his shoulder. Her one hand, he could feel, was at his waist, beneath his nightshirt.

The experience had been very new for him too. From the age of nineteen he had always chosen his mistresses on the basis of their reputation as skilled courtesans. He had been taught all he knew about the pleasures of the body from those mistresses, having been a virgin himself when he employed the first.

He had not realized that there could be something erotic and deeply satisfying about making love to an innocent, to a woman who lay still on the bed beneath him and confessed to not knowing what to do.

He smiled as he remembered Abigail admitting just that when he first kissed her.

He lifted his free hand to smooth back the hair from her face. A shaft of light slanted across the bed from a chink in the curtains. There was nothing at all beyond the ordinary about her, except her hair, of course, and her eyes. Her breasts were firm and feminine but not large. Her waist was not unusually tiny or her hips particularly shapely. Her legs, though slim, were not long. There was nothing about her that could be called truly beautiful.

And yet he had found the bedding of her wonderfully satisfying. Perhaps it had been the strange novelty of knowing that no other man had been where he had gone. Or perhaps the even greater strangeness of knowing that she was his wife, that he could allow his seed to spring in her without having to be careful not to impregnate her. Or perhaps the new luxury of being able to bed her in the familiar surroundings of his own home.

He did not know what it was. But he did know that

for her sake he must remove himself to his own room. She was his for a lifetime. He must not demand service of her more often than once in a night.

He was up on one elbow, his palm beneath her head, when she opened her eyes and gazed sleepily up at him in the near darkness.

"Was I sleeping?" she said. "I thought I would never sleep again."

"I hurt you badly?" he asked.

"No." Her hand was still at his waist. "But it was all very strange. It astonished me that you were able to fall asleep immediately after."

He smiled. "You should have woken me," he said. "I promised to leave you to relax and rest alone."

"I must have fallen asleep before I could think to do so," she said.

He chuckled and lowered his head to kiss her. Her mouth was relaxed and warm from sleep. He lingered over it, nudging her lips apart with his own.

He should go. She was not a mistress, to be kept awake and busy at all hours of the night or day. She was his wife. But it was their wedding night, a night that could be expected to be different from all others. Perhaps tomorrow night he could set the pattern for the rest of their married life.

"Are you sore?" he asked her.

"Sore?"

"Here." His hand ran down her side and touched the cloth between her legs.

"Oh," she said. Her voice sounded breathless. "No."

He lowered his mouth to hers again and pushed the cloth back against the mattress. She was warm, slightly moist. His hand stroked her, played with her, parted her.

This time when he lowered himself on top of her, she opened her legs for him and even lifted them to twine them about his. She did not wince when he put himself inside her, though she did inhale slowly and deeply.

She lay still and felt comfortable beneath him. She had one hand in his hair, one arm loosely about his waist. He rested his cheek against her temple and felt the soft moist heat of her. He wanted this encounter to last for a good long time, he decided, beginning a slow shallow rhythm that he would quicken and deepen when his need outpaced his control.

She neither moved nor spoke during all the minutes that followed. And yet it was not his own isolated pleasure that pounded with the blood through his body and lodged in his mind. Sexual activity had always been for himself. Much as he had appreciated the beauty and charm of his mistresses, much as he had enjoyed the skill of their performances, it had always been just for himself.

But this time, with his wife, on their wedding night, he was very aware of the woman with whom he coupled, very aware of her warm and supple body, of her quiet surrender. He wanted to give her something in return.

"Abby," he said, moving his head so that his mouth was against hers. "I am going to make you happy. I am going to make you forget your years of loneliness and servitude."

And he brought himself swiftly to completion, sorry that he had given in to self-indulgence by taking her for a second time.

"You have a greedy husband, my dear," he said to her after disengaging himself from her body and sitting up at the side of the bed. He lowered her nightgown to the knees. "Forgive me?" He touched her cheek with light fingers. "Sleep well. I'll not expect you up before noon. I shall leave word that you are not to be disturbed."

She said nothing as he raised the blankets up over her shoulders, stooped to pick up his dressing gown from the floor, and let himself into her dressing room and through to his own, closing the doors quietly behind him.

He was going to be very well pleased with his marriage, he thought, yawning and climbing into his own cold and empty bed.

He already was very pleased.

Abigail was just the kind of wife he wanted. And more. A good pleasurable deal more.

FORTUNATELY ABIGAIL HAD had the forethought to send a small trunk of clothes to Grosvenor Square the morning before. Otherwise, she thought, descending the stairs and looking about her in search of the breakfast room, she would have been forced to wear her wedding dress again, and a pale blue muslin dress with flounces was hardly suitable attire for breakfast.

"This way, my lady," a footman said, bowing to her.

"Ah, Alistair," she said, giving him a big smile. "Is it so obvious that I am lost?"

He grinned at her and opened the door. She was feeling quite comfortable, clad in a brown dress with white trimmings, her hair pinned back in its coiled braids. Well, almost comfortable, she thought, putting a spring in her step and smiling at the butler, who stood at the sideboard. Her husband was at the table, a newspaper spread before him. She felt breathless. He got hastily to his feet.

"Good morning, Mr. Watson," she said. "Good morning, Miles." She set her hand in his outstretched one and allowed him to seat her at the table.

"I was not expecting you up for hours," he said. "Could you not sleep?"

Abigail blushed, very aware of the butler standing at the sideboard behind her.

"I slept like the dead after you left," she said, and blushed even more hotly.

"Watson," the earl said, looking up, "you may serve her ladyship and leave. I shall ring when we are finished."

Abigail nodded her head to the eggs and ham and toast and refused the kidneys and sweet cakes and coffee.

"I am always up early," she told her husband. "I believe there is a mental clock inside my head that cries 'Cuckoo' at a certain time, no matter how late I was to bed. Besides, the morning is the loveliest time of day, though it is not always apparent in town, with its buildings and traffic. In the country there is no time like morning. Unless it is the evening after a day's work—just when the wind has died down and the dusk has begun to fall. Why is it that the wind always stops blowing when evening comes? Have you noticed?"

Her husband had folded his paper and set it beside his plate. He was smiling at her in some amusement.

"Do you like the country?" he asked. "I intend to

take you to Severn Park in Wiltshire for the summer. I believe you will enjoy being there."

"I have something to tell you," she said in a rush. "I ought to have told you right at the start, and certainly before you married me. In fact, I should not have called upon you at all. I did so under false pretenses."

"Ah," he said, resting one elbow on the table and supporting his chin on a lightly clenched fist. He looked at her very directly from his blue eyes. "Confession time?"

"Don't smile, Miles," she said. "You will not be amused when I have told you all. Perhaps you will even cast me off. I am sure you will wish to do so."

His eyes continued to smile, but he said nothing.

"I am not your relative at all," she said, and felt her heart pounding up into her throat. She had not planned to tell him. Not yet, in any case. She drew breath to continue.

"Yes, you are," he said quietly. "You are my wife."

"But apart from that," she said. His eyes were disturbingly blue. She wished he would not look at her. And she was very glad that it had been dark during the night when he had . . . She could feel herself flushing. "Well," she continued lamely, "only very distantly related anyway, Miles. I ought not to have called myself your cousin."

"And this is your greatest confession?" he said, smiling at her.

No, it was not. That was not it at all. But she had turned craven. And perhaps she need never tell him. No one else knew. When her father had died, she had been the only one left to know. Perhaps she need not tell him? What if no one had ever told her? She would be none the wiser, would she? She would not know that she was deceiving him.

"No," she said, "there is more. There are more of us."

"More like you?" he said, reaching across the table for her hand and squeezing it. She had not realized until he touched her that her hands were like blocks of ice. "You are one of triplets? Quadruplets?"

"Oh, heaven save the world," she said. "No. But there are Boris and Bea and Clara."

"Tell me about them," he said. He was using his fatherly voice again, talking to her as if she were a child. He sat back in his chair, rested his elbows on the table, and steepled his fingers beneath his chin.

"Boris is my brother," she said, and swallowed. That was not quite the truth, but she no longer had the courage to tell him the truth. She should have done it, if she was going to do so, as soon as she had sat down at the table and before looking at him. "Beatrice and Clara are my half-sisters. They are still just children. They are Papa's and my stepmother's, but she . . ." She picked up a fork from the table and played absently with it. "She passed on." That was not a total untruth, she thought.

"Where are these children now?" he asked.

"Bea and Clara?" she said. "They are with a great-aunt in Bath. Their great-aunt, not mine. But they are not happy there. She took them in only because there was no alternative, and she subscribes to the ridiculous notion that children are to be seen and not heard."

"You are fond of them?" he asked.

She glanced down at her hands and replaced the fork beside her plate. She was surprised to see that the plate was empty of all except a few crumbs.

"They are almost like my own children," she said. "After their mother lef . . . er, was gone, I had the full care of them because Papa was . . . well, indisposed. It broke my heart when I had to set them on the stage and see them on their way to Bath. They have never had a happy life, but at least I used to be there to love them and to allow them to get dirty and to shout and run once in a while."

"Your brother inherited," he said, frowning, "and would not care for either you or your sisters?"

"Oh, there was nothing to inherit," she said, "except debts. Papa was . . . ill, you know, for a long time and was unable to pay his debts. We sold everything and still did not pay them all. Boris is here in London somewhere—I rarely see him. He is determined to make his fortune the quick way."

"Gambling?" he asked.

"He wants to pay our debts," she said. "He always wanted something better than Papa would . . . Well, Papa was ill and Boris did not have a chance to do any of the things he would have liked to do."

He looked at her without speaking.

"Miles," she said. She was fidgeting with her fork again and set it down. "I thought . . . When you asked me to marry you, that is, I thought . . . That is, everyone knows that you are as rich as Croesus." She looked up at him in dismay and flushed. "And that is something else you should know about me. I sometimes do not hear the words I am going to speak until my audience is hearing them too. I did not mean to say that. It is none of my concern."

"It is," he said. "You are married to a man whom everyone knows to be as rich as Croesus. What do you want me to do for your brother and your sisters, Abby?"

"Oh," she said, looking up at him in an agony, "I want them to live with me, Miles. The girls, that is. I want them back with me. Is there a large house at Severn Park? I will wager there is. You need never see them. I will keep them out of your way. And they will not be overly expensive, I promise you. They are not accustomed to wealth and will not be demanding. And I will not expect any expensive schooling for them. Indeed, I would not want them away from home to go to school. I would teach them myself."

"Abby." His hand was over hers again, his fingers curled under her palm. "Stop arguing with yourself. Of course we must have your sisters back with you. Will their great-aunt be willing?"

"Oh, yes, indeed," she said. "She has made it very clear that they live with her only on sufferance. May they come, Miles? You will not mind terribly?"

He smiled at her and squeezed her hand.

"Oh!" she said, staring at him but not really seeing him. "Yes, of course. Oh, of course. I marvel that I did not think of it before. It could not be more perfect. If the idea had a fist, it would have punched me on the nose long since."

He was looking amused again.

"That eel," she said. "That toad. That snake. It was she he was molesting, not me, you know. He knew better than to try molesting me. I told him the very first time he tried smiling at me that if he did it just one more time he would be wearing his teeth in his throat."

The earl threw back his head and shouted with laughter. "Abby," he said, "you did not. You are quite incapable of saying anything so ungenteel. But what on earth and whom on earth are you talking about?"

"Mr. Gill," she said. "It was Laura he was molesting because she is so very pretty and too afraid of losing her post to stand up against him."

"And yet you lost your position?" he said.

"I told him that if . . ." She paused and flushed. "I told him to leave her alone," she said, "and the next thing I knew, I was accused of ogling their son and was dismissed. If you had ever seen Humphrey Gill, Miles, you would know how indignant I was to be accused of such a thing. The very idea! It should be funny, but it is not."

"And what was perfect?" he asked. "What should have formed a fist and punched you on the nose?"

"Laura is a governess," she said. "She can teach the children and get away from that dreadful house and that lecherous man. Don't you think it is a wonderful idea, Miles? May I ask her?"

She thought he was going to refuse. He looked at her consideringly for some time. And the silence was loud. Oh, dear, she thought, she had decided that she would remain quiet for at least a few days. But she had been prattling, hadn't she?

Miles looked, she thought, as he had looked that first afternoon—was it only three days before?—and as he had looked the day he took her shopping. He looked handsome and immaculate and remote. It was hard to believe that he was the same man who had done those shockingly intimate things to her the night before. She could feel the color creep up her throat.

"Would it be wise?" he said. "If she is being abused, we must certainly take her away from there, Abby, or at the very least I must have a serious talk with Mr. Gill. But will she appreciate being your employee when she has been your friend, on a footing of equality with you?"

"She will be my friend," she said, "helping me by teaching the girls what I know nothing about."

"And living on your charity?" he said. "Will she like that, Abby?"

"Charity!" she said. "She will think no such thing. Am I living on your charity because you took me from that house and have given me a home here?" She felt the color mount all the way into her cheeks. "Am I?"

"You are my wife," he said, "and belong with me. You have a right to my care. Don't speak with Miss Seymour just yet. Let us take time to consider." He smiled. "Are you always so impulsive?"

"Yes," she said. "Always. I'm sorry, Miles. I am afraid you are going to find that I am not the wife you said you wanted and thought me to be."

"So far," he said, laughing, "you are just the wife I want. Now, I need your help."

She stared at him.

"My mother is on the way to London," he said, "with my two sisters. My mother and Constance, my younger sister, are coming from a lengthy stay with Lord Galloway and his family, friends of my mother's. Prudence is traveling with them, though she is married. Her husband will be joining her here later."

"And you are wondering how you are going to explain me to them?" Abigail asked. "They will die of shock, won't they?"

"I hope nothing so drastic," he said, grinning at her. "But yes, the moment may be an awkward one. I am afraid they all dote on me because I am the only male in the family. And while that situation has its definite advantages, it also has one distinct drawback. They all think they own me and know far better than I how my life should be lived."

Abigail nodded. He had said something similar before. She understood that he had married her so that she would be some sort of buffer between him and his female relatives. Quiet, sensible, and good-natured. Oh, dear. Poor Miles!

"When?" she said. "When are they coming?"

"Perhaps today," he said. "Certainly within the next few days. Will it put a great strain on you to meet them so soon?"

"There will probably not be nearly so great a strain

on me as on them when they have met me," she said. "I, after all, have some prior warning."

"You are very brave," he said. "You make a great effort to overcome your shyness, don't you, Abby? I noticed that yesterday. I just hope that meeting my mother under such circumstances will not prove too much for you. I have been very selfish, haven't I? But don't answer that, please. I know I have been selfish.

"And I have been delighted to find this morning," he said, getting to his feet and coming up behind her chair to rest his hands on her shoulders, "that you are not quite silent after all, Abby. It is difficult to make conversation with someone who has nothing whatsoever to say."

Not quite silent. Did he realize that he had just made the understatement of the century? Abigail stared meekly at her plate.

He bent and kissed the back of her neck.

"Do you think we could have fallen violently and insanely in love when you called here three days ago?" he said.

"What?" She turned in her chair to look into his face, which was still bent over her.

"For my mother's benefit," he said. "It will make matters a great deal simpler than if we tell the truth."

"Yes," she said. "Yes, it will. I can see that."

"You will do it, then?" he asked. He was grinning at

her, his blue eyes dancing, his dimple pitting his cheek, his teeth very white and very even—she had not particularly noticed that perfection before.

"Yes," she said. "Better that than have her think us quite insane."

He bent his head closer and kissed her lightly on the lips. "You are a good sport, Abby," he said. "Shall we spend the day together? There is a great deal we have to learn about each other, as I think we have both realized this morning. How does a drive out to Kew Gardens sound?"

"Quite splendid," she said. "I have never been there."

"Run upstairs and fetch your bonnet, then," he said. "I shall have my curricle brought around."

Abigail ran, forgetting on her way her earlier plans for talking with Mrs. Williams and exploring the house. Her father had never taken either her mother or her stepmother anywhere except to the occasional assembly, from which he had always returned home drunk. Mr. Gill never took his wife anywhere.

But Miles was going to take her to Kew Gardens. And he had suggested that they spend the day together. It was still quite early morning.

IT WAS LATE AFTERNOON by the time they returned, having strolled at their leisure in Kew Gardens and admired the flowers and the trees and lawns, and having exchanged more information about their families.

Abigail kept hearing herself doing most of the talking and clamped her teeth together every time she became aware of it. But a minute or so later her husband would ask a question that would set her going again. And he smiled at her and laughed at much of what she said, so that she began to feel that after all it was not such a terrible thing to be so talkative.

She did not tell him a great deal about her father. And nothing at all about her mother or Rachel, her stepmother. Despite all her chatter, she was selective in what she said.

They met two groups of people whom the earl knew, and he stopped and introduced Abigail to them as his wife. The news was greeted with surprise, smiles, laughter, much handshaking, and some chagrin by two ladies, who hid their feelings behind smiles and hugged Abigail. But she was not deceived, even if her husband was.

"By tonight everyone will know," he said to her when they were walking alone again. "I might have saved myself the trouble and expense of sending notices to the *Post* and the *Gazette*. Tomorrow you will be public property, Abby. We will have to drive to Hyde Park if the weather is kind. And there is Lady Trevor's ball tomorrow night that I have promised to attend.

You will come with me, of course. Will you mind very much? If I hold your arm very firmly through mine and do not let you go, will you be able to face the ordeal?" He was smiling at her, that gentle look on his face that always made her feel that she was being mistaken for a child.

"I have not danced for years," she said, "and then only at country assemblies. I have never waltzed. Mrs. Gill always called it a 'shockingly vulgar display of wantonness, Gardiner.' " She puffed out her chest and imitated the breathless nasal voice of her former employer.

The earl laughed. "I will teach you," he said. "Tomorrow. There will be no one to play the music. We will have to sing. Do you sing?"

For some reason that neither could explain, considering the fact that she did not answer the question, they both spent the following minute laughing merrily.

They had a late luncheon at a tavern that the earl was familiar with. They called at Bond Street on their way home in order to direct Madame Savard to have the Brussels-lace ball gown delivered in time for the next night's ball, and came away with two day dresses that were finished already.

They arrived home finally to be informed by the butler that Lady Ripley was in the drawing room with Mrs. Kelsey and Miss Ripley. Master Terrence and Miss

Barbara Kelsey were upstairs in the nursery with their nanny.

"Ah," Lord Severn said, turning to his wife and taking one of her hands in his. "I was hoping for at least one day's grace for your sake, my dear."

She smiled at him.

"Go upstairs," he said, "and put on one of the new dresses. Will you? Come down to the drawing room when you are ready. I will not let them devour you, I promise." He raised her hand to his lips.

"Give me fifteen minutes," she said. "I will not be any longer, Miles."

But heavens, she thought as he led her up to the first floor and she ran up the stairs to the second while he took a deep breath and opened the doors into the drawing room, there was a strong temptation to start knotting bedsheets in her room in order to take flight out through the window.

This was not an encounter to be looked forward to with relish. She immediately discarded the delicate pink muslin in favor of the bolder yellow.

6

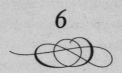

$\mathcal{M}$ILES. THERE YOU ARE." LADY RIPLEY rose from her chair and came hurrying across the drawing room, both hands outstretched to her son. Her dark hair was now turned almost completely silver, but she had kept her slim figure, and her face was still handsome. "And looking very well, dear."

The Earl of Severn ignored her hands and took her straight into his arms. He hugged her.

"Mama," he said. "I would have come home earlier if I had known for certain that you would arrive today. Connie?" He turned to hug his younger sister. "You did not suffer your usual sickness during the journey? Your color is good. Pru." He paused and looked down before hugging his elder sister. "Is it to be triplets this time?"

"I sincerely hope not," she said. "But I am rather large, am I not? And there are almost two months to go yet unless the doctor has miscalculated."

"Let me pour you some tea," his mother said. "I ordered up the tray, as you can see. It is so good to be back in London, Miles. The country was beginning to pall on us, was it not, Constance? And Dorothy and Frances, of course, have been able to think of nothing but the coming Season for weeks past." She handed him a cup.

The earl had not sat down. "I have something to tell you, Mama," he said.

"Have you?" she said. "This is new china, Miles? Or was it in the house when you came? It is very elegant. Lord Galloway is organizing a ball for Frances, to take place less than two weeks from now. It is not to be her come-out, though. Lady Trevor—Lord Galloway's sister, you will remember—has agreed to make her ball tomorrow night a come-out for her niece. Is that not gracious of her? It is all very rushed, of course. Dorothy and Frances are in a fever, as you can well imagine. You must spread the word among your acquaintances, my dear, that it is the event to attend. Though I daresay it will be a squeeze anyway, Lady Trevor being very fashionable."

"I will do so, Mama," he said. "I—"

"You will, of course, dance the opening set with Frances," she said. "You will bring her into fashion by doing so."

"I think that hardly necessary, Mama," Prudence

said. "Frances is like to take the *ton* by storm. She has a great deal of beauty and presence."

"All the more reason for you to dance the first set with her, Miles," Constance said with a smile. "Everyone will see that you have a prior claim to her affections."

"But I do not," the earl said. "Mama—"

"Pru and I think Lord Galloway's ball should be a betrothal ball," Constance said. "How splendid that would be, Miles, and you do intend to betroth yourself to her before the Season is out, do you not? But Mama thinks it would not be quite proper for Frances to make her come-out and be betrothed all in such a hurry." She laughed. "Mama believes in doing things properly."

"Besides," Prudence said with a smile, "I would rather like to be at your betrothal ball, Miles. Will you have enough patience to wait for two months or so for this little monster to put in an appearance? Theo will be in town within the month. He would not wish to miss the birth—or your betrothal celebrations, for that matter."

"There is no question of Lord Galloway's ball being a betrothal ball," the earl said firmly, "or—"

"Of course not," his mother said soothingly. "Drink your tea, dear, before it gets cold."

The earl sipped—and had that old familiar feeling

of being a small boy again in a household of women, totally subject to their will. It was a feeling he had not had all day, even though Abigail had surprised him by talking almost nonstop during their outing.

"This is a very elegant house," Prudence said. "What I have seen of it, anyway. I was in it only once when you were here for a few days after the funeral, Miles. Of course, one would not expect a house on Grosvenor Square to be anything less than splendid."

"But it does need a woman's touch," Lady Ripley said.

"Frances will enjoy herself here," Constance said, "as well as at Severn Park. I know you are always reluctant to talk of such matters, Miles, but do tell. When do you plan to marry? While the Season is still in progress? During the summer? The autumn? Not the winter, I hope. It is so difficult for guests to travel during the winter."

"Lord Galloway will want St. George's with all the *ton* present, you may be sure," Lady Ripley said. "And so do I. I have only one son, after all, and his wedding must be celebrated with all due pomp and circumstance. But we are making you nervous, Miles. Men are so foolish about such things. I suppose you are getting cold feet. But you and Frances dealt so famously together in the country that I almost expected you to make your offer there. I am glad you did not, since she has not yet been presented at court. But I am sure she will be expecting a declaration daily now that she has arrived in town."

"Then she will have to stop expecting," the earl said, setting his cup and saucer down resolutely on a table. "Or at least change the identity of the suitor. He will not be me."

There was a small silence.

"Oh, Miles," Prudence said fondly. "You really do have cold feet, don't you? Theo has told me since our marriage that he almost fled to France the day before the wedding, never to return. The prospect of being an exile for the rest of his life seemed infinitely more appealing than that of being a married man, he said."

The three ladies laughed heartily.

"But look at him now," Prudence said. "A fonder husband or a more doting father one could not hope to find. Your feelings are quite natural, Miles. But you must not give in to them."

"Besides, dear," his mother added, "your declaration has all but been made. Everyone expects it. It would be too embarrassing for words if you were to renege now."

"A declaration cannot be *almost* made, Mama," he said. "It is either made or it is not. And I made no declaration to either Frances or her papa. And never will do, either."

There was a chorus of protests from the ladies.

"If you will all just be quiet for a moment and remain quiet," he said with such firmness that they all complied and looked at him in surprise, "I have something of some importance to say."

Finally he had their attention. Finally, after more than thirty years. And it had been accomplished with some ease. One merely had to tell them to be quiet, using a suitably firm tone as one did so, and they were quiet.

"There is a reason why I cannot marry Frances," he said. "Something of great importance has happened in my life in the past two months."

He paused to notice the effect of his words on his audience. They were looking at him politely and with some curiosity.

And then the door opened and the reason he had spoken of and the something of great importance walked into the room, a spring in her step and a smile on her face and a muslin dress of vivid sunshine yellow on her person.

"Darling," she said, her eyes sparking into his, "I was as quick as I could be. Have I taken forever?"

She took the hand he had reached out for hers and raised her face for his kiss. He kissed her—on the lips—and was aware that no one else in the room had moved.

"Mama," he said, gripping Abigail's hand, dazzled by the ray of sunlight she had brought into the room with her, stunned by the way she was putting into practice the suggestion he had made at the breakfast table, "may I present Abigail to you?" He saw the blank look on his mother's face. "My wife."

Abigail smiled at Lady Ripley and curtsied. "I see you have been taken completely by surprise, ma'am," she said. "Had Miles said nothing to you before my arrival? How very slow of him. And I was rushing abovestairs to change into a more becoming dress, thinking that you would be impatient already with the long wait to make my acquaintance."

The earl squeezed her hand more tightly. "My mother, Lady Ripley, my love," he said, "and Pru and Connie, my sisters." He indicated them one at a time.

"I am very pleased to meet you," Abigail said, curtsying again. She smiled at Prudence. "You are Miles's married sister, aren't you? He has told me about his nephew and niece. He did not tell me that there is to be another soon. How excited you must be."

"Your wife?" Lady Ripley was setting her cup back onto its saucer, her movements slow and deliberate. "Your wife, Miles?"

His two sisters seemed to have been permanently silenced for once in their lives, Lord Severn thought.

"We should have waited, I suppose," he said, gazing

down into Abigail's eyes as if he longed to devour her, "knowing that you would be here sooner or later, Mama. But it seemed too good an idea to waste no time but to marry by special license without delay." He raised his wife's hand to his lips.

"We were impatient to be together," Abigail said. "We could not bear the thought of even one day's delay."

Lady Ripley set her cup and saucer down carefully and got to her feet.

"You are married, Miles?" she said, her voice unnaturally calm. "This is your wife? It is not one of your more bizarre jokes?"

Lord Severn could not remember indulging in any kind of joke with his mother, bizarre or otherwise.

"And when did this . . . event take place?" she asked.

"Yesterday," he said. "We were married by special license yesterday morning, Mama."

"And this has all happened within two months, Miles?" Constance had found her tongue again. "You did not even know Miss . . . er, your wife before that time?"

"We met three days ago," Abigail said with a bright smile one moment before the earl could say that it had been six weeks. "We fell violently and insanely in love, did we not, Miles?"

He grinned at her, feeling a flash of quite inappropriate amusement. They were his very own words, but they certainly had not been intended for his mother's ears.

"Yes, my love," he said, drawing her against his side with one arm about her waist. "We did."

"Three days ago." Lady Ripley's voice was steady, expressionless. "Four days ago you did not know each other, yet now you are married? And you fell insanely in love, you say? I believe you."

"You are angry with Miles," Abigail said, "and have a disgust of me. That is quite understandable, ma'am. I can hardly blame you. And if Miles had told me before this morning that you were expected in town so soon I would have persuaded him to wait, hard as it would have been for both of us. But you must not blame him entirely, you know. Doubtless he would have waited for you and for the banns too if I had not been about to be thrown out bag and baggage on the street from my place of former employment."

The earl closed his eyes briefly and inhaled slowly. He should have spent part of the day, he realized now, agreeing to some plausible story with Abigail.

"But what about your other plans, Miles?" Constance said, her voice gaining strength. "Did you completely forget? Does Miss . . . does your wife know about them?"

"My wife's name is Abigail, Connie," he said. "And I had no other plans, you know, apart from spending some time with you and Mama and Pru when you all arrived. My marriage will not prevent my doing that. We will both spend time with you. Won't we, my love?"

"Oh, dear," Abigail said, drawing away from the earl's side and smiling brightly. "This is a difficult moment, is it not? I perceive that you are all quite ready to throttle Miles and to boil me in oil. Shall we all sit down and discuss the matter sensibly? I shall ring for fresh tea."

"I am quite capable of ringing, thank you," Lady Ripley said icily.

Abigail smiled at her. "Do sit down, again," she said. "It is my duty to entertain you, ma'am, now that I am Miles's wife and Lady Severn."

The earl pursed his lips and waited for the explosion. And he watched in some fascination as his mother sat down, her back ramrod straight, and Abigail pulled the bell rope and smiled and looked as thoroughly at her ease as if she had been his countess for twenty years. His sisters were regarding her rather as if she were a fascinating sideshow at a country fair.

"Do sit down, darling," his wife said to him, looking at him with that glow in her eyes that proclaimed her a master actress—a mistress actress? "Take the sofa so that I may sit beside you. And you must give your mother and your sisters a full account of the past three days. And none of us will interrupt you even once, for after all, you are the man of the house and the head of the family. You and I will answer questions when you are finished."

His mother's and his sisters' attention was riveted on her, the earl saw with a glance at each of them. None of them spoke a word.

"Alistair," his wife said, smiling again when the door opened, "you may take this tray back to the kitchen, if you please, and instruct Cook to prepare us a fresh pot of tea and some cakes if she has been baking today. Has she?"

"Yes, my lady," he said. "Currant cakes and scones. Cook's scones are the best in London, my lady."

"Mmm," she said. "A plate of each, then, Alistair, if you please."

She waited until he had picked up the tray and disappeared from the room with it.

"I am starved," she said. "I hope Alistair's boast was no idle one. Now, darling." She sat down close beside her husband and took his hand in hers. She looked up at him almost worshipfully.

He laced his fingers with hers, cleared his throat, and began speaking. His mother and his sisters had never ever been such a quiet audience. The only interruption during the next several minutes was caused by the arrival of the tea tray and his wife's smiling but silent indication to the butler and footman that it be placed before her and the plates of cakes and scones handed around.

ABIGAIL HAD TAKEN for granted that her mother-in-law and her sisters-in-law would be taking up residence at Grosvenor Square. But it appeared not. Lady Ripley had her own establishment in town, and Constance stayed with her there. Mr. Kelsey had rented a house for the Season and was to join Prudence and their two children there within a month.

"The only reason I brought the children visiting with me this afternoon," she explained to Abigail before she left, "was that we are newly arrived and I thought Barbara would be frightened if I drove off without her. And if I were to bring Barbara, then it seemed only right to bring Terrence too."

Prudence was the one who thawed most noticeably before taking her leave. She even kissed Abigail's cheek and asked for the name of her modiste.

Constance was polite, though she protested to both the earl and her mother that she could not remember any Gardiners in the family.

"Yes, there were some," her mother said unwillingly. "Though we never had any dealings with them, Constance."

Lady Ripley herself accepted the inevitable with a cold graciousness. "This will appear like a ramshackle affair," she said. "I must take you about with me, Abigail, and see to it that you are presented to the right people. It must seem that this match has my approval."

"I hope it will not merely seem so," Lord Severn said. "I hope our marriage will have your approval, Mama, once you have recovered from your shock."

Abigail smiled determinedly. "When you see how I love Miles, ma'am, and how I will use every effort to make him comfortable," she said, "then perhaps you will be less unhappy. It must be dreadful to lose a son to a stranger—and so suddenly. I am sure I would not wish it to happen to any of my sons."

She blushed at the implications of what she had said. Her husband, who was holding her hand at the time in preparation for escorting their visitors to the door, squeezed it tightly.

"Well," the earl said to her after the door had closed behind his mother and younger sister and they had ascended the stairs back to the drawing room, "that ordeal is over. You did very well indeed, Abby. I was proud of you."

"They are used to running your life for you, aren't

they?" she said, and watched his rather shamefaced grin bring the dimple to his cheek. "But I think it will not happen any longer, Miles. You stood up to them beautifully and forced them to be quiet and listen to you. I am glad you decided to tell them the full truth instead of making up a more plausible-sounding story that they would have been bound to discover was a lie. I was afraid that you would say perhaps that we had met several weeks ago. But you had the courage to admit that it has been only three days."

"I think it was you who said that," he said, still grinning.

"Was it?" she said. "But I could see that that was what you wanted. Miles, you have spent the whole day with me. But you must not feel obliged always to do so. You must go out this evening if you wish. Do you belong to any of the clubs? I am sure you must. You would feel more comfortable spending an evening at one of them, would you not, and relaxing with your friends? I will be quite happy to find the library and take my embroidery there. I shall find a good book and not feel at all neglected."

"What I would really like to do," he said, "is spend the evening in the library with you, Abby. A nice quiet read sounds like the perfect way to relax. Will you mind my company?"

"What a foolish question," she said. "This is your home, after all."

"And yours," he said.

And so they spent the evening together, exchanging scarcely a word once they had adjourned from the dining room to the library, which was all wood and leather and brandy bottles and masculine coziness. Abigail loved it.

She could not, after all, read, she found. Her brain was teeming too actively with all the new facts and events of her life. She had never been an avid needlewoman, though she had been forced to acquire a taste for embroidery when living with Mrs. Gill. The woman spent most of her days indoors and inactive.

But she enjoyed stitching that evening and looking about her at this most cozy room of her new home and at the sprawling and oblivious figure of her husband, his attention entirely focused on the large tome that was open on his lap.

She was beginning to feel less intimidated by his good looks. After two days and a night spent in his company, she was growing more familiar with him and more comfortable with him.

She was seated at her dressing table, brushing her hair, when he came through his own dressing room later that night. She was thankful that it was not the night before—very thankful. This night she could look forward to with some pleasure. She smiled at him and set down her brush and preceded him into her bedchamber. She lay down on her bed while he removed his dressing gown and blew out the candles.

"I think perhaps your mother and your sisters do not wholly dislike me," she said. "They will get used to me, won't they, once they have got over being vexed with you for marrying without consulting them and once they have recovered from their disappointment in not having a chance to help you choose a bride. That is what their plans were for this Season, weren't they? That is what they were referring to?"

"Of course they did not dislike you," he said, joining her on the bed and settling one arm beneath her shoulders. "Why should they? They do love me, after all, and you put on a splendid show of being deeply infatuated with me, Abby. You had me almost convinced. Are you less nervous tonight?"

"Oh, yes," she said. "I was very foolish. It scarcely hurt at all, and even then only for a moment." She lifted her hips so that he could raise her nightgown to her waist. "It was more the fear of pain than pain itself—the feeling of 'Oh, oh, here we go—pain on the way,' and then the realization that it was over already."

He found her mouth in the darkness and kissed her. "I am glad," he said. "Hurting you is the last thing I would wish to do, Abby."

His hand had slid up beneath her nightgown and was fondling one breast. His thumb was rough against her nipple, his palm warm as it covered the hardened tip and made circular movements over it.

"That feels good, Miles."

"Does it?" he said, moving his hand to perform the same magic on her other breast.

"And as for its being unpleasant," she said, "that is so much nonsense. I heard it from wives when I was still living at home, and I heard it from Mrs. Gill and her friends. They would sit for hours conversing about their children and the miserliness of their husbands with money and of how very tedious and unpleasant *that* part of marriage was—always spoken with nodding heads and widened eyes and lowered voices and a significant emphasis on the *that*. One woman actually commented once that she pitied mistresses since they have to perform the duty ten times as often as wives. But she received such a look from the other women present that it is amazing she was not immediately transformed into an icicle."

He was laughing softly against her mouth. "Abby!" he said, while his hand moved down between her thighs and his thumb found a part of her and rubbed lightly over it and sent that sharp ache shooting up into her throat again.

"Ah," she said. She enjoyed the sensation for a few

silent moments and parted her legs slightly to give room to his hand. "I think those women were silly. I don't find it at all unpleasant, Miles, and certainly not tedious. And it is silly to call it a duty, like dusting the furniture or emptying the chamber pots."

He was doing a great deal of laughing, she thought as he brought his weight over on top of her at last and she parted her legs for him, bending her knees and sliding up her feet to rest on the mattress on either side of his hips, lifting her own so that he could slip his hands beneath her.

"Do you have a mistress?" she asked a moment before gasping as he came into her.

"Why do you want to know?" he asked, his mouth against her ear.

"Just idle curiosity, I suppose," she said. "Though perhaps more than that. I would not like the idea, Miles. And if it is just this that you go to her for, then I would prefer that you do it with me."

"Would you?" he said, beginning to move in her as he had the night before and creating that growing physical excitement that had been the only disappointing part then because it had led nowhere and had forced her to spend several minutes after he was finished, imposing relaxation on her body. "Even if I wanted you several times during the day and several times during the night?"

She thought for a moment and almost lost the trend of her thoughts in the pleasure of what he was doing to her body, though he was moving slowly and without the depth that she had particularly enjoyed the night before.

"During the day?" she said. "Is it not embarrassing?"

"Because we would see each other?" he said. His voice sounded amused. "I don't think either of us has a body we need feel ashamed of."

"Well," she said briskly, "I would rather a little embarrassment, I suppose, than the knowledge that you also did this with a mistress."

"Abby," he said, his mouth finding hers again, "I have no mistress, my dear, and have no intention of doing this with anyone but you for the rest of my life. Can we discuss the other possibilities you have brought up at some other time? I find it somewhat difficult to hold a conversation and make love at the same time. And if one of those activities has to go, I would prefer it to be the conversation."

"And so would I," she said.

She lay still and quiet with her eyes closed, enjoying the physical sensations of his lovemaking, hoping that it would not end for a long time, not at least until she had reached beyond the achings and yearnings that were quite out of her control.

But it did not happen. And perhaps it never would,

she thought sadly, putting her arms about him as he lay still on her finally, the whole of his weight relaxed on top of her. Perhaps there was nothing else. Perhaps it was that fact that had soured those silly women in Mrs. Gill's parlor.

But no. They had spoken with some disgust about the necessary but unwelcome male attentions that were a lamentable part of marriage. Not with regret and longing, but with disgust.

He moved away from her with a sigh of what sounded like satisfaction and drew her with him, onto her side, against his relaxed warmth.

At least, she thought, he was going to stay for a while. Perhaps if she remained very quiet and very still he would stay for a long while. Perhaps he would do it again.

"But you have had mistresses, haven't you?" she said.

He sighed again. "I was not a virgin last night, Abby," he said.

"I must seem very inexperienced and unsatisfactory," she said.

"Inexperienced, perhaps," he said. "But if you think I am not satisfied with you, Abby, you have not been paying attention. This is not to be a lengthy conversation, is it?"

"No," she said, "not if you do not wish for it."

"I don't," he said. "Something has made me tired. I cannot imagine what."

"My tedious conversation, perhaps," she said.

"Perhaps." He laughed softly and pecked her on the nose with his teeth to take any sting from the word. "Go to sleep, Abby."

"Yes," she said. "I will."

"I don't have a mistress, I promise you," he said. "And at the moment I have no hankering for one, either. None whatsoever. Now, will you sound less forlorn and go to sleep?"

"Yes," she said. "I didn't plan to say a word. I wanted you to fall asleep before you remembered that you should go back to your own bed."

"Did you?" he said. "You would rather I slept here?"

"Yes," she said.

"You are going to have to be quiet, then," he said, "or I shall flee screaming to my own rooms."

She chuckled.

"Go to sleep," he said.

"Yes, my lord."

She slept almost immediately.

7

*W*ELL, THE SMUG BRIDEGROOM." SIR Gerald Stapleton stopped in the doorway of the reading room at White's, strolled inside, and peered over the top of the *Morning Post* at his friend. "You are looking very pleased with life, Miles."

The Earl of Severn folded his paper and got to his feet. "Let's find a room where we don't have to strain our voices whispering," he said. "And why should I not be feeling pleased with myself, Ger? A two-day bridegroom, the notice in this morning's papers for all the world to see, and everyone eager to offer congratulations."

He stopped to shake hands with a well-wisher to prove his point.

"And after two full days you have been driven to finding more congenial surroundings," Sir Gerald said. "I must confess I was looking for you all day yesterday. I was obliged to go to the races with Appleby and

Hendricks and to spend the evening with Philby and his crowd. You might have saved yourself the expense of the notices in the papers, Miles. I told everyone your sad story and they all commiserated."

The earl chuckled. "The confirmed cynic," he said. "I left Abby composing a letter to a relative in Bath and tickling her nose with the quill and ordering me from the room because she could not think with me there and finds the writing of letters difficult under the best of circumstances."

His friend looked at him dubiously. "Oh," he said. "And you left meekly, Miles—not only the room but also the house? Driven from your own dwelling after only two days? Not an auspicious beginning, old chap."

Lord Severn laughed. "I was also excused from an outing to Bond Street later this morning," he said. "One of Abby's new dresses is ill-fitting and needs some alterations."

"Doubtless you will be happy to be at some distance when she gives the dressmaker the length of her tongue," the other said. "So, Miles, are you finding that your bride is exactly as you expected—quiet, demure, very ordinary, someone to be largely ignored, in short?"

"Do I detect a note of malice?" the earl asked. "You will be pleased to know, then, my friend, that Abby could probably talk nonstop from dawn to midnight without once running short of a topic or an opinion if no one insisted on having his say or if she did not occasionally notice that she is talking too much."

"Ah," Sir Gerald said. "I suspected as much on your wedding day, together with the fact that she is quite good-looking enough to cause you trouble if she so chooses. I am sorry, Miles. But you cannot say that I did not warn you."

"No," the earl said with a grin, "I cannot say that, Ger. She set Mama and the girls in their place quite magnificently yesterday."

"Your mother?" Sir Gerald said, impressed.

"Told her to be seated and not to trouble herself about running my life," the earl said, "now that I have a countess to take precedence over her."

"She said that?" Sir Gerald sounded awed.

"Actually," Lord Severn said with a laugh, "she told my mother to sit down while she rang for a pot of fresh tea. But the other was what she really meant. I think my wife has backbone after all, Ger."

"In other words, she will be running your life just as the females in your family have always done," his friend said gloomily. "You have jumped from the frying pan into the fire, Miles. And you continue to grin like an imbecile and look as if the world is your oyster—to mix metaphors quite atrociously. You will be a poor abject thing before the year is out. Mark my words."

The earl threw back his head and laughed. "I think she will suit me, Ger," he said. "I think she will. Despite the talkativeness, which has taken me by surprise, I must admit, there is a basic shyness, I believe, and an eagerness to please. I like her."

"Eagerness to please?" Sir Gerald said. "Enough to compensate you for the loss of Jenny, Miles?"

"Now, that," the earl said, raising one finger to summon a waiter, "is privileged information, Ger."

"Did you know that Northcote and Farthingdale are fighting over Jenny?" Sir Gerald asked. "And that her price is going up and up? It is doubtful that Farthingdale can afford her anyway. Though he is more personable than Northcote, of course, and Jenny is quite discriminating."

"How is Prissy?" the earl asked. "Still threatening to move back home to the country?"

"Some rejected swain wants her back," his friend said, "even knowing what she has become. She should go, I keep telling her. She does not really suit the life of a courtesan. It's time I found someone else anyway. A year is too long to spend with one mistress—makes them too possessive. How about a stroll to Tattersall's this afternoon, Miles? I have my eye on some grays."

"I have promised to take Abby driving in the park,"

the earl said. "And before that I will be giving her waltzing lessons."

His friend stared at him.

"She has never waltzed," Lord Severn explained. "And Lady Trevor's ball is this evening. I promised to teach her."

"Good Lord," Sir Gerald said. "I see the noose tightening with alarming speed, Miles. I strongly advise you to tell your good lady quite firmly that you are going to Tattersall's. Better still, send a note."

"You play the pianoforte," the earl said. "You confessed as much to me in one rash moment, Ger. Come and play for us. Otherwise I will be reduced to singing a waltz tune. I don't think Abby sings. At least, when I asked her, she dissolved into peals of laughter, had me laughing too, and never answered the question."

"Don't try dragging me into this cozy domestic arrangement you have," Sir Gerald said with an exaggerated shudder. "If your wife wants to waltz, Miles, hire her a dancing master, and take yourself off about some more manly pursuit while the lessons are in progress. You'll be sorry if you don't, mark my words."

"I knew you were a true friend," the earl said, getting to his feet. "We will expect you at three, Ger?"

"I say," his friend said.

"Don't worry if you are a little early," Lord Severn said. "My wife and I will both be at home."

He grinned, turned to shake hands and exchange greetings with another pair of well-wishers, and made his way from the room and the club.

Gerald could be right, he thought as he made his way home. Abby was certainly not the quiet, timid creature he had taken her for on first acquaintance. Perhaps she would in time try to dominate him and he would have to exert himself to be master in his own house, as he had never done with Mama and the girls.

But he did not think so. Despite her talkativeness and her firm and clever handling of his mother the day before, he believed there was a certain innocence and basic shyness in Abby. And he had spoken the truth to Gerald: in two days she had shown an eagerness to please him, refusing to demand his company, entering wholeheartedly into the scheme to convince his mother that they had fallen deeply in love, wearing her hair as he liked it at night.

And she had made no protest against anything he had done to her in bed, claiming in that unexpectedly candid way that always had him laughing that she found it not at all unpleasant, though he had touched her more intimately than he had expected to be allowed to do with a wife and had prolonged his love-makings beyond the limits he would have expected her willing to endure. She had not complained about being taken a second time on both their wedding night and the night before. He had restrained himself at dawn that morning, when he had wanted her again.

She had even said that she wished him to sleep in her bed. He had plans for taking her into his own that night, making it a permanent arrangement. She could use her own room during the daytime when she needed rest.

Yes, he thought, he had unwittingly made the wisest move of his life when he had impulsively asked Miss Abigail Gardiner just four days before to marry him.

She was going to make his life comfortable, he suspected. And to hell with Gerald, who warned him differently. What did Gerald know about marriage, anyway?

ABIGAIL HAD AN UNEXPECTED VISITOR during the morning. Who would it be? she wondered as she hurried down the stairs to the yellow salon, where she herself had waited just four days before. Her mother-in-law or one of her sisters-in-law? But no, they would have come up. Laura? Mrs. Gill? Some stranger who had read the marriage announcement in the paper that morning?

She felt apprehensive. But when she stepped inside the salon and saw who her visitor was, she cried out in delight and went hurtling across the room.

"Boris!" she cried, hugging the tall, thin young man

who stood where she had stood on a previous occasion. "Where have you been? I have not seen you in an age. How did you know I was here? Did you read the announcement of my marriage? What do you think of it? Were you ever so surprised in your life? I would have liked to tell you before the wedding, but I never know where you may be found. Have you come to congratulate me? How thin you are! You are not eating well, are you? Are things not going well for you? Have you—?"

"Abby," he said, with a firmness of voice that seemed well accustomed to breaking into her monologues, "hush."

"Yes," she said, smoothing her hands over the lapels of his coat. "It is just that I am so very pleased to see you, Boris. Miles is from home. What a shame! I do so want you to meet him. He is our kinsman, you know. Did you know that the old earl was dead? Or did you think I had married a white-haired old man?"

"Abby," he said, and she could see at last that he was not sharing her delight, "you did not come begging to him, did you?"

"Begging?" she said. "No. Not for money, anyway. Mrs. Gill dismissed me from my post, Boris, and would not supply me with a character. I thought the earl would give me a letter, he being our cousin and all. That is all. It was not really begging."

"He is not our cousin," he said. "Even the old earl was not, not really. The connection was very remote, and you know very well that he would not have acknowledged any connection at all with us, Abby. We have always been disreputable."

"No," she said, all the joy gone out of her morning. "Only Papa, Boris, and he could not help it."

"Not to mention Rachel," he said.

"Our stepmother?" She spread her hands before her and examined the backs of them. "Perhaps she had good cause too, Boris. Papa was not easy to live with."

"We are off the point," he said. "Why did he marry you, Abby?"

"He fell in love with me?" she said, looking at him inquiringly, eyebrows raised, willing him to believe her.

"Nonsense," he said impatiently. "This is real life."

"He needed a wife," she said, "and wanted to marry before his mother and his sisters arrived to try to arrange a dazzling match for him. He wanted someone quiet and sensible and good-natured—those are his exact words. And so he asked me."

"Quiet?" he said. "Sensible? Come on, Abby. Was he born yesterday? Did he tell you that he had an understanding with Lord Galloway's daughter?"

"Who?" she said, frowning.

"The Honorable Miss Frances Meighan," he said. "Reputed to be a rare beauty. A friend of the family. All the right connections and an enormous dowry. He didn't tell you, did he? He married you out of pity, that's what, Abby."

"He did not," she said indignantly. "That is not true, Boris. Men don't marry women out of pity."

"Why, then?" he asked.

"I don't know why," she said, "apart from what I have told you. Don't spoil things, Boris. You always do that. Just when I am happy, you always come along and try to convince me that I am being unrealistic."

His shoulders slumped suddenly. "I'm sorry, Abby," he said. "You are happy with him, then? How long have you known him, for goodness' sake? I have never had wind of it. Come and be hugged, then. Yes, I wish you happy, of course I do. Oh, of course I do, Ab." He hugged her tightly. "You of all people should have an eternity of happiness. And of course you are right. He would not have married you out of pity. People just don't do that. He has probably been wise enough to discover just what a gem you are."

"He can help you," she said eagerly, pulling away to look up into his face. "You are not doing well, are you, Boris? You really are very thin—and marvelously handsome. Are all the ladies swooning over you?"

"Oh, yes," he said with the boyish grin she remembered from earlier days. "Women have a habit of swooning over penniless adventurers."

"They do," she said. "You never did understand women, Boris. "I am going to ask Miles—"

"No!" he said sharply. "Absolutely no, Abby. I am going to find my own way in life, do you hear me? I am going to pay off Papa's debts if it is the last thing I do. And then I will find something to do with the rest of my life—without your help and without Severn's help. If you try getting him to assist me, Ab, I will disappear entirely from your life and you will never see me again. Understand?"

She sighed and pushed a lock of fair hair back from his forehead. "I have just written to the girls' Great-Aunt Edwina," she said. "I am going to have them back, Boris. Miles said I might."

"I'm glad," he said, smiling fondly at her. "They belong with you, Abby, and you with them. I had better be on my way."

"Stay to luncheon?" she said.

He shook his head and reached out to touch her cheek with one knuckle. "Mad, mad Abby," he said. "How long did you know him before you married him, anyway? You did not answer my question."

"Two days," she said. "It is four days now."

He stared at her for a moment before chuckling softly.

"Well," he said, "it is about time life started to turn

around for you, Ab. I will just hope that this is it. I'll see you again."

She could not persuade him to change his mind about staying. She stood at the door a minute later, watching him striding down the street. And she raised a hand to brush a tear from her cheek.

NOW WOULD COME the main test, Abigail thought, taking a deep breath and resisting the urge to reach out a hand to cling to her husband's sleeve. Now and this evening.

It was true that she was wearing another new outfit, a dress and pelisse of spring green and a straw bonnet trimmed with spring flowers that one would swear were real, though they were not. And true too that Miles had taken her by both hands before they left the house, squeezed them, and declared that she would cast all the other ladies in the park quite in the shade.

But bridegrooms were supposed to pay such lavish and foolish compliments to their new brides. The *ton* would doubtless see her as very plain and ordinary and wonder what on earth the very handsome Earl of Severn had seen in her to marry her, considering the fact that she was a nobody and had had nothing by way of a fortune to bring to the marriage.

The Earl of Severn was turning the heads of his

horses through the gateway into Hyde Park, which was already crowded with horses, carriages, and pedestrians. It was right on the fashionable hour.

This was it, Abigail thought. The notice of their marriage had appeared in the papers that morning, and the *ton* must be agog to see Miles's bride. The ladies must be all poised and ready with their spiteful tongues and their cats' claws. And who could blame them? Miles had doubtless been the most eligible and the most desirable bachelor in London just four days before.

She would probably die of the ordeal ahead of her. Her very best plan would be to remain quite silent and to smile and nod graciously at anyone to whom Miles chose to present her. That was what she would do, she decided.

"I feel like a performing bear tied to a post," she said. "Very conspicuous and very much in danger of being torn limb from limb."

"Do you?" The earl turned to smile down at her. "We will just take one turn about, then, Abby, and go home again. But it will make things a little easier for you tonight if you are familiar with at least a few faces."

"Sir Gerald Stapleton," she said. "Your mother and your sisters. That sounds like plenty of faces, Miles. I really don't think I dare try doing the waltz, do I? That is, assuming that anyone asks me, of course. But you will, won't you? And with you I can do it, Miles. You have the remarkable ability to keep your feet from beneath mine. I did not tread on them more than three or four times, did I? And that was at the beginning, when we were both laughing so hard and Sir Gerald was playing so many wrong notes that we were not concentrating at all."

"Staying away from your feet is called good leading, Abby," he said. "Most gentlemen are quite skilled at it, I assure you. You need not be afraid."

"Did you mind my inviting Sir Gerald to spend the summer at Severn Park?" she asked. "I realized as the words were coming from my mouth that I should have asked you first, Miles. But it seemed such a splendid idea for you to have a friend with you. If your mother and Constance come, with me that makes three ladies—not to mention Bea and Clara—and you all alone."

"I did not mind," he said. "I thought it a good idea, Abby, and was glad that it came from you. Here are Lord Beauchamp and his wife. Easy, dear. They are a friendly couple."

They were. Abigail launched into speech after the introductions had been made and continued to talk and smile and laugh when Mr. Carton and Mr. Dyke and his sister, all on horseback, joined them. And when the Beauchamps finally drove away, after Lord Beauchamp had asked her to reserve a set for him at Lady Trevor's ball, Lady Prothero and her two daughters stopped their carriage, and she chattered away to them too. And Sir Hedley Ward stopped to be presented and to exchange a few pleasantries, though he did not introduce the young lady on his arm.

"She must be his mistress," Abigail said in a quiet aside to her husband as the couple walked away. "She is pretty, is she not?"

And she turned back to talk with the little crowd of people that had gathered around the curricle, and continued to converse with several others who stopped for varying lengths of time.

"I did say we would make one turn about the park, did I not, Abby?" her husband said at last, when there was a lull in the crowd. "I thought I was doing your shyness a favor, and expected that we would be on our way out through the gates ten or fifteen minutes after coming through them. That was more than an hour ago."

"Everyone is very kind," she said. "I have promised four sets for tonight. I am not going to be quite a wallflower after all."

"Did you expect to be?" he asked.

"Oh, yes," she said. "It is strange, Miles. I have driven here twice before with Mrs. Gill, when not a single person so much as turned a head to look our way. It is the clothes you have bought me, of course, and the fact that I am the new Countess of Severn. I am not so vain as to think that I have suddenly become a belle. Oh!"

"What is it?" he asked as she turned her head sharply to peer back through the crowd.

"Nothing," she said, frowning. "I just thought I saw someone I knew, though I do not know who it was I thought I saw."

"Shall we turn back that way?" he asked.

"No," she said. "Will you mind if I invite Laura into the country for the summer too, Miles? I have been thinking about what you said, and you are quite right. I cannot offer her employment, though I suppose you could use your influence to find her something more suitable than what she has. But I could find her a husband, couldn't I?"

He grinned at her. "You have someone picked out already?" he asked.

"Of course," she said. "Sir Gerald Stapleton. I think he is handsome enough for Laura. She is very lovely."

"Gerald has a horror of marriage," he said, "and an incurable distrust of women. He thinks of leg shackles and mousetraps and such things whenever the subject is broached."

"But Laura is very sweet," she said. "If they are

together for the summer, he will change his tune. You mark my words."

"Are you a matchmaker too, Abby?" he said.

"Too?" She looked up at him. "In addition to what?"

"In addition to caring about other people's happiness," he said. "You do care, don't you?"

"Wanting to match one's friends is part of it," she said. "Don't you think it a splendid idea, Miles?"

"Invite your friend, by all means," he said. "But don't start hearing wedding bells, Abby. Invite your brother too if you wish. I am sorry I was from home when he called. Did you get your letter written to your satisfaction this morning?"

"Yes," she said. "The girls' Great-Aunt Edwina will be glad to be rid of them. I do not foresee any problem. And I can scarce wait to have them back. It will be a good idea for them to come straight to Severn Park when we remove there, Miles, rather than come here, won't it? You are going to be swamped with females, aren't you?"

He smiled.

"I just hope our first child is a son," she said.

He turned his head to look directly into her eyes, and she flushed painfully.

"Do you?" he said. "Just so that numbers will be stacked more in my favor, Abby? I hope our first child will be healthy. Will you welcome the experience?"

"Yes," she said, acutely embarrassed and wishing that they had not already turned out through the gates onto the busy street beyond the park. She wished someone else would come along and interrupt their conversation. "I did something very impulsive this morning. I hope you will not be annoyed."

"Did you?" he said. "Is that not unusual for you?"

"You sounded quite like Boris then," she said. "He always likes to mock me."

"What did you do, Abby?" he asked.

"I hired myself a personal maid," she said. "I did not really need one because you provided me with one, though I do not think that Alice has any real ambitions to be a lady's maid and I am sure Mrs. Williams will be quite willing for her to resume her former duties."

"Abby?" he prompted.

"I don't believe Madame Savard is a pleasant person to work for," she said, "and if you will not mind very much, Miles, I will not patronize her anymore. She does make lovely clothes, but I don't believe that employers who treat their employees with less than courtesy should be allowed to prosper. Do you?"

"No, I don't," he said. "What happened?"

"There is a seamstress there who is perhaps a little slow and a little clumsy," Abigail said. "And she is very thin and very anxious-looking, Miles. I can well imagine what would become of her if she were ever dismissed. Madame Savard had the girl in tears this morning, blaming her because the bodice of my pink muslin dress did not fit quite perfectly. Though I did not go in there to accuse anyone or be angry with anyone, just to have the adjustments made. And I do not think it kind to reduce an employee to tears in front of a customer, do you?"

"You have hired the girl?" he asked.

"You guessed?" she said. "Yes, I did, Miles. When Madame turned away to talk with another customer and we were left alone for a few moments, I asked Ellen—her name is Ellen—if she would like to come and work for me. And her eyes lit up, Miles. She is going to work out a week's notice and then come. Are you angry with me?"

"I have the feeling," he said, "that I had better not take you into the poorer quarters of London, Abby, unless I have you in a closed carriage with all the curtains drawn. I might find my home bulging at the seams with waifs and strays."

"You *are* angry," she said.

"On the contrary." He smiled at her. "Are you sure this girl can do your hair and perform all the other duties of a lady's maid?"

"I have never had a maid," she said. "I am very used to doing for myself, Miles. If I do not like the way she does my hair, I shall wait until she has left the room, not to hurt her feelings, and do it again the way I like it. Nothing could be simpler."

The Earl of Severn threw back his head in the middle of a busy street and roared with laughter. "Abby," he said, "where have you been all my life? I don't think I ever laughed until four days ago—or perhaps three. You were very demure on that first day."

"Well," she said stiffly, not knowing whether to be hurt or to join him in his laughter, "I am glad I amuse you, Miles, I am sure."

She joined in his laughter.

8

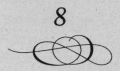

THE EARL OF SEVERN WAS FEELING amused. He seemed to have misjudged his wife on every count, and the realization might have alarmed him, given the fact that he had married her two days after meeting her and drawing all the wrong conclusions about her. But he was not alarmed. He was amused.

For one thing, he thought after he had tapped on the door of her dressing room the evening of the ball and let himself in, she was not plain. She was wearing the evening gown that had been his favorite from the start, even before it had been made. The underdress of pale green silk glimmered through the overdress of white Brussels lace. The gown was low at the bosom, revealing the tops of her firm breasts. Her long gloves and her slippers matched the underdress. Her maid had dressed her hair becomingly in a style similar to that she had worn on their wedding day. The color was high in her cheeks and her eyes sparkled.

No, she was not plain. She was not beautiful either, of course, not in the way that Frances, for example, was beautiful. She was perhaps something better. For while he found Frances beautiful yet unappealing, he could see that all of Abigail's loveliness came from within. She was clearly enjoying the occasion even before they left the house.

And she was not timid and shrinking, as he had rather expected her to be. Or at all shy, for that matter, though he had clung to the belief that she was for a few days. She could be nervous, and became highly voluble when she was, but once into a situation, she appeared to be thoroughly at ease. He smiled at the memory of the way she had held court in Hyde Park that afternoon for a whole hour, with almost no assistance from him.

He was not even sure he could cling to the hope that she was sensible. He thought of her plans for Gerald and of her hiring herself a maid when she did not even know if the girl could dress hair, and had to make an effort to repress a grin.

He should feel alarm. It was becoming increasingly obvious that she was nothing even remotely like the ideal wife he had described to Gerald less than a week before.

"I think I look quite gloriously splendid," she said to him, twirling before the full-length pier glass. "And I am determined to enjoy admiring myself while I may. I am quite sure that as soon as we set foot inside Lady Trevor's house and I see all the other ladies, my vanity will be instantly deflated." She laughed merrily.

Alice curtsied and left the room quietly.

"You will be the belle of the ball," he said. "You look very lovely."

"Thank you, sir," she said, curtsying deeply, "but you lie through your teeth. Oh, you match me, Miles. You are all silver and green. Did it take you forever to tie your neckcloth that way?"

"I have a valet," he said, "who fancies himself an artist. Turn around."

"Like this?" she said, turning her back on him and extending her arms to the sides.

"Like that," he said. He reached into the pocket of his satin evening coat and drew out the diamond necklace he had bought that morning before returning home. He placed it about her neck and secured it. "A wedding present, Abby." He kissed her just below the clasp of the necklace.

"Oh," she said, fingering it and turning to look in a mirror. "Oh, it is beautiful. You bought it for me, Miles? As a wedding present?" She whirled about to look at him. "But I have nothing for you."

He smiled at her. "One does not give gifts in order to

receive something in return," he said. "I wanted to buy you something."

"Thank you," she said, and her eyes were suspiciously bright for a moment. "No one has bought me a present for years." She hesitated, took one step forward, threw her arms up about his neck, and kissed him hard on the lips. "And now I will be squashing you and earning the eternal enmity of your valet. I was wondering what to wear to fill the bare expanse between my chin and my bos . . ." She flushed. "I was wondering what to wear and realizing that I had only one choice—Mama's old pearls, which are not real pearls at all, though they are a quite convincing imitation, and are too heavy and too long for this gown. Or nothing at all. No jewelry, that is. But now I have these. They are gorgeous, Miles. They must have cost you the earth."

"The earth and half a star," he said. "Shall we go?"

"If my stomach would just turn itself the right way up again," she said, "and the bones return to my knees. I have never been so frightened in my life."

"You, frightened?" he said, smiling. "Is it possible?"

"It is," she said. "But I lied. I have been more frightened before—when I came to call on you that first time, though I was expecting the old earl, of course. I would have died outright if I had known it was you I must face. I thought you were his secretary at first.

And on our wedding day. And when I had to walk into the drawing room alone to meet your mother and your sisters."

He laughed and offered her his arm. "Let's see you through one more ordeal, then," he said. "Soon you will have faced all the terrors that life has to offer, Abby, and there will be nothing left to do but enjoy what remains of it."

"There will be at least one more to face," she said. "I once had to watch a woman suffer through labor pains and give birth."

The earl looked down at her as she stopped talking abruptly. She was deeply flushed. Even her neck and bosom were rosy. He grinned at her, though she did not turn her head to note his expression.

And if she was frightened, he thought, then he was feeling decidedly nervous himself. Foolishly he had forgotten when he had accepted his invitation to Lady Trevor's ball that she was Frances's aunt. And as luck would have it, Frances had arrived in town in time for the event and it had suddenly been transformed into her come-out ball.

Nothing could be less fortunate or more awkward: Frances and Abigail making their debut into society on the same evening and at the same event.

He had called on Lord Galloway that morning. Lady Galloway and Frances had been nowhere in sight. But

Lord Galloway had known about his marriage and was very civil in his congratulations. Nothing had been said about any imagined arrangement with Frances. Perhaps it was all in his mother's head, he thought hopefully.

But the evening was not one he greatly looked forward to, despite his eagerness to show Abigail off to the *ton*.

He turned his head to watch her as they descended the stairs and Watson opened the front door. Yes, he thought as she smiled at the butler and thanked him, she was very different indeed from the demure, sensible, rather dull young lady he had taken her for just four days before. He had married her for all the qualities she appeared not to have.

He supposed he should be sorry, to say the least. Perhaps he would be, in time. He had not wanted a prattler or a manager of a woman who would force her way into the very forefront of his life. Abigail appeared to be all three.

And yet he was not sorry. Not yet, at least.

He even thought he was beginning to be a little in love with his wife.

ABIGAIL HAD NOT LIED about boneless knees and a stomach that stood on its head. What she had not realized until they had entered Lady Trevor's hallway and climbed the stairs and passed the receiving line and were standing inside the ballroom was that her hands would also be cold and vibrating and her head swimming and her heart thumping.

And though she had known that everyone would be curious to see the bride of such an illustrious personage as the Earl of Severn, she had not expected to be quite such a focus of attention. It seemed—and she was sure she did not imagine it—that every eye and quizzing glass and lorgnette in the room was directed their way and that the buzz of conversation was buzzing more energetically after they had stepped inside the doors.

It did not seem right when a young lady was making her come-out that evening and had a right to expect to be the center of attention. Of course, the young lady in question was still in the receiving line. Perhaps the situation would change when she arrived in the ballroom to lead the opening set.

The young lady was the Honorable Miss Frances Meighan, she thought with another lurching of the stomach. An extremely beautiful young lady, who was wearing a white lace and satin gown that was far more becoming to her blond and fragile beauty than was Abigail's own. Miles had taken her hand in both of his and raised it to his lips. Miss Meighan had looked at her as if she were a worm that had dared to wriggle into the house.

She would not think of it. Miles had married her quite freely. And of course men did not marry women out of pity. Not when they could far more easily give a letter of recommendation.

"Don't remove your arm for at least another five minutes, please, Miles," she begged, her jaw feeling stiff from the effort it was taking her to stop her teeth from clacking together. "If you do, I shall collapse in a heap on the floor." His arm felt reassuringly solid and steady beneath her hand.

He smiled at her, showing his very white teeth and his dimple, his blue eyes crinkling at the corners, and she could almost feel all those eyes and quizzing glasses and lorgnettes swiveling from her face to his.

"And yet you seemed so very much at your ease as you talked your way along the receiving line," he said. "Here come Gerald and Pepperidge. You will feel better once you have someone other than just me to talk with."

She did. She chattered happily with Mr. Pepperidge after Sir Gerald had reserved the second set with her— he would dance once, he said, before taking himself off to the card room for the rest of the evening. He definitely needed Laura's touch, Abigail decided, and stored the thought for future planning. And Lord and

Lady Beauchamp came to exchange pleasantries and brought with them Lady Beauchamp's young sister and brother-in-law, the Earl and Countess of Chartleigh. The countess appeared as eager to converse as Abigail herself.

Abigail was surprised to find after a very few minutes that her arm was no longer resting on her husband's but that she was still on her feet nevertheless. He was standing a few feet away from her, talking with Sir Gerald and another young man.

"Sorenson has brought Mrs. Harper with him, I see," Sir Gerald was saying, looking across the ballroom, his quizzing glass to his eye. "Lady Trevor must have turned purple when she saw her. Not quite good *ton* to bring her to a gathering like this, is it?"

"Then Lady Trevor ought not to have invited Sorenson," the unknown young man said. "He takes her everywhere these days."

The earl caught his wife's eye and winked at her.

Abigail followed the direction of Sir Gerald's look, but the ballroom was already crowded and several couples were promenading about the room. For a moment she had that same strange sensation of having spotted someone familiar that she had had that afternoon, but her attention was diverted to Lady Beauchamp, who was flushing and looking uncomfortable.

"Georgie!" she said to her sister, reproach in her voice.

"Did I say something wrong?" the countess asked. "But there is only Lady Severn to hear, Vera—or did you imagine that I had not told Ralph yet? And I am sure Lady Severn will not have a fit of the vapors to know that you are increasing and that I am wondering if you will be dancing the more strenuous sets."

Lord Beauchamp was grinning, and had set one arm loosely about his wife's waist. "I warned you not to tell Georgie until the evidence was staring her in the face, Vera," he said. "Though why you should be embarrassed, I have no idea, unless you are afraid that people will be imagining the process by which you have come by this state."

"Roger!" his wife said while he laughed down at her. "I am so sorry, Lady Severn. If my sister and my husband do not drive me to an early grave, perhaps I will live to a ripe old age."

"I envy you," Abigail said, smiling reassuringly at the baroness. "I hope to be in the same state myself before many months are past."

Her husband's hand was at her waist, she felt as she was speaking.

Lord Beauchamp chuckled. "Now, there is a challenge for you to take up, Severn," he said. "Ah, the dancing is about to begin at last. Vera, my love?"

"Abby?" The earl was smiling at her. "It is a quadrille, not a waltz, so you can put away that look of blank terror for a while."

Abigail laughed. It felt very splendid, she thought, to be led into the opening set by the gentleman who was not only her husband but also without a doubt the most gorgeously handsome man in the room. Her own claim to great splendor had already been relinquished to fifty other women, but she would continue to bask in the glory of being Miles's wife.

After a few minutes of dancing, she was caught again by that feeling of familiarity about someone across the ballroom. She turned her head sharply and looked again.

It was a woman—a woman with black hair and a daringly low-cut red gown that clung to her generous curves just as if it had been dampened. And undoubtedly it had been—Abigail had heard that several bold ladies did that.

Her hair had been a light brown when Abigail had known her, and her figure had not appeared quite so generous. But her identity was unmistakable. She was laughing up at a dark-haired, heavyset gentleman, her dancing partner, apparently enjoying herself greatly. She had not often looked happy when Abigail had known her. Not toward the end, anyway.

Their eyes suddenly caught and held across the

room, and her stepmother raised her eyebrows and smiled at her.

Abigail jerked her head back to stare at the intricate folds of her husband's neckcloth.

"I am sorry," she said as she trod on his foot.

"No harm done," he said, "I managed not to scream out loud and you are not so very heavy anyway. You are not really nervous, are you, Abby? You look as white as a ghost."

"I have only three spaces on my dancing card," she said. "Everyone has been most obliging."

"Have you reserved a waltz for me after supper?" he asked.

"Two spaces," she said. "Are you permitted three dances with me, Miles? I thought two was the limit."

"Since you are my bride of two days," he said, "I think I will be forgiven."

Abigail glanced again at the woman in red. But there was no mistake. She was Rachel, all right.

THE EARL OF SEVERN was feeling well pleased with his first appearance in public with his wife. She was taking well.

His mother and Connie, he was relieved to find, had treated her civilly after their late arrival, his mother actually seeking them out after the opening quadrille was finished and offering her cheek for Abigail's kiss and his own.

A large number of people had come to be presented to her and had remained to be charmed and amused by her conversation. The two empty unreserved spaces on her dancing card were quickly filled.

Lord and Lady Galloway had been courteous in the receiving line, and Frances gracious. He had reserved a set with her sometime before supper.

His wife was dancing the same set with the young Earl of Chartleigh, he saw. At least she would be able to talk uninterrupted with that very quiet gentleman. He smiled and wondered not for the first time how Abigail had succeeded in appearing so quiet on that first morning and during their shopping trip the next day.

"I am to be presented next week," Frances was saying. "Of course, Mama did wonder if it was quite proper for me to make my come-out tonight before my appearance at court, but Aunt Irene assured us that it would be quite unexceptionable to do so. I do believe that sets during a ball should be shorter, do you not agree, my lord? Then one would be able to dance with more gentlemen and there would be fewer disappointed at finding that one's card is full already."

"You are a great success, then, Frances, as I knew you would be," he said.

"Mama says we will have vouchers for Almack's by next week," she said. "It is a great bore there, so I have heard, but of course it is the thing to do to appear there. Doubtless within the next week or two I will be permitted to waltz too. It is very provoking to be prohibited from performing the dance until one has had the approval of one of the old ladies from Almack's."

"I am quite sure you will not have long to wait, Frances," he said.

And he suddenly realized why he had always found Frances's prattling tedious while he was amused by Abigail's. Frances was incurably conceited. Abby was not. When she had admired her appearance earlier that evening, she had done so with a merry laugh and the acknowledgment that she would be outshone as soon as she was in other female company.

And yet she was not outshone, he thought, glancing at her once more.

"It was very kind of you to marry Lady Severn," Frances said, and his eyes focused on his partner again.

"Kind?" he said.

"And greatly condescending," she said, "to marry a poor relative to save her from destitution."

"There is a very distant connection of blood between Abby and me," he said. "And I married her because I wished to do so, Frances."

She smiled kindly at him. "She was in service?" she

said. "With a cit? And was dismissed for excessive familiarity with her employer's son, though I am quite sure the charge was unjust. She would have found it difficult, if not impossible, to find another post, of course. And so you married her, my lord. It was very noble of you."

Galloway had certainly done his homework, the earl thought. Had he told Frances merely to reassure her, to make her feel less humiliated by the loss of a prospective suitor? Or did he mean to cause mischief?

He smiled. "You have omitted one detail, Frances," he said, "and the key one too. I fell in love with her."

"Oh, dear," she said, looking over his shoulder. "Aunt Irene was very upset when that woman walked along the receiving line with Lord Sorenson and we were all obliged to be civil to her. Perhaps Lady Severn knew her before you elevated her socially, my lord. Or perhaps she does not know that it is not the thing to associate with her."

The earl turned his head to look at his wife, who was no longer dancing with Chartleigh but was standing close to one of the windows with Mrs. Harper.

"Or perhaps they are merely exchanging courtesies," he said. "What are your plans for the coming weeks, Frances?"

He knew the girl well enough to understand that

answering that particular question would occupy her for the rest of the set.

They were not merely exchanging courtesies, he saw in another glance across the room. They were deep in conversation.

"I HEARD ABOUT YOUR MARRIAGE," Mrs. Harper was saying to Abigail. "I was delighted for you."

"Thank you." Abigail had excused herself from completing the set of country dances with Lord Chartleigh, having seen that her stepmother was standing alone by one of the windows, smiling at her. On closer view she could see that Rachel was wearing cosmetics. And surely one shrug of the shoulders would expose her bosom entirely. Abigail could feel herself flush. "Rachel, what are you doing here?"

"Dancing most of the time," Mrs. Harper said. Her voice was lower-pitched than it had used to be, Abigail thought. It sounded seductive. "And enjoying myself, of course. These private balls are always quite lavish affairs."

"But where did you go?" Abigail said. "What have you been doing all this time? We did not hear one word from you, even after Papa died."

"Well," her companion said, smiling, "I did not believe he would have left anything to me, Abigail. And I cannot pretend that I was consumed with grief at his death. I had wished him dead a hundred times when I lived with him."

"He was ill," Abigail said.

Mrs. Harper laughed. "Yes, I suppose he was," she said. "Some people would be less kind, of course, and say that he merely drank himself to death."

"Have you been in London all the time?" Abigail said. "But what have you been doing? How have you lived?"

"Very well, as it happens," the other said. "I have prospered, Abigail."

How old was she? Abigail thought. Thirty? Yes, thirty—six years older than she was herself. Rachel had been only eighteen when she had married Papa out of defiance of her father, who had whipped her one night after she had danced with Papa and walked with him in the garden at one of the local assemblies.

She had suffered many more whippings after her marriage. But Abigail shut the thought from her mind. Rachel looked older than thirty. The dyed hair and the cosmetics had the opposite effect from the one intended.

"And you have fallen into the lap of luxury," Mrs. Harper said. "The Countess of Severn, Abigail! Should I curtsy down to the ground? Perhaps I can hope for a similar good fortune for my girls."

The girls. The two reasons why Abigail had never been able to forgive Rachel for running away. Her life had been wretched with Papa, of course. But then, Beatrice and Clara had often been the butt of his drunken rages too, though they had been only two and four years old when Rachel had left six years before. Abigail had had to take on the task of protecting them.

"They are at Aunt Edwina's?" Mrs. Harper said.

"I am going to have them to live with me again," Abigail said. "Miles has said I might. When we move to Severn Park for the summer, they will be coming too."

"How kind of you and of him," the other woman said.

"Kind?" Abigail said indignantly. "I love them, Rachel. It broke my heart when I had to send them to your aunt after we sold the house. I love them as if they were my own. I can hardly wait to see them again."

Her stepmother smiled. "I have something of a hankering to see them again myself," she said. "They must be quite grown. I have even considered having them to live with me now that I am settled and doing well."

Abigail felt herself grow cold.

"I am their mother, after all," Mrs. Harper said. "Though I can understand your feelings, Abigail. You were always good to the girls, even when they were babies. Perhaps at some other, more convenient time we can discuss where it would be best for them to live. But now it is almost time for a new set, and time too to enjoy ourselves again. I shall send you a note?"

Abigail could see her husband approaching. "Yes," she said. "Yes, do that, Rachel."

"I am Mrs. Harper, by the way," her stepmother said with a smile from beneath darkened lashes for the Earl of Severn.

"Abby," he said, reaching out one hand, "this is my waltz, I believe."

"Yes," she said. "Do you know Mrs. Harper, Miles?"

"Ma'am?" he said with a half-bow.

Mrs. Harper smiled and waved a fan before her face.

"Abby," he said as he led her into the dance a minute later, "do you know who Mrs. Harper is?"

She did not answer him.

"She has a house in a respectable neighborhood," he said. "All is respectable on the surface and she is received by some—and by all, I suppose, when they are given no choice. But the house is reputedly a gaming hell. Darker dealings are rumored to go on there too. She is not someone I would wish you to associate with, dear."

"I am being ordered to stay away from her?" she asked.

"Ordered?" He looked down at her with a laugh. "With a big stick and a ferocious frown? I would not express it quite so strongly, Abby. I don't plan to start giving you orders. But I can give you advice, can I not, express my preferences to you? I would prefer that you stayed away from her. Is that better?"

"Perhaps circumstances forced her into this way of life," she said. "Perhaps she had no choice. Perhaps she made a great mistake in her youth and could never get herself untangled from its effects."

He was grinning at her. "I am not likely to find her in our house wielding a feather duster or checking the addition in my account books, am I?" he asked. "If so, you had better warn me, Abby."

"No, of course not," she said irritably. "Would I be likely to do such a thing without first consulting you?"

"In a word, yes," he said, still grinning. "Are you cross with me?"

"No," she said.

"Then why are you frowning and answering in those clipped tones?" he asked her.

She looked up into his smiling eyes. "For no reason," she said. "I am counting my steps. One two three, one two three. Imagine how it would drive you insane if I did it out loud, Miles. I am doing it silently."

"Then I will not talk and confuse you," he said.

She was feeling cold about the heart. Almost panic-stricken. Rachel was running a gaming hell and perhaps a house of ill repute too. And she was thinking of visiting her children, even taking them to live with her, perhaps.

Would it be allowed? Could a woman abandon her own children and return six years later and take them away with her? Would not a court of law stop her?

She wanted to ask Miles, but she was afraid of what his answer would be. Besides, she did not want to tell him who Mrs. Harper really was. She should have told him right at the start, even before their marriage, just how disreputable her family was. She still planned to tell him. But in her own time and in her own way. Not like this.

And she could not lose Bea and Clara when she was so close to having them back again.

"Abby?" She was being drawn closer to her partner so that her bodice was almost touching his coat. "What is it?"

It was only when she looked up into his face that she realized that her vision was blurred.

"Nothing," she said, smiling. "I am just over-whelmed by it all, Miles. At first I was terrified and now I am happy. I could sit down on the floor right here and bawl."

"You had better not," he said, his voice amused. "Someone might put the wrong interpretation on your actions and think that I have been treading all over your feet. That would be most unfair."

He had danced her close to the doorway. He took her by the elbow and guided her out into the hallway and along the corridor to a small lighted anteroom, which was empty, most of the guests either dancing or assembling for supper.

"Are you telling me the truth?" he asked. "There is nothing wrong? No one has been unkind?"

"What nonsense," she said. "Everyone has been just the opposite. It is all very splendid, Miles. Until a few days ago I could only dream of attending such an event. And I keep seeing my new gown and feeling my diamond necklace at my throat and remembering that it is a wedding present from you. I am very happy. Really I am."

"We should go in search of supper, then," he said. "Are you hungry?"

She thought for a moment. "No," she said, "but I will probably be able to eat a bear when I see all the food."

"I don't think bear is on the menu," he said.

And quite unexpectedly he set his hands at her waist, drew her against him, and lowered his head to kiss her.

"Abby," he said, "you are the belle of the ball after all."

"Oh, nonsense," she said. "There are fifty ladies lovelier, and no one at all more beautiful than Miss Meighan."

"Ah," he said, "perhaps you are right. My claim was only that you are the belle of the ball."

He kissed her again, drawing her right into his arms, opening his mouth over hers, tasting her with his lips and his tongue. Abigail could feel her temperature rising and found her arms about his neck when he finally lifted his head.

"Wouldn't anyone who walked in think it was peculiar to find you kissing your wife?" she asked.

"Better that than finding me kissing someone else's wife," he said with a grin. "I am moving you into my own bed for tonight and all future nights, by the way. If you meant what you said about liking to have me sleep with you, that is. What an interesting shade of scarlet."

"It is because I am embarrassed," she said. "Yes, I did mean it. Is it what you want too?"

"What a strange combination of shyness and boldness you are, Abby," he said. "Have you worked up an appetite for that bear yet?"

She nodded and smiled at him.

9

$\mathcal{T}$HE EARL OF SEVERN SMILED AT HIS wife, folded his newspaper, and set it beside his plate. He might have known that she would be up for breakfast despite the fact that they had not arrived home until the early hours of the morning and even then he had kept her awake for another half-hour, making love to her. He got to his feet and handed her to her place at the table.

"Good morning, Abby," he said. "Aren't you tired?"

"I must be," she said. "I did not hear you get up. Was it long ago?"

She had indeed been very fast asleep, curled into his body like a kitten, one hand beneath her cheek. He had lain awake for all of ten minutes before getting up, wondering how severely it would distress her to be made love to by daylight. He had decided finally not to put the matter to the test quite so early in their marriage.

"Not long," he said. "I am still at breakfast. I have an appointment with my tailor this morning and would like to go to Jackson's again afterward to see if I can find someone to punch the cobwebs off me. Will you mind a morning alone? I thought we might drive out to Richmond this afternoon."

"You have forgotten," she said, "that I promised your mother and Constance last night that I would go visiting with them this afternoon. I had better go."

He grimaced. "Yes," he said. "The theater tonight? Do you like watching plays?"

"I have never been," she said, her eyes glowing at him, "but wild horses would not keep me away. Do you have a box?"

"Large enough for guests too," he said. "Should we invite my mother and Connie, do you think?"

"How about Laura?" she asked, brightening. "And Sir Gerald? We can have them to dinner first, Miles, and then go together to the theater. I know Laura would be as excited as I. And if we throw them together a few times here in town, they will be more ready for a romance to flourish when we move into the country, won't they? Why are you grinning like that? Have I said something funny?"

He laughed outright. "We will invite them, by all means," he said. "But don't be disappointed when you have no success with your scheme, Abby. Gerald is a confirmed bachelor. What are you planning for this morning?"

"I am going to spend it with Mrs. Williams," she said. "I want to find out all about the workings of the house. Until two years ago, you know, I was used to running a house almost single-handedly."

"No, I don't know," he said, smiling. "You have told me remarkably little about your home and your life there, Abby. We will sit down sometime and you can tell me about it."

"Yes," she said, and looked over her shoulder. "May I have more coffee, please, Mr. Watson?"

Her cup was still three-quarters full, her husband noticed. He got to his feet, squeezed her shoulder, and took his leave of her, promising to see her before dinner.

"I will speak with Gerald," he said. "You will see to inviting Miss Seymour?"

"Yes," she said.

For someone who clearly liked to talk, he thought as he left the house and took himself first to his friend's rooms to issue the invitation for that evening, his wife really had said remarkably little about her home life before the death of her father.

She had run the household almost single-handedly, she had told him just that morning. Had there been no servants, then, or very few? Her stepsisters were almost like her own children, although she must have been only twenty-two when her father died. How long before that had the stepmother died? And her father had been very ill for a long time before his death. Had Abigail nursed him too? Her brother was younger than she.

Somehow the father had got into debt, so deeply in fact that they had lost everything after his death. And now the brother was living by his wits in London. Abigail was clearly very fond of him if her reaction after his visit the morning before was anything to judge by.

And she herself had been forced to send her sisters away to a great-aunt while she went into service.

She had had a hard life, it seemed. He looked forward to making it all up to her.

Though that might not be so easy, he discovered when he arrived at Sir Gerald Stapleton's rooms to find his friend looking pale and disheveled.

"I just got home half an hour ago," he said with a groan, one hand going to his head. "Do me a favor, Miles? Drive out to the coast and see if I really did drink the sea dry last night. I think I must have."

The earl clucked his tongue. "And this is the idyllic bachelor life you cling to so tenaciously?" he said.

Sir Gerald lowered himself gingerly into a chair and ran a hand over the bristles on his chin. "Priss has gone home to her swain," he said. "Cried all over me yesterday afternoon, wouldn't let me touch her beyond allowing her to cry all over me, that is, and left. What else was there to do last night after the ball but drown myself?"

"What you need is a wife," Lord Severn said. "I am beginning to agree with Abby after all. You have grown fond of Prissy, haven't you?"

"Habit," Sir Gerald said. "Sheer habit. Lady Severn hasn't turned her attention to my eternal happiness, has she? Confound it, Miles, can't you control her? Isn't it enough that she has you wrapped about her little finger?"

"Careful," the earl said. "I have all due respect for the state of your head, Ger, but you are likely to find your nose on a collision course with my fist if you say anything disrespectful about my wife."

Sir Gerald clutched his head with both hands. "See what I mean?" he said. "You are a lost cause already. I had something to tell you. Something to do with Lady Severn. Confound it, couldn't Priss have waited until the summer, when I would have been leaving town anyway?"

"What about Abby?" the earl asked.

Sir Gerald frowned. "Something to do with Galloway," he said. "Ah, got it! Can't imagine how I could have forgotten. Did you know that he and his good lady were putting it about last night that Lady Severn was in service with a cit and was dismissed for dallying with the son?"

The earl frowned. "Well, it is true," he said, "except that the charge was false, of course. I haven't been trying to hide the fact, Ger."

"You left early," Sir Gerald said, "with the Chartleighs and the Beauchamps. Lady Trevor's was buzzing with the information before the evening was out, Miles, and the conjecture that you had taken your lady away early because you were ashamed of her."

The earl clucked his tongue again. "What utter nonsense!" he said. "I don't even want to listen to such rubbish, Ger. Why would I have taken her in the first place if I was ashamed of her?"

"You had hoped to hush it all up," Sir Gerald said. "If you must cluck, Miles, do you think you could do it a little more quietly, old chap?"

"I shall take myself off and cluck all the way along the street," Lord Severn said. "I am already late for my tailor's. I would lie down for an hour if I were you, Ger. Did I tell you that you are to come for dinner tonight and then to the theater?"

"Who is the fourth?" Sir Gerald asked. "No, don't tell me. Let me guess. The auburn-haired governess. Am I right? Lady Severn is going to get the two of us leg-shackled. Have you warned her that she is doomed to failure?"

The earl grinned. "Yes," he said, "but Abby is undaunted."

His friend groaned. "Priss had a way with headaches," he said. "I don't suppose you would care to take my head in your lap and stroke my temples, would you, Miles? Ooh, I wish I had not said that," he added, as both men bellowed with laughter.

The Earl of Severn did not carry his laughter beyond his friend's room. The Galloways were having their revenge, it seemed, and would make life uncomfortable for Abby if they could.

Over his dead body, damn their eyes!

ABIGAIL SPENT a thoroughly pleasant morning, first of all with Mrs. Williams and then in the kitchen.

Mrs. Williams, she felt, was somewhat disappointed with their lengthy talk and tour of the house. The old earl had been a bachelor, and so had Miles until three days before. The housekeeper had hoped for an ally in his new countess, someone who would approve her schemes for making the house a more feminine place.

But Abigail liked the house as it was, especially the library, her husband's favorite room, with its old leather and wood furniture, the old paintings, and the heavy velvet draperies. She did not like the sound of the colorful chintzes and the cushions and frills with which Mrs. Williams wished to brighten and add comfort to the room.

"I want my husband to be comfortable here," Abigail said. "I do not want him to feel that his home has been invaded by women and that he must search out comfort in his clubs."

And besides, she thought more selfishly, she was comfortable there. She felt more at home after three days in Grosvenor Square than she had in almost two years at the Gills', despite all the splendors of the nouveaux riches that that house boasted.

The cook was thrown into consternation at first when Abigail arrived unannounced in the kitchen to discuss the menu for dinner that night. However, she was soon set at her ease and began telling her new mistress about the French chef next door who cooked foods so fancy that everyone was too awed to eat them.

"The cats are getting fat on them, my lady," she said, and proceeded by some strange progression of thought to describe the veins in her legs and the difficulties she sometimes had standing on her feet for any length of time.

"Then you must take more time to sit down and put your feet up," Abigail said. "You must delegate more of your tasks. I know how difficult that is to do sometimes. It is easier just to do everything oneself, is it not?"

She picked an apple out of the barrel by the door, bit into it, smiled at Victor and tossed one to him too, and sat down on a kitchen chair to have a comfortable coze with the cook. She set an arm about the child's waist as they ate their apples.

"Do you go out much, Victor?" she asked when there was a lull in the conversation.

"To market with Sally, m'lady," he said.

"Do you enjoy it?" Abigail asked. "You may come shopping with me too when I go, if you wish. You may carry some of my parcels and get some fresh air. Would you like that?"

The child nodded.

"Do you know your letters or your numbers?" she asked him. "Does anyone teach you?"

He shook his head.

"He is just a poor little waif, my lady," the cook said fondly. "He is fortunate to have a home."

"He is also a child," Abigail said. "I shall teach you some things, Victor, when I have time. You shall learn to read books. Will you like that?"

The child stared at her with open mouth.

She would ask Miles if she might take the child into the country for the summer, Abigail decided later when she was upstairs getting ready to drive to her mother-in-law's house. He was too pale and thin for a child. He needed country air and country food and some small tasks, perhaps in the stables rather than in the kitchen. And she would let him learn some lessons with Bea and Clara.

In the meantime she had an afternoon of visiting to prepare herself for. She did not much relish the thought. She had spent almost two years as companion to a woman who did almost nothing else in the afternoon but visit or be visited—and gossip endlessly. But at least it would be easy. She had already faced the ordeals of her first meeting with Lady Ripley and Constance and her first drive in the park and her first ball. Now she could relax.

It was not to be as easy as she had anticipated, however. Her mother-in-law offered a cheek for her kiss when Abigail arrived, and both she and Constance were clearly ready to go out. But neither smiled.

"We are going to call on Lady Mulligan, Mrs. Reese, and Lady Galloway," Lady Ripley said. "If we can carry off those visits, Abigail, then all may be well after all. It will be best if we are quite frank about your circumstances before you married Miles. Constance and I, of course, will express our delight at welcoming you as a daughter- and sister-in-law."

Abigail raised her eyebrows and looked at Constance.

"The story is out," Constance said. "It was, even before you and Miles left last evening, Abigail, but it was unfortunate that you left early. It was the main topic of conversation after you left."

"The Earl and Countess of Chartleigh invited us to their home for an hour," Abigail said, "since the countess had not finished telling me all about their son during supper and Lady Beauchamp was feeling too fatigued to continue dancing. And what story is out?" She grew cold as she remembered Rachel's presence at the ball. She should have told Miles herself, she thought, not let him find out this way, the whole *ton* knowing before he did.

"That you have been in service with a man who is not even a gentleman," her mother-in-law said. "And that you were dismissed for dallying with his son."

"Oh, is that all?" Abigail said, laughing with relief. "But I had no wish to hide those facts, ma'am. And anyone who had seen Humphrey Gill would realize how absurd that charge was. He is nineteen years old and has pimples."

Constance smiled fleetingly but grew serious again. "Even so, Abigail," she said, "the *ton* does not take kindly to welcoming into its numbers someone whose past has been sullied in any way. Miles, of course, has great influence, but we must be careful. Mama and I will do our best for you this afternoon."

"If the *ton* does not take kindly to me," Abigail said hotly, "then I shall not take kindly to the *ton*. I shall certainly lose no sleep over their disapproval, believe me."

"Abigail." Her mother-in-law's voice was cold. "Miles has done you the great kindness to bestow the prestige and security of his name on you. A few days ago you had nothing. Now you are the Countess of Severn, the wife of one of the wealthiest gentlemen in England. I believe you owe it to him to care."

Abigail clamped her teeth together and felt herself flush. It was true. There was no argument against such a truth, especially when it was spoken by Miles's mother. But she would see herself in Hades before she would grovel to the *ton* or tiptoe about them. She had groveled once in a lifetime and was married as a result. She did not plan to lower herself ever again.

"Shall we go?" Constance slipped an arm through Abigail's and smiled at her. "That is a very becoming dress, Abigail. Have you thought of having your hair cut? Short hair is all the crack, you know, and so easy to care for. It would suit the shape of your face."

"I can't," Abigail said curtly. "Miles has ordered me not to cut it. He likes me to wear it loose at night. Besides," she added, smiling and forgetting something of her chagrin, "if he had ordered otherwise, he would have to drag me by the hair to a hairdresser's."

Constance smiled uncertainly and glanced at her mother.

Abigail realized immediately on their arrival why her mother-in-law had chosen Lady Mulligan's as a place they must visit that afternoon. She was hosting an at-home, and her drawing room was filled with fashionable ladies, all of them balancing delicate cups and saucers in one hand.

Lady Ripley linked an arm through Abigail's as they entered the drawing room and smiled graciously as she presented her daughter-in-law to their hostess and the group of ladies surrounding her.

"So provoking for you, dear Lady Ripley, to miss the nuptials by one day," one lady said. "Young people are far more impatient than they used to be in our day, are they not?"

"But I had all the delight," Lady Ripley said, "of meeting a brand-new daughter-in-law as soon as I arrived in London, without having all the headache of a wedding to arrange. Imagine my delight!"

A few of the ladies joined in her laughter.

"Besides," Abigail said, "Miles and I were so deeply in love that we could not wait even one day longer."

The ladies tittered again as her mother-in-law squeezed her arm.

"You were a Gardiner, I understand, Lady Severn?" another lady said. "Would that be the Gardiners of Lincolnshire?"

"Sussex," Abigail said.

"And our kinsmen," Lady Ripley added. "An illustrious branch of the family."

One lady had raised a lorgnette to her eye and was viewing her through it, Abigail noticed. And all the other ladies were looking at her in that polite, arctic way that Mrs. Gill and her cronies could also do to perfection when they wished to establish their superiority over another poor mortal.

"Also an impoverished branch," she said, smiling and looking easily about her. "Did you ladies know that I was forced to earn my own living for the past two years? I was companion to a wealthy merchant's wife." She laughed. "I was very fortunate to meet my husband when I did, and even more fortunate that he fell as deeply in love with me as I with him. I had been dismissed from my post without a character for objecting rather pointedly to the attentions my employer's husband was paying the unwilling governess. He could not tell his wife that that was the reason, of course. She would doubtless have smashed a chamber pot over his head."

A few of the ladies were smiling. Two laughed out loud.

"He convinced his wife that I was sighing over his nineteen-year-old son," Abigail said, "whose chief claim to fame at the moment is that his face is all over spots, the poor boy. His doting mama believed all, of course, and I was given a week's notice. And then along came Miles."

"It is quite a Cinderella story," one very small lady said.

"And certainly has its Prince Charming," Lady Mulligan said. "You have done all the other young ladies of the Season a great disservice, Lady Severn, I do assure you."

"My husband's second cousin was forced into service for a whole year," another lady said, "before being fortunate enough to inherit a competence from her maternal aunt. Then she married Mr. Henry. Ten thousand a year, you know, and property in Derbyshire. They do not come to town very often, I'm afraid."

Lady Ripley squeezed Abigail's arm again and they moved on to another group.

"My dear Abigail," she said later, when they were in the carriage on the way to Mrs. Reese's, "it was a very near-run thing. I thought I would have the vapors when you began to speak so very candidly. It was more fortunate than I can say that Lady Murtry found your story amusing. When she laughed, everyone else followed suit. But do be careful. It would be wise to allow me to do the talking for the rest of the afternoon."

"I thought I would die," Constance said. "But you did make it sound so funny, Abigail. I could just picture your employer's wife smashing a chamber pot over his head."

"That detail must certainly not be repeated," Lady Ripley said hastily. "Some people may consider it downright vulgar of you to say such a thing, Abigail."

Abigail held her peace. But if Mrs. Reese tried freezing her out with that look, she thought, then she would not be answerable for what she might say. And it was indeed fortunate that the ladies at Lady Mulligan's had found her words funny. She had not meant to amuse them. She had meant to give them a collective and blistering setdown.

She was glad it had not worked that way. For Miles's sake she was glad. She would not wish to embarrass him by any vulgar display or by making an enemy of the whole of polite society. She would keep her mouth closed for the rest of the afternoon, she decided. She would smile meekly and allow her mother-in-law to thaw any chilly atmosphere that might greet her.

LORD SEVERN CALLED on his mother before returning home to change for dinner. It had been a long day, he reflected as his mother's butler preceded him to the door of her sitting room. He had had luncheon at White's, read the papers there for a while, having recalled that he had not had a chance to read at breakfast, and joined a few acquaintances in a walk to Tattersall's, though he had no present interest in buying any horses.

How long had he been married? he thought with a frown. Three days? Could it be that short a time? Had he really known Abby for less than a week? And was he already losing interest in his typical bachelor pursuits?

She was not really dominating his life, was she? How had Gerald put it? Did she really have him wrapped around her finger?

No, of course she did not. It was just that by some good fortune he had chosen a bride with a character that interested and amused him. And with a person that even more unexpectedly attracted him.

"Good afternoon, Mama," he said after he had been announced, taking both her hands in his and kissing her offered cheek. "Connie? How has your day been?"

"Busy," his mother said.

He smiled at his sister. "I noticed you dancing twice with Darlington last evening, Connie," he said. "I thought that came to an end last year. Is there still a spark there?"

"I am to be one of his sister's party to Vauxhall next week," she said. "If our family is still being received by then, that is."

He raised his eyebrows. "Is there any reason why we would not be?" he asked.

"Miles," his mother said, "I was prepared to keep an open mind, dear, because the deed was done already and there was no choice but to make the best of the matter. But you really must take your wife in hand before it is too late—if it is not too late already."

Lord Severn clasped his hands behind his back. "What has Abby done that is so bad?" he said.

"She was already under a cloud," she said, "after word of her background leaked out at Lady Trevor's last evening. I chose the places we should visit with great care this afternoon and instructed Abigail to let me do the talking. I told her that both Constance and I would give her our full support."

"Under a cloud, Mama?" he said quietly. "I think not. It is no crime, nor disgrace either, to be poor and to work for an honest living."

"She is already influencing you," Lady Ripley said in some distress. "Miles, she told a large group of the most influential ladies at Lady Mulligan's that her employer's wife would have smashed a chamber pot over her husband's head if she had known the truth about him and the governess. Fortunately—very fortunately—Lady

Murtry laughed, and so everyone else considered the story enormously witty. The ladies at Mrs. Reese's were not amused. I was very vexed. I had pointedly instructed Abigail on the way there not to speak in such a vulgar fashion."

The earl was chuckling. "Did she repeat the detail about the chamber pot?" he said. "To Mrs. Reese? Poor Abby."

"It was not funny, Miles," Constance said. "Mama had to work very hard to smooth over the moment. And remember that Mr. Reese is a cousin to Lord Darlington."

"Well," Lord Severn said, "if she was being given the tabby treatment, I cannot say I am sorry to hear that she defended herself."

"She need not have insulted Frances," Lady Ripley said coldly. "If you could know how provoking it was to sit there, Miles, with both of them in the same room—your wife and the lady who should have been your wife—you would not be displaying any amusement at all. I think the woman must have you bewitched."

"How did she insult Frances?" he asked.

"She told her that eighteen-year-olds who have lived sheltered, privileged lives could be permitted to be silly for a few years longer," Constance said. "Frances was speechless, Miles."

"Yes," he said, "I can imagine she would have been. What had she said to provoke such a setdown?"

"She merely commented that it was kind of you to marry Abigail under the circumstances," his mother said.

" 'Under the circumstances,' " he said. "I will wager that Frances injected a whole world of meaning into those words, Mama. I am with Abby, I must admit. I would say she showed admirable restraint in saying so little."

Lady Ripley made an impatient gesture. "Miles," she said, "I have always loved you. You know that. But you have always been easily led. I have tried for years to influence you for the good. I have spent a great deal of time and energy in arranging matters so that you could marry Frances, who would have managed your home and your life well and been an impeccably well-bred hostess. But it seems I have failed and you have fallen under the influence of a vulgar, ill-disciplined fortune hunter."

"Mama," Constance said, "don't upset yourself, pray."

The earl clasped his hands more tightly at his back. "She is my wife, Mama," he said, "and if you have a quarrel with her, then I am afraid you have one with me too. It sounds to me as if she was severely provoked this afternoon."

"We were trying to help her, Miles," Constance said.

"Can you not see that? It will be a dreadful thing for all of us if the most influential people of the *ton* decide to turn their backs on her. It will affect all of us."

"I have to go," he said. "We are expecting dinner guests. Good day to you, Mama. Connie."

He was sorry he had called. He had already been angry at what Gerald had told him that morning and at the opinion he had expressed about Abigail. Now this!

He was bewitched, was he? He had fallen under the influence of a vulgar fortune hunter, had he? He should control her, both his mother and Gerald had told him. He was easily led, his mother had said. He knew that to be partly true—he had been dominated by her and his sisters for years.

Was he now dominated by Abigail?

The idea was foolish. He would not think of it. His steps quickened as he neared home. He wanted to see her. It seemed a long time since breakfast.

10

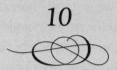

*A*BIGAIL FULLY INTENDED TO TELL HER husband about the events of the afternoon. It was not in her nature to keep secrets and she was already burdened with too many from her past.

When he came to her dressing room before dinner, however, he returned her smile in the mirror, bent to kiss the back of her neck, and clasped a string of pearls about it.

"Because your mother's are too large and heavy for evening wear," he said.

"Oh." She covered the pearls at her throat with one hand and gazed at him in the mirror. "They are quite gorgeous, Miles. And I will wager that they are real too."

She watched laughter crinkle the corners of his eyes and dimple his cheek.

"How was your afternoon?" he asked, touching her shoulder.

She opened her mouth and closed it again. She remembered what her mother-in-law had said about the kindness Miles had done her in marrying her. And she remembered the way she had chosen to defend herself that afternoon and the strong possibility that what she had said was vulgar. She remembered that not all the ladies who had listened to her story had been amused by it. She remembered the setdown she had given Frances Meighan.

"It was good," she said, smiling brightly. "I have met a large number of people in the last two days, Miles. What did you do today?"

She would tell him later, she thought. Perhaps after they returned from the theater.

Laura was embarrassed by the invitation, Abigail found later.

"But, Abby," she said on her arrival when they were alone together, "it was different on your wedding day. Now you are the Countess of Severn. Are you sure his lordship does not resent my being here?"

"How preposterous!" Abigail said. "As if Miles is high in the instep, and as if I had changed in four days. You are my dearest friend, Laura, and I intend that you will remain so. Now, tell me: have Mr. Gill and Humphrey been behaving themselves? Before I left the house, I enjoyed giving Humphrey that friendly advice on how he might treat his spots. I particularly enjoyed assuring him that it was a youthful malady and would surely disappear as soon as he reached manhood."

Laura smothered a laugh. "Mr. Gill has been in the schoolroom once since you left," she said. "I am afraid I quite shamelessly mentioned my dear friends the Earl and Countess of Severn. He did not stay long."

Abigail took her arm and led the way into the drawing room, where her husband and Sir Gerald were enjoying a drink before dinner.

Conversation at the dinner table fell mainly on Abigail's shoulders, the earl being unusually quiet, Laura shy, and Sir Gerald content to be an amused spectator. She talked almost without stopping.

"I have never been to the theater," she confided at last. "I was never more excited in my life."

"Never, ma'am?" Sir Gerald asked. "That is rather an extravagant claim."

Abigail thought for a moment. "I suppose I was just as excited when I attended my first assembly at home," she said. "Though it turned out to be a poor affair, and I was not nearly the belle of the ball I expected to be. I was sixteen and invisible to all the young gentlemen. Only the grandfathers danced with me." She laughed merrily.

"I do not believe you will be invisible tonight," Sir Gerald said gallantly.

"And I suppose I was as excited on my wedding

day," Abigail said. "But I was also terrified and cannot even remember the excitement. Laura had to help me unroot my feet from the floor of my bedchamber."

They all joined in her laughter.

Before she could think to rise and summon Laura to the drawing room while the gentlemen drank their port, the earl rose to announce that it was time to leave for the theater if they did not wish to be late.

Abigail flushed and glanced at her husband as he drew back Laura's chair for her to rise. She really must learn more behavior before he took her in total disgust. But perhaps it would be too late once she confessed about the afternoon's events.

She sighed quietly and smiled up at Sir Gerald, who was drawing back her own chair.

NEITHER HIS WIFE nor Miss Seymour had ever been to a London theater, the Earl of Severn had discovered at dinner, and yet there was a predictable contrast in their behavior when they entered his box. Miss Seymour, on Gerald's arm, looked about her with quiet interest and allowed him to seat her. Abigail gripped his own arm more tightly and stood quite still, letting out an audible "Ooh!"

"Now, is it the theater itself that has you in awe,

Abby?" he asked. "Or is it the splendor of the audience?"

"Oh, both," she said. "This is quite as magnificent as last night's ball. Will the performance equal it?"

"The play is of secondary importance, as you must learn," he said. "One comes to the theater to see and be seen."

"Absurd!" she said, flashing him a smile before seating herself on the chair he had moved out for her and looking about her again. "What a foolish thing to say. It is not true, is it?"

He laughed. "That you must discover for yourself," he said. "Everyone is certainly doing a good deal of looking about at everyone else at the moment, wouldn't you agree?"

And their own box was receiving more than its fair share of looks, he had noticed as soon as they entered the box. It seemed that yesterday's drive in the park and last night's ball had not been sufficient to satisfy the curiosity of the *ton*.

Since the night before, of course, most of them would have learned that most delicious of all details about the new addition to their numbers—that perhaps she was not quite respectable. And if his mother was to be believed, Abigail had done nothing to allay those suspicions during the afternoon.

Why had she said nothing to him when he had

asked before dinner? He had expected all the details to come pouring out. He had expected that they could have laughed together, that he could have kissed her and assured her that it was all nonsense and would be forgotten about as soon as the hint of some other scandal gave fresh food to the gossips.

But she had said nothing. Perhaps she had not even noticed that she was being shunned.

"Keep talking to me," she said to him now very quietly. "I think Laura and Sir Gerald are getting along together famously, aren't they?"

"They are both well-bred enough to make conversation with each other," he said, smiling at her. "But I would not expect any interesting announcement before the evening is out if I were you, Abby."

"Perhaps not," she said. "But stranger things have happened."

Yes indeed, he thought. Stranger things had happened. He had met Abigail less than a week before, married her two days later, discovered that she in no way resembled the woman he had taken her for, and yet grown fond of her. But he did not know her at all. He was suddenly appalled by his own ignorance of the person she was, of all the events and forces and persons who had shaped her into the woman he had married.

His mother thought her vulgar. Gerald thought her

managing. And he? He was amused by her, attracted to her. But he did not know her.

"Oh, look," she said eagerly, pointing down to the pit in a manner that would have had his mother cringing. "There is Boris."

"Which one?" he asked.

"In the green coat," she said. "With the fairish brown hair. The one who is too thin. Next to the gentleman in lavender ogling the ladies in the box opposite through his quizzing glass. How rude of him! But one of the ladies likes it. She is smiling back and fluttering her fan. Do you see?"

"I see your brother," the earl said at the same moment as Boris Gardiner turned his head, looked into their box, smiled, and raised a hand in greeting. "He has seen you."

She waved vigorously back, her face lighting up with a smile.

He did know something about her, the earl thought. She was eagerly awaiting the moment when she could be reunited with her sisters—her half-sisters. And she lit up like a candle at the mere sight of her brother. One fact about her past was very clear: she was dearly fond of her family. They must have been a close-knit group before the death of the father.

"May we go down there to talk with him?" she asked.

"At the interval," he said. "The play is about to begin."

It was not the best performance he had ever seen. And he found that the loud comments and guffaws of laughter from the gentlemen crowded into the next box—acquaintances of his, though not close friends— destroyed his concentration.

But both Abigail and Miss Seymour were enthralled, he saw at a glance, and met the amused eyes of his friend over the latter's head. Abigail was staring wide-eyed at the stage, one bare arm resting on the velvet edge of the box before her. He took her other hand in his and she curled her fingers about it, though she did not move her eyes from the actors.

He smiled and wondered if it were so essential to know another person—to know about that person's past life, that was. He had known Abigail for almost a week and he liked her. To hell with the opinions of those who did not and who tried to warn him against her.

He liked her and he was falling a little in love with her. And surely that was all that mattered.

ABIGAIL LOOKED UP when the actors left the stage, and realized, in something of a daze, that it was the interval.

"Oh, so soon?" she said. "It seems that it has just started."

But she remembered Boris and looked eagerly down into the pit, only to discover that he was no longer in the place where he had been.

"Perhaps he is on his way up here," the earl said. "Let's stroll out into the corridor, and perhaps we will meet him. Ger? Miss Seymour? Are you coming for some air?"

Abigail would have preferred to leave them alone in the box together, but both got to their feet quite willingly. Laura looked particularly fetching that evening, Abigail thought, with her auburn hair dressed in curls and with her blue dress, which was not quite unfashionable.

Miles had been right. They met her brother almost as soon as they stepped out of the box.

"Boris," she said, throwing her arms about his neck and hugging him. "Is it not a wonderful performance? I feel quite as if I had been transported into another world."

"Tolerable," he said, patting her waist.

She took his arm and presented him to her husband and to Laura and Sir Gerald. She smiled up at him while they all conversed for a few minutes.

"Miles was sorry to miss you yesterday morning," she said at last. She brightened at a sudden thought.

"We want you to come for dinner tomorrow, don't we, Miles? And Laura and Sir Gerald must come again. And we will invite a few other people—perhaps your mother and Constance will come, Miles, and Prudence too if she is not too embarrassed about her condition, though I think she will not be at a small informal dinner party, do you? We can have cards afterward or charades, perhaps. Sir Gerald can play for us on the pianoforte—he plays well, Boris, and did so yesterday afternoon while Miles taught me how to waltz. And Laura can sing. She has a very sweet voice."

"Pardon me, ma'am," Sir Gerald said, "but I regret to say I have another engagement for tomorrow evening."

"Oh," Abigail said. "What a shame."

"But you must certainly come, Boris," the earl said. "And you too, if you will, Miss Seymour. We will decide on our other guests later, my love."

Boris's arm was rigid beneath her hand in that way he had always had at home before ripping up at her. Laura was flushing and looking decidedly uncomfortable. Oh, dear, Abigail thought. Oh, dear. Had her mouth run away with her again?

Her husband was smiling, she saw when she looked up at him. "As you can tell," he was saying to Boris, "we had decided that we would invite you the moment Abby next saw you. And, Miss Seymour, being my wife's closest friend, I am afraid that you must accustom yourself to being a frequent guest in our home. Abby refuses to be without you, and I refuse to disappoint her."

Boris's arm felt more like an arm again. Laura visibly relaxed. Abigail gazed at her husband with renewed respect. He had smoothed over an uncomfortable moment and made it appear as if her words had not been so impulsive after all.

Sir Gerald offered Laura his arm and they began to stroll along the crowded corridor. The earl saw an elderly couple some distance away to whom he wished to pay his respects.

"Are you coming with me, Abby?" he asked. "Or do you wish to stay here with your brother for a few minutes?"

"I shall stay," she said. "Don't let me stop you, Miles." She turned to her brother as he walked away.

"Well, what do you think?" she asked eagerly. "Have I made a good marriage or haven't I?"

"I don't suppose you had really discussed with him the idea of inviting me to dinner the very next time you saw me?" he said.

"But he did not mind," she said. "You are my brother."

"And your friend was mortified too," he said. "Abby!"

"Don't scold," she said. "Don't, Boris. I am so very happy that we can be together occasionally again. You must come to Severn Park with us in the summer and we can all be together again—the four of us. The girls will be ecstatic to see you."

"You see?" he said. "You are at it again. Don't, Abby. Severn may tolerate it now because you are new to him. But he will not enjoy having you organize his life, believe me. But yes." He patted her hand and his expression softened. "I will try to see the girls when they come to you. Two years ago it did not seem that we would ever be together as a family again, did it?"

"Oh, Boris," she said suddenly, her eyes widening. "Guess whom I saw at Lady Trevor's ball last night? Rachel! I swear it. I even spoke with her."

"Ah," he said quietly. "You have seen her, have you?"

"You are not even surprised," she said. "You knew she was here?"

He nodded.

"Boris," she said, "her hair is black and her face was painted."

"Yes," he said. "It would be best if you forgot about her, Ab. I had better be getting back to my seat. The play must be almost ready to start again. Shall I take you to Severn?"

"No," she said. "I shall return to our box. He will be there soon. You will come tomorrow?"

"I will," he said. "But no more invitations without consulting Severn in private first. Promise me?"

"I promise," she said. "If I remember, that is." She smiled brightly at him as he clucked his tongue, opened the door to the box for her to enter, and took himself off back to the pit.

Abigail sat down quietly and watched the people milling about in the boxes opposite. Boris was quite right, she thought. She must learn to curb her tongue, or at least to know what she was about to say before she actually said it. It would not do for Miles to develop a disgust of her and think that she was thoroughly lacking in conduct.

". . . the delectable Miss Meighan if I had a chance," one of the gentlemen from the next box was saying.

Abigail's eyes pricked up at the familiar name. She felt instant guilt at the setdown she had given that young lady earlier in the day. Though, of course, the girl had asked for it.

"He said he was tired of managing females and tired of beautiful females too," another man said with a chuckle.

"He can talk," someone else said indignantly, "when he has the beautiful Jenny to visit every day of his life, and every night too, for that matter. I wouldn't mind being able to afford her."

"She wouldn't have you if you had a king's ransom

to lavish on her," the first voice said, and there was a loud burst of guffaws from the other occupants of the box. "Jenny may be a courtesan, but she likes her men handsome and well-formed and sweet-smelling."

Oh, goodness, Abigail thought, they were talking about someone's mistress. How scandalous. She considered coughing, but decided it would be better to leave the box quietly again to find her husband.

"I suppose it might have been too much to have Miss Meighan as Lady Severn and Jenny as mistress too," the second man said. "A mite exhausting, wouldn't you say?"

There was more laughter as Abigail froze in her seat.

"I wouldn't mind suffering that sort of exhaustion," someone else said. There was a moment of silence. "No. No need for alarm. They are not back yet."

"Anyway," the second speaker's voice said, "you haven't heard the best of it yet. He told Stapleton that he was quite determined to avoid the match. He vowed he would marry the very next plain and dull woman he met. Someone he could take into the country during the summer, get with child, and leave behind him. Someone to fade into the background producing an heir while he was left free for Jenny and her successors. And the very next morning he met just such a woman and kept his vow."

"We had better lower our voices," someone who had not spoken before said. "They are going to be back any minute."

"He chose well," the first voice said. "In addition to everything else, she is also a nobody and inclined to vulgarity, if my Aunt Prendergast is to be believed. Severn is going to regret giving up Miss Meighan yet, the idiot."

Abigail got to her feet and rushed blindly for the door. She yanked it open and collided hard with her husband's chest.

"Abby?" he said. "I did not realize you were alone. I am so very sorry, dear. Your brother has returned to his seat?"

"Yes, he has," she said. "I was just coming to see where you were, Miles. The play is about to resume, and I was sure you would not wish to miss the beginning and perhaps lose the trend of the plot. Though probably you have seen it before and know very well what happens, do you? And Laura and Sir Gerald are not back. I thought I would call to them, for I know very well that Laura will not wish to miss a single moment. Ah, but here they are now. Are you enjoying the play, Laura? I have not had a moment to speak with you since the interval began. Was it not fortunate that we met Boris here? I have been wanting you to meet him for so long, but there has never been a chance. Tomorrow—"

"Abby." Her husband had her by the elbow and was speaking quietly to her. "The play is starting, dear."

She sat down and folded her hands in her lap. She fixed her eyes on the stage and did not move them for the rest of the performance, though she saw not a single action and heard not a single word.

ABIGAIL HAD SENT ALICE to bed. She was not used to having a maid and had no wish to be undressed by one that night, just as if she did not have hands and fingers of her own. And she did not wish to have someone else brush out her hair. She would do it herself.

She sat before her mirror brushing and staring at her reflection. Plain. Dull. Someone to be taken into the country and left there and forgotten about. Someone to be got with child. To bear an heir. To be bred just as the cows and the sheep were bred. Someone to fade into the background. Beautiful, expensive Jenny. A nobody. Vulgar. Plain. Dull.

It was all true. All of it. She had never had any illusions about her looks or her charm. And she had known that there was something strange about the haste of his offer to her. He had admitted that he wished to be married before his mother arrived in town. He had never pretended any personal regard for her.

There was nothing hurtful in what she had heard. She had known it all before.

Except about beautiful, expensive Jenny, that was. He had told her he had no mistress.

Had she thought that her own charms could hold him? Miles, the most beautiful man she had known?

She set her brush down and picked up his pearls from the dressing table. She ran a finger lightly over a few of the smooth beads. Because her mother's pearls were too long and too heavy to be worn with an evening gown. A gift. Something to keep his dull wife satisfied and quiet. Something to make her feel of value. Like the diamonds. A wedding present. Something to give her the illusion of beauty.

She turned suddenly and hurled the necklace with all her strength across the room. And then she scurried after it and picked it up and examined it. By some miracle, the string had not broken and none of the pearls had been damaged. She closed her hand over them.

She would wager they were real, she had said, and he had laughed. Money, of course, was something the Earl of Severn had in great abundance.

He could afford the beautiful Jenny.

She sat down heavily on the stool again, set the

pearls down, and braided her hair with hasty and determined fingers.

She finished only just in time. There was a tap on her dressing-room door, and her husband came in without waiting for her answer.

"Are you coming to bed?" he asked with a smile. "I thought perhaps you had fallen asleep in here."

"No," she said.

"Oh, Abby," he said, "you have braided your hair."

"It is easier to comb in the morning," she said.

"What's the matter?" he asked, coming up behind her and setting his hands on her shoulders.

"Nothing," she said.

He smiled. "When you answer in single words, Abby," he said, "there is something very wrong. It has been a tiring day for you, hasn't it? I called on Mama on my way home this afternoon. Some of the old tabbies gave you a rough time?"

She could no longer feel dismay that he had known all evening what she had kept from him herself. "Nothing that I did not give right back again," she said. "Your mother has told you how vulgar I was, doubtless."

He squeezed her shoulders. "If you spoke up for yourself," he said, "then I am with you, Abby. May I ask one thing of you?"

She looked at him in the mirror.

"It is difficult to adjust to the married state, is it not?" he said. "It is hard to stop thinking as an individual and start thinking as a couple. I did not have anything definite in mind for tomorrow evening, though I planned to ask if you wanted to go to Mrs. Drew's soiree. In future shall we discuss our plans together before making them public? I am sure that I will slip up too before much time has passed, and find myself arranging things before I remember to consult you. It is a difficult adjustment."

Abigail raised her chin and stared steadily back at him in the mirror. "Yes," she said. "I am sorry I embarrassed everyone over tomorrow's dinner. I shall try to remember to consult you on all issues, Miles." *I will try to fade into the background.*

He lowered his head and kissed the side of her neck. "I have hurt you?" he said. "Come to bed, Abby. You are tired."

She wanted to go to her own bed. She wanted to be alone. She did not want him to touch her. But of course there was an heir to be begotten.

She hoped as she allowed him to lead her through his dressing room into his bedchamber that she would have a dozen daughters and no sons at all. She hoped she would be quite barren.

"Don't be angry with me," he said after he had blown the candles out and climbed into the bed beside her and taken her into his arms. "We must tell each other, Abby, if there is something about the other we do not quite like, or we will only grow apart and come to resent each other. And I am not really criticizing you. I shall look forward to our dinner party."

"Who is Jenny?" she asked.

He went very still. "Why do you ask?" he said.

"I overheard some men at the theater saying that she is your mistress," she said. "They said she is very beautiful and very expensive."

He swore under his breath. "They used the wrong tense," he said. "She *was* my mistress, Abby, and their description was quite accurate. I settled with her after deciding to marry you and before our wedding. I did not lie to you on our wedding night."

She lay with closed eyes, inhaling deeply.

"Is that what was bothering you?" he asked. "I knew you had something on your mind. Put it from you, Abby. I will be answerable to you for the present and the future, but I cannot answer for the past. And there is nothing in the present that would dishonor you, I swear to you, and will be nothing in the future. Is that all? Do you feel better now?"

"Yes," she said.

She swallowed and lay still. And when he lifted her nightgown and came over on top of her and entered her without any of the usual kisses and caresses, she bit down on her lower lip and stayed still.

And for the first time there was no excitement, no physical response at all to what he did to her. Just a dispassionate observing of his movements.

But no response was needed. Only her womb was needed to receive his seed, not her mind or her emotions. There was really no need at all for a wife to feel excitement or even pleasure while she was being impregnated with her husband's heir.

She resisted the pressure of his arm, which would have drawn her onto her side and against him after he had finished with her, and turned away from him. And she pretended to be asleep when he reached a hand over her shoulder and touched one knuckle softly to her cheek.

"Good night, Abby," he whispered.

She lay awake for a whole hour after his breathing told her that he was asleep. She lay awake until her head spun from so much thinking and every bone in her body ached from lying so still and so tense.

She turned finally and looked at him in the near-darkness, his face relaxed and handsome in sleep, one lock of dark hair fallen across his forehead and over his nose.

She inched closer until finally she gave in altogether to temptation and snuggled up against him and butted her head up under his chin until she could rest it on his shoulder.

He grunted in his sleep and adjusted his arm until it was about her, and moved his head until his cheek was more snug against the top of her head.

He was warm and comfortable, and he smelled of the cologne he always wore and of plain masculine goodness.

She would not think anymore. She was too tired to think. She burrowed one hand up between them to spread against his chest.

And finally she slept.

11

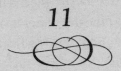

"SHALL I SEE TO INVITING MY MOTHER and Pru and Connie?" the Earl of Severn asked his wife at the breakfast table the next morning. "I'll ask Darlington too, if you don't mind, to even the numbers a little more. He is a friend of Connie's."

"Yes," Abigail said. "Do that, Miles."

"Would you like to ask the Beauchamps and the Chartleighs?" he asked. "It is rather short notice, but perhaps they will be free to come. And you like them, don't you?"

"Yes," she said. "I will send the invitations immediately after breakfast."

He looked at her, but she had no more to say. After a minute of silence he set his napkin beside his plate and rose to his feet.

"Will I see you at luncheon?" he asked. "Would you like to visit the Tower this afternoon?"

"No," she said. "I have to be busy."

He set a hand on her shoulder as he passed. "I shall see you later this afternoon, then," he said.

"Yes." She balanced her knife on her forefinger and spun it. It clattered to the floor after the door had closed behind her husband.

So he did not care for her, she thought with none of the bleak despondency of the night before. She was plain and dull, and she had turned out to be unexpectedly and unpleasantly talkative. She had been married because he did not want to be bothered with a beautiful and vibrant woman in his life and because he needed an heir. She was to be impregnated during the spring and then taken to Severn Park and left there forever after.

So. Was there anything so very dreadful in all that? She had known from the start that she was being married for convenience, and heaven knew that her mirror had been telling her for twenty-four years that she was no beauty. She had married him for convenience too. She had married him to avoid destitution. It was as simple as that. It was quite irrelevant that he had compelling blue eyes and a knee-weakening dimple and all those other attributes that she would not depress herself by enumerating at the moment. She probably would have married him if he had looked like a frog.

She would enjoy being left alone at Severn Park. She would have Bea and Clara with her, and perhaps Boris would be less reluctant to come there for extended visits if he knew she was alone. It would be quite like old times, except that Papa would not be there. It would be like heaven.

And if she did her duty properly and was a nice, obedient, uncomplicated wife, then there would be a baby to bring up too—a daughter, she fervently hoped. If it were a girl, of course, he would doubtless come back to try again. But she would not think of that.

She got up resolutely from the breakfast table. There were things to be done. She was not going to sit around all day brooding. And she was no longer going to care what anyone said about her, including Miles Ripley, the Earl of Severn. He did not like her anyway, so why try to please him? It was a pleasant, liberating thought.

She knew the first thing she was going to do—after writing invitations to the Chartleighs and the Beauchamps, that was. She would be punishing herself as well as him, of course, but she was going to do it anyway.

All her plans were thrown somewhat awry when a footman in the hallway bowed to her and handed her a note that had just been delivered. She took it into the morning room, where she planned to write the invitations.

"Come for a stroll with me this afternoon," Rachel

had written. "Meet me in St. James's Park at two o'clock. Your affectionate stepmother, R. Harper."

Abigail folded the note and tapped it on her palm. She did not want to see Rachel again. She really did not. She had been fond of her and sorry for her unhappiness and horrified by the rough treatment she had had at Papa's hands. She had been bewildered and upset and angry when Rachel had run away and left her daughters to the mercy of her drunken and frequently violent father. She wanted to leave it at that. She did not feel in any mood to reopen an old story or aggravate old wounds. She did not want to discover that perhaps Rachel was still a woman to be pitied.

But there were the girls and Rachel's ominous suggestion that she would like to see them again and perhaps even have them to live with her.

She must go, she thought with a sigh. In the park? In such a very public setting? But of course, she did not care what anyone thought of her any longer. She would go.

An hour later Abigail had written and sent off the invitations, changed into a new carriage dress, which had been delivered the day before, and was on her way to Oxford Street. There were a few hairdressers to choose among. She knew none of them but picked one at random. And she emerged one hour after that with short curly hair beneath her bonnet, and knees that felt turned to jelly and a stomach that felt as if it wished to relieve itself of her breakfast.

She went home and spent the short remainder of the morning giving Victor his first reading lesson. It was not going to be easy, she discovered. It was not as simple as opening a book on his lap and pointing out to him what each word was. How did one teach a child to read? Victor knew all about A and B and C by the time she sent him back to the kitchen for his luncheon, but she was not at all sure that he realized the significance of those letters or the depressing fact that there were twenty-three others to grow familiar with.

RACHEL HAD CHOSEN the time with care, Abigail discovered later. The morning walkers and riders had left long before, while most of the afternoon strollers had not yet arrived. The park was almost deserted.

"Abigail," Mrs. Harper said, "I knew you would come." She linked her arm through Abigail's. "Have you cut your hair? I thought you never would. Severn wishes you to be fashionable, does he? I can understand that a woman would wish to please Severn. You did well for yourself. How did you do it?" She laughed in that low, seductive way that Abigail found unfamiliar and thoroughly unpleasant.

"Rachel," she said, "why did you leave home? I could never quite understand."

"Why?" The other laughed. "He probably would have ended up killing me if I stayed. He had given me bruises enough. I chose life, Abigail. Is that so incomprehensible?"

"But you left the children behind," Abigail said. "They were little more than babies. How could you have left them to Papa?"

"It was not easy." The other woman shrugged. "But I knew you would look after them, Abigail. You were fond of them, and you always had a way with your father. He never laid a violent hand on you, did he? And Boris was growing up. I thought he would protect them."

"You were their mother," Abigail said. "And you did not leave alone, Rachel."

"John Marchmont?" Rachel laughed. "He was just my means of getting away. You cannot know how helpless I felt, a woman alone, and how good it was to have someone who appreciated me. I was still only twenty-four—your age now. Don't judge me. Life became intolerable and I had only two alternatives—to take my own life or to run away. I ran."

"Bea and Clara did not have those alternatives," Abigail said. She noticed that even in the daylight her stepmother wore cosmetics. She turned her head to look away. Rachel had been a beautiful girl when she married Papa.

"Well." The other woman's manner became brisker. "The past can be amended yet. I have been thinking of writing to Aunt Edwina and taking the stage down to Bath. Though I daresay I could persuade Sorenson to take me down in his carriage. Do you think it would be a good idea to go, Abby? Would they like to see their mother again?"

Abigail swallowed. "What do you do in London, Rachel?" she asked. "Is it true that you run a gambling hell? Are you Lord Sorenson's mistress?"

Mrs. Harper laughed. "I have a respectable home in a respectable district," she said. "I like to entertain. And you know what gentlemen are. They like to play cards, and they cannot enjoy a game unless they are playing deep. And I am no one's mistress except my own. Do you think I would allow any other man to have power over me as your father did? I learned my lesson many years ago, Abigail. One should use gentlemen for one's pleasure and convenience and discard them without hesitation when they become possessive, as they always do. You would do well to remember that, though of course you were never one to allow yourself to be bullied. I always admired that in you."

"I'll take the girls," Abigail said quietly. "I have Severn Park to offer them, Rachel, and all my time and devotion. I can offer them proper schooling and respectable marriages when they grow up. I am sure Miles will give them suitable dowries. They can be happy. They were attached to me emotionally, you know, before I was forced to send them away to your aunt's. And I was happy with them. We will recapture that happiness."

"And what about my happiness?" Mrs. Harper asked. "Don't you think I deserve some, Abigail? I bore them, after all. I suffered all the discomfort for nine months with each one of them and all the pain at the end of it. For what? For nothing? I have a hankering to see them again."

"Rachel." Abigail stopped walking and disengaged her arm from her stepmother's. "You do not need my permission to go down to Bath. As you say, they are your children, and I have no legal custody of them. Why have you arranged this meeting? What do you want of me?"

Mrs. Harper laughed. "That is something else I always admired about you, Abigail," she said. "You always liked everything out in the open. Very well, then. My life is at a crossroads. I am thirty years old—a restless age. A little frightening. What do I do? Do I recover my children and settle down to a cozy domestic life with them? Or do I travel to other lands and taste all the delights that the world has to offer before I really am too old?"

Abigail said nothing. She continued to look steadily but warily at the other.

"But I fool myself to believe that there is a choice," her stepmother said with a shrug. "There is none. How could a woman like me afford a year or so on the Continent? One does not earn enough from . . . the means I have of earning a living."

"Is that it, then?" Abigail asked. "If I can provide you with the means to go, you will do so and leave the children to me?"

Mrs. Harper shrugged. "I did not suggest it," she said. "Could my daughters mean that much to you, Abigail?"

"Exactly how much are we talking about?" Abigail asked.

"I suppose five thousand would be just sufficient," Mrs. Harper said. She laughed. "It is always so delightful to dream, is it not? Shall we walk on?"

"I shall get it for you," Abigail said recklessly. "By next week? One week from today? Will that be soon enough?"

"Abigail!" Mrs. Harper laughed again. "You cannot be serious."

"You know I am," Abigail said. "Give me your address, Rachel. I shall bring the money there within the week. You will promise to go as soon as you have it?"

"How could I resist?" the other said. "But how naughty of you to have me dreaming like this. Where would you come by five thousand pounds? You surely cannot have Severn so firmly wrapped about your finger, can you? But you always had a way with you. I always marveled that your father would do what you told him even when he was in one of his worst rages."

"Give me your direction," Abigail said.

"I don't think Severn would be delighted to have you seen entering my house," Mrs. Harper said.

"No one will see me," Abigail said. "Your direction, Rachel."

Mrs. Harper shrugged. "You really mean it, don't you?" she said. "Very well, then, Abigail. But remember that this was all your idea."

"Yes," Abigail said. "I think it is a good bargain, Rachel."

THE EARL OF SEVERN ARRIVED home early, though a group of his acquaintances had tried to persuade him to attend the races with them. He wanted to see Abigail and make his peace with her.

The night before had been something of a disaster,

and she had still been cross with him that morning. She had said scarcely a word at breakfast.

Being married was not easy, he was discovering. Abigail was impetuous—endearingly so, but she could embarrass other people as she had the evening before, when she had decided so obviously on the spur of the moment to invite everyone for dinner.

He had tried to handle the matter tactfully. He thought he had done so, but his mild reproof had left her tight-lipped and snappy. Of course, he might have known that it would be best to allow that occasion to pass by and have his talk with her the next time. He had known perfectly well that she had had a rough afternoon.

He had not known, of course, what she had over-heard about Jenny. Damnation to Philby and his crew in the next box. Could they not have kept their infernal mouths shut until they were well away from the the-ater? What had they said about him and Jenny, any-way, apart from the fact that she was his mistress and lovely and expensive?

He had a great deal to learn about women and mar-riage, it seemed. He had thought the matter at an end as soon as his explanation had been made, and had proceeded with what he had been looking forward to all evening, though he had eliminated the preliminar-ies, knowing that she was tired. But she had lain as still as a board beneath him and had turned away from him as soon as it was over.

Hell and damnation, he thought as he handed his hat and cane to his butler and took the stairs two at a time. Hadn't he married Abigail deliberately so that he would not have to worry about tiptoeing about her feelings? So that he would not feel that he had lost control of his own life?

Of course, he thought, he had woken in the night to find her curled up against him in her usual kittenlike position.

"Abby," he said after tapping on the door of her sitting room and letting himself in. "I have come home to have tea with you. I'm glad you are not out. *Abby!*"

She set her book aside and rose to her feet, her cheeks flaming.

"Oh, Lord," he said with a groan. "What have you done?"

"I have had it cut," she said in that curt little voice she had used the night before and at the breakfast table, "because I wanted to."

He crossed the room and took her hands in his. They were quite cold.

"To punish me for Jenny?" he said. "Is that why?"

"What nonsense," she said.

He held her hands and looked closely at the cropped curls and the flushed, wide-eyed face beneath.

"It was to punish me for Jenny," he said, smiling at her slowly. "Because I have given you only one command since our wedding and you had no choice over which one to disobey. Abby! You look like a pixie. And you have failed miserably, dear. It looks, very, very pretty."

And she looked startlingly pretty too.

"What a bouncer," she said, pulling her hands from his. "You need not feel obligated to pay me compliments, Miles. I am glad you came home. I wished to talk with you."

"That sounds serious," he said. "Will you ring for tea? Connie and Pru will come tonight, by the way, though Pru is very apprehensive about being seen puffed out with her triplets. Mother had another engagement. Have you heard from the Chartleighs and the Beauchamps? Are they coming?"

"Yes," she said, crossing the room to pull the bell rope.

The earl watched her with some appreciation. She looked altogether daintier and prettier with the new haircut. He felt an unexpected stab of desire for her.

"Come and sit down," he said, gesturing to a settee, "and tell me what is so important."

She seated herself straight-backed on a chair and folded her hands in her lap. The earl sat down alone on the settee.

"It is about money," she said abruptly, and flushed again.

"I have been meaning to talk to you about it myself," he said. "I am sorry you have had the embarrassment of having to broach the matter to me, Abby. I cannot expect you to have to refer all bills to me, no matter how small and petty, can I? I shall settle a quarterly allowance on you so that you may feel more independent. All your larger bills, of course, you may have sent directly to me. I want you to have pretty clothes and bonnets and such. You must not feel constrained."

"How much?" she asked.

"How much quarterly?" he said, his eyebrows raised. "I do not have experience with such matters. How does a thousand pounds a quarter sound?"

She thought for a moment. "Fifteen hundred would sound better," she said. "And could you pay it yearly, in advance?"

He looked at her closely. Her clasped hands, which looked relaxed enough, were white-knuckled.

"You want me to give you six thousand pounds now?" he said.

"And then you would not have to worry about me for a whole year," she said. "You can afford that much, can't you?"

"Abby," he said, "do you have a special need of the moment that I can help you with? A debt?"

"No," she said, and licked her lips. "Yes. Something to do with the girls. Something I wish to . . . to buy for them before they come from Bath. They have never had a great deal, and in the past two years life has been dreary for them. I want them to have a happy life from now on. I want to take care of them. I . . ."

"What is it that you wish to buy them?" he asked. "Can it be a gift from both of us? I am their new brother-in-law, after all. You do not need to spend all of your own money."

"No," she said. "It is nothing. Nothing that they . . . Nothing that you . . . Ah, here is the tea. I hope there are some scones again. I am starved. Did I tell you that I was going to teach Victor to read, Miles? The little servant boy, that is. I spent a whole hour with him this morning, only to discover that I do not know at all how to teach someone to read. It is not easy. I shall have to ask Laura how it is done. I think Victor must have thought that I was a little crazy. And perhaps he is right. I have been meaning to ask you—may we take him into the country with us when we go? He is rather pale and puny. I am sure the country air and a little more of the outdoors would help him greatly. He can even—"

"Abby," he said. "Yes. I think it a very good idea. And it is typical of you to have thought of it. But we will need a whole cavalcade of carriages to take everyone when it comes time for us to leave. How have you spent your day apart from having your hair shorn? Tell me about it."

She launched into a tale of having her hair cut and wandering up and down Oxford Street afterward and running into an old acquaintance of hers—companion to a friend of Mrs. Gill's—and making arrangements to go walking to St. James's Park with her in the afternoon. With the companion, that was, not with the friend of Mrs. Gill. There followed an account of that stroll and every strange and eccentric character they had passed on the paths.

What was it? the earl wondered, listening to her rapid speech, watching her pretty, mobile face, and sipping on his tea. What was it that had set her at a distance from him? Was it just Jenny? Was he going to have to have patience and give her time to realize that Jenny was no longer a part of his life? Or was there something else?

Why did she have a sudden need of six thousand pounds? It was an enormous sum for a woman who a few days before had been a former lady's companion facing destitution. What sort of a gift for her half-sisters did she have in mind? And why could she not share the idea with him?

"Oh, Miles," she said suddenly, looking up from pouring him a second cup of tea. "I don't suppose there is a vacant steward's position or bailiff's position on one of your estates, is there? Or I don't suppose you have felt the need of a secretary?"

"No to all three," he said, looking into large and anxious gray eyes as she crossed the room with his cup and saucer. "Did you meet a beggar in St. James's Park, Abby? Or a destitute duke on Oxford Street? Or was it the person who cut your hair?"

"You are laughing at me," she said.

"Forgive me." He smiled at her. "I was teasing you. Who needs a job?"

"Boris," she said. She sat down on the edge of her chair again and leaned toward him. "Did you notice how thin he is, Miles? He used not to be so thin. We paid off as many of Papa's debts as we could after we had sold the house and all the furnishings. But there are still some, and Boris swears he is going to pay them all. I thought it would be easier for him if he had regular employment."

"Abby," the earl said gently, "from my brief meeting with him last evening, I had the impression that your brother is a proud young man."

"But if the idea came from you," she said. "If you could plead with him to help you out of a nasty situation. If it seemed that I had not spoken to you at all about him. If it could seem that he was doing you a favor instead of the other way around." She sat back suddenly and lifted her cup so jerkily to her lips that she spilled some tea into the saucer. "I am asking too much, am I not? I am too demanding. I have not been married to you for a week yet. I am sorry."

"It is not that." He set his cup and saucer down on a side table and got to his feet. "I just think your brother would not accept charity, Abby. And he would see through any of those schemes you suggest in a moment. I don't imagine he is defective in understanding, is he?"

"No," she said. "It was rather stupid of me, was it not?"

He took the saucer from her hand and set it on the tray. He held out a hand for one of hers and drew her to her feet.

"Concerned and loving of you," he said. "Why did your father have so many debts?"

She stared at him. "He was sick," she said. "For several years. There were medicines and other things."

"It's none of my business," he said, seeing her discomposure. "Leave the matter of your brother with me, will you, Abby? I shall see if there is some way I can help him without his knowing it. It will have to be a devious scheme, I'm afraid. He will not accept your six thousand, by the way."

She swallowed awkwardly. "I know," she said.

He smiled at her. "It really is very pretty, you know," he said, "your hair."

"Oh, don't mention it," she said, "or I shall start to bawl."

He laughed. "Abby," he said, "did you give yourself even a moment to consider?"

"I planned it," she said, "for all of three hours. It was not an impulsive thing at all."

He laughed again and drew her into his arms. "I like it," he said. "Promise me that you will not braid it tonight."

She giggled a little nervously.

He lowered his head and kissed her, opening his mouth over hers and rubbing the tip of his tongue across the seam of her lips until she drew back her head and looked up at him a little uncertainly.

He kissed her again more briefly and firmly, and reluctantly let her go. He did not want to ruin a very precarious peace between them by committing the *faux pas* of trying to make love to her during the day.

Although at that particular moment he would have liked nothing better.

12

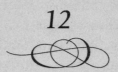

*Y*OU AREN'T FOXED, ARE YOU, GER?" The Earl of Severn stepped past his friend's manservant into his somewhat untidy parlor. "This early in the day?"

"Foxed?" Sir Gerald Stapleton said indignantly and nasally. "I have the devil of a cold and have been sprawled here all day feeling sorry for myself. Have a seat."

"Thank you," the earl said, seating himself as his friend blew his nose loudly. "I thought perhaps you had taken yourself out of the country. Haven't seen you for almost three days."

"That is hardly surprising," Sir Gerald said, "when you have been tied to your wife's apron strings all that time."

"Jealousy, jealousy," Lord Severn said. "You should set your face over a bowl of steaming water, Ger, and throw a towel over your head."

"I've tried it," the other said. "It doesn't work. It did once when I had a chill and went to Priss. But this time it doesn't."

The earl grinned. "Still missing her?" he said. "Is that why you are like a bear at a stake?"

"Talking about getting foxed," Sir Gerald said, "there are no drinks in here. I'll ring." He lurched to his feet.

"Not on my account," the earl said, raising a hand. "I can't stay, Ger. I am just a messenger boy this afternoon. Abby wants you to join us in a picnic to Richmond. Miss Seymour will be there too, of course. You had better come. Perhaps she will take your mind off Prissy." He grinned.

"Absolutely and definitely no," the other said irritably. "You might as well have married Frances Meighan, Miles. This wife has you just as firmly in tow. And Frances would have been prettier to look at." He frowned at the fraying tassel that he had just pulled.

"Careful," the earl said.

"And this one is like to be many times more expensive," Sir Gerald said. "You need to take her in hand from the start, Miles, before you find that it is too . . . Oof!" His shoulder glanced off the mantel and he went crashing and sprawling across the hearth and among the fire irons. He pushed himself up into a sitting position and felt the left side of his jaw gingerly. "What the devil was that for?"

The Earl of Severn stood over him, fists clenched at his sides. "You know very well what it was for," he said through his teeth. "You were speaking of my wife, Gerald."

"So she is going to destroy our friendship too, is she?" Sir Gerald said, flexing his jaw and wincing. "I hope you haven't broken it, Miles. How am I supposed to explain the bruise?"

The earl reached down a hand to help him to his feet. "If it is the new clothes and the diamonds and the pearls that have you fearing for my financial ruin," he said, "they were all my idea, Ger. And the clothes and the jewels I buy my wife are none of your damned business. And neither is her beauty or the amount of time I choose to spend with her. If our friendship is ruined, it will be nothing to do with Abby—or with me either."

"You should not come here quarreling with me when I have a head the size of a hot-air balloon," Sir Gerald said, sinking into his chair again and prodding at his jaw with his fingertips. When the door opened, he directed his manservant to bring the brandy decanter and glasses. "I didn't mean to insult Lady Severn, Miles. I'm sorry. But you yourself said you had chosen her because she was plain and would not intrude into your life. Devil take it, but I feel wretched."

"A word of advice," Lord Severn said. "Don't drink

any brandy, Ger. Your head will explode into the blue yonder just like a burst balloon. What did you mean when you said that Abby would be expensive?"

"Nothing," his friend said. "Forget it."

"What did you mean?"

"Look, Miles," Sir Gerald said, first sniffing and then blowing his nose again, "I felt deuced miserable enough before you decided to practice one of Jackson's best punches on my jaw. Go home to your wife, will you, and leave me alone to die? God, I wish Priss were still in town."

"I'm leaving." The earl got to his feet. "But tell me first what you meant."

"Did you know she was at Mrs. Harper's yesterday?" Sir Gerald asked.

"At Mrs. Harper's?" The earl frowned.

"Fox saw her there," Sir Gerald said. "Sudden wealth must have gone to her head, Miles. She will gamble your fortune away if you don't be careful. You will be fortunate if she doesn't start asking you for large sums of money any day. But, sorry." He held up a hand. "You don't need any comment from me, do you? Perhaps it was Lady Severn's double. Or perhaps it was a social call. Maybe Mrs. Harper is her maiden aunt or something—though she would not be a *maiden* aunt, would she? Who knows? It's none of my business. But Fox was sniggering over it. And you must know that

Lady Severn's reputation does not stand on very firm ground as it is."

"There will be a good explanation," Lord Severn said quietly. "Abby's brother has been doing some gambling, I gather. Abby is probably trying to save him from the sharks. I'm on my way. Try that steaming bowl again, Ger. And leave the brandy alone. You won't come to Richmond, then?"

"Oh, yes, I'll come," Sir Gerald said irritably. "You are my friend, Miles, and I had better start liking your wife, hadn't I? I think you are growing fond of her."

"Abby will be happy," the earl said with a grin. "Though if she could just see beyond the end of her nose, she would have noticed a few evenings ago that her brother and Miss Seymour were exchanging more than a few appreciative glances. You may have competition for the fair little redhead, Ger."

Sir Gerald Stapleton blew his nose loudly as his friend laughed and let himself out of the room.

His smile faded as he ran down the stairs and walked out onto the street. Abby at Mrs. Harper's? And not a mention to him of having been there, though she had given him an exhaustive account during dinner the evening before and during their drive to the opera of all she had done during the day.

And Abby had asked him for six thousand pounds, a year's allowance in advance.

For her brother? Had his guess been right? Or was she too gambling to try to pay off the family debts? It would be quite like her to try it and lose six thousand pounds at a sitting. Though of course, if she had asked him for the money three days before and called on Mrs. Harper yesterday, then she might have made more than one visit to the tables.

Her father must have been a gambler too. He had guessed that several days before. Was it a family weakness?

He knew so little about his wife, he thought in some frustration. In some ways it was almost impossible to believe that they had been married for only a week. In other ways it seemed that they were still total strangers, though they had been together and on intimate terms physically for a week.

And of course a week had been quite a long-enough time in which to fall in love.

ABIGAIL HAD had a quite happy day. She had spent part of the morning planning her picnic in Richmond and part with her husband on Bond Street, choosing a sapphire-and-diamond ring as a gift for their first anniversary.

"One week," he had explained to her when she had

looked at him in incomprehension. "We have been married for a week, Abby. Had you forgotten?"

And he had insisted on buying her the ring though she had assured him that it was a quite pointless extravagance and had reminded him that he had already given her a diamond necklace and her pearls.

"But I cannot let our first anniversary go by unheralded," he had said with a smile.

Even after a week his smile was still turning her weak at the knees. And she still wished that he had brown or hazel eyes.

It had ended up with her buying him a matching sapphire-and-diamond pin.

"A combined wedding and anniversary gift," she had told him.

And so a considerable dent had been made in her remaining thousand pounds, all that she had to last her for a year—or fifty-one weeks, to be exact.

She had begun the afternoon calling upon Lady Beauchamp and strolling with her in the park, having sent her husband on his way to invite Sir Gerald Stapleton to the picnic. If she threw them together often enough, perhaps he and Laura would be betrothed even before the summer came. They were very obviously perfect for each other.

In the park, they had met Lord and Lady Chartleigh and their young son, who was racing along ahead of them when he was not falling flat on the grass. The four adults strolled together for a while.

The Chartleighs must have been very young when they married, Abigail guessed. The earl in particular looked far too young to be a father. And yet despite his extreme quietness and his wife's vivacity, there was clearly a strong bond of affection between them.

Perhaps there was hope for her, she thought. And yet the Countess of Chartleigh was very pretty. And perhaps the earl had not expected her to be quiet and to disappear into the background of his life. Perhaps he had loved her and her vivacity when he married her.

But she would not think of her problems, she had decided. Soon Rachel would be on her way to the Continent, and soon Boris would be out of his difficulties. Miles had promised to help him, and she had had an idea of how it might be done so that Boris would never know that he had been helped. By the time spring turned to summer, she would be at Severn Park with her sisters and perhaps she would be with child too. Certainly Miles must be very eager for it to happen without delay. In the week of their marriage he had coupled with her twice each night except for that one night when she had been upset at learning the brutal truth of their marriage.

She had accepted that truth. And really it was not so very dreadful. He had married her and saved her from a nasty situation, and he had not been unkind since except when he had reprimanded her over their dinner party. If she was to be taken to Severn Park and left there when he returned to town, well, then, so be it. She would think of that when the time came.

"I have been married for longer than a year," Lady Beauchamp was telling her, "and I wept at the end of each month for eleven months before the miracle happened. I am afraid I have been a sore trial to Roger, Lady Severn. He has been foolishly assuring me that it will not wreck his life to remain childless and that of course he does not regret marrying me. And I can't tell you how envious I have been of Georgie and Ralph, who had to wait no time at all after their marriage. But it has been worth the wait. The sun seems a little brighter each day now that I know I have new life inside me." She squeezed Abigail's arm. "You will know what I mean soon enough."

"I hope so," Abigail said.

"I am afraid you will find me a dreadful bore this spring," her friend said contritely. "I can think of nothing but babies, Lady Severn. Roger laughs at the fact that in private I talk of nothing else, whereas in public I become very flustered if it is so much as mentioned."

"I believe I would feel compelled to stand up and make the announcement myself at the very next social function I attended after finding out," Abigail said, "whether it was a ball or the theater."

Lady Beauchamp looked startled, and laughed. "You sound just like Georgie," she said. "I do hope I have a son this first time, though Roger laughs at me when I say that, and becomes quite outrageous." She laughed again. "He says he will tolerate daughters for the first six times, provided I get serious the seventh time and present him with his heir. I used to dislike Roger quite intensely, you know, when we were first acquainted, because he used to delight in outraging me. He still does."

Abigail was feeling quite cheerful by the time she arrived home. The day had been pleasant, and there was another ball to attend that evening—her second.

But there was a note awaiting her. Her heart sank as she took it from the butler's hand and made her way straight toward her sitting room. Everything had been settled the day before. What else could Rachel possibly want?

It seemed that there was a further problem. Abigail was to call at Rachel's house the following day.

But she did not wish to go. Even though the house was in a respectable neighborhood, there was something about it that made her uneasy. And she had not gone unseen the day before. Although Rachel had taken her directly to an office, they had passed the open door of a salon, and there had been a group of gentlemen and one lady inside. One of them had called to Rachel as she passed.

There could be only one reason for Rachel's wishing to see her again. She wanted more money. Abigail had feared it, but hoped that her stepmother was still basically decent. It seemed that perhaps she was not.

But she had very little more money to give.

And even if she had plenty, she would not give it, she decided. She would not give in to perpetual blackmail. If Rachel was not content with the five thousand pounds, well, then, they would have to see. Abigail did not believe that her stepmother had any real intention of taking her daughters into her own home.

She folded the letter hastily and slid it beneath a cushion as there was a tap on the door and her husband came inside.

"Am I in time for tea?" he asked. "Hello, Abby."

She smiled at him and her stomach lurched in the way that was becoming quite customary with her. His dark hair was tousled from the outdoors and his hat.

"I was about to ring," she said.

"Gerald will come to your picnic," he said. "I'm afraid he was like a lion in a cage this afternoon. He has a bad cold."

"I should call on him and take him some powders," she said, "and make sure that he stays in bed and drinks plenty of hot lemon. And I should get him to set his head beneath a towel and over a bowl of steaming water. That would do wonders for him."

He laughed. "You would too, wouldn't you?" he said. "You would march into a bachelor's rooms close to St. James's, rout the manservant, and proceed to take charge."

She looked at him warily. "I had the charge of my father and brother and two sisters for several years," she said. "I am afraid I had to become a managing female, Miles, or we might not have survived. As it was, Papa did not. I suppose Sir Gerald is sitting in a stuffy room sniffing and running a fever and drinking liquor."

"I told him about the bowl and towel," he said. "I tell you what, Abby. If I have caught the chill from him, you may coddle me to your heart's content and I shall not utter a word of complaint."

"You are laughing at me," she said. "I know you did not want a managing wife, Miles. I should have confessed during the first day and told you what I was really like."

She had sat on the settee. He came to sit beside her, and took her hand in his.

"Tell me about your life at home," he said. "You really did play mother, didn't you? For how long? When did your stepmother die?"

It struck her suddenly that she could tell him the

truth. Nothing could be simpler. She could tell him everything, even about the five thousand pounds, and they could go together to Rachel's the next day. He would help her. He would frighten Rachel off if she were planning further blackmail.

But if she told the truth, he would know what a ramshackle family she came from. He would know that Rachel had run off with another man, leaving behind her two daughters, because she was being beaten and abused at home. He would know that her father had been a drunken, brutal man and a heavy gambler, so that they had all lived more by their wits than by honest money for the last few years. He would know that Mrs. Harper, gambling hell owner and courtesan, was her stepmother.

And he would know that the marriage he had made was even more of a disaster than he already realized. She would see that knowledge in his face.

But she was growing to love that face and the person to whom it belonged.

"Six years ago," she said. "Clara was two and Beatrice four. Boris was sixteen."

"And you eighteen," he said. "And so at a time when there should have been parties and balls for you and suitors, there was an ailing and grieving father to tend to and two small children to bring up. What was wrong with your father?"

"He had stomach problems," she said vaguely. "He was bedridden for the last year."

"He had a nurse?" he asked.

She smiled fleetingly. "Me," she said.

He squeezed her hand.

"Your brother," he said. "Did he go to university or want to do so?"

She shook her head. "He wanted passionately to go into the army," she said. "But he could not. Papa . . . Papa needed him at home."

But talking of Boris reminded her. Her face lit up.

"I have thought of how we may help him," she said. "Boris, I mean. You do want to help him too, don't you, Miles, even though he is just my brother and really you scarcely know him at all? But, of course, he is your relative even apart from our connection, isn't he? I wish I could help him myself, but of course I cannot, partly because I do not have the means, and partly because he would not knowingly accept help from a living soul, even me. He is so very proud, you know. And I am afraid that unless he has help soon, he will go to his grave as an old man with Papa's debts unpaid and nothing whatsoever made of his own life."

"Abby," he said, taking her free hand into his and squeezing them both. "Tell me your plan, dear. I confess, I am at my wits' end."

"We must find out where he goes to do his gambling," she said. "I am sure he gambles, though he was never addicted to it at home. Indeed, he had something of an aversion to it. But he is desperate for money now, and a great deal of it too, so I believe he must gamble."

"And then what?" he said.

"You must find someone who cheats," she said. "It might be difficult to find such a person, but there are men who cheat and make a handsome living from doing so, are there not? Would you know how to find such a person, Miles?"

"I daresay it might be done," he said, his lips twitching. "But why?"

"He must be persuaded to allow Boris to win a large sum," she said. "And then Boris will pay off all Papa's debts and perhaps have some left over to begin a decent life on his own account. And he will never know that he does not owe his good fortune to his own efforts and to luck. Don't you think it a splendid idea?"

He looked at her for a long while in silence. "People who play cards regularly can usually spot a cheat without much effort," he said.

"But someone who is cheating to lose?" she said. "Who would ever suspect?"

"I shall have to think about it," he said. "It is an interesting idea, Abby."

She beamed at him. "Do you think so?" she said.

"People usually think my ideas quite shatterbrained, though they always make perfect sense to me."

"Abby," he said, "you have so much love in you. Your family was fortunate indeed to have you to see to their well-being. You have not heard from Bath yet?"

She shook her head. "But it is easy to be generous with someone else's money," she said. "You do not know how much money Boris needs, Miles."

He raised one of her hands to his lips. "You shall tell me some other time," he said. "The sum is quite unimportant. The tray arrived five minutes ago. Are you going to pour?"

"Oh," she said, looking blankly at the tea tray. "I had not noticed."

"You enjoyed yourself, Abby?"

The Earl of Severn turned his head to look down on his wife's tousled curls. She was seated beside him in his carriage, her arm linked through his, their fingers laced together, her head resting against his shoulder. Both of her slippered feet were resting on the seat opposite, an inelegant but quite endearing pose. She was humming tunelessly.

"Mm," she said, and paused in order to yawn. "I love dancing. I have realized that it is the only musical accomplishment that I can boast about in even the most modest of ways. I cannot hold a tune, and my fingers develop a will of their own when I try to marshal them on a keyboard. But I can dance tolerably well."

He laughed and rubbed his cheek against her curls. "What typical feminine accomplishments do you have?" he asked. "What hidden talents have I not discovered yet?"

"Oh, dear," she said, turning her toes out and wiggling them, "I am afraid I have none, Miles. I embroider tolerably well, though the silk has a habit of tangling itself hopelessly just as I am drawing it through the cloth. I have tried knotting, but it seems that only my brain will tie itself into knots. I am tolerably good at watercolors, but I think I must keep my brush too wet, because the colors will keep running down the paper."

"I have married a woman without accomplishments?" he said.

"I am afraid so," she said apologetically. "But I know how to treat chills and headaches and stomachaches and bruises and cuts and bleeding noses. And I know how to put an end to fights and quarrels and tears. And I know how to tell stories without having to have a book open before me. And I know how to—"

"Abby," he said, squeezing her hand, "I believe you, dear. I will have to give you a dozen children so that you can enjoy using your skills."

She turned her face into his shoulder.

I love you, he wanted to tell her as he kissed her curls. *I love you*, he had thought all evening as he had watched her dance with other men and glow with vitality and enjoyment. *I love you*, he had wanted to tell her when he had waltzed with her and she had turned her face up to him and talked without stopping, telling him all the details of her other partners' lives that they had confided to her.

It was absurd. He had known her for a little longer than a week, and he was still fully aware that he knew her scarcely at all. He had married her so that he could have all the advantages of having a wife with none of the inconveniences and obligations that would have come with marrying a socially prominent young lady like Frances.

And yet he found that he had to force himself away from Abigail for a few hours each day. He was becoming quite alarmingly besotted with her.

He closed his eyes for a few moments to gather together his resolution. He had gone home to tea in order to confront her with his knowledge that she had been to Mrs. Harper's the day before. And yet he had said nothing after their conversation had moved to her family and her brother.

He had meant to talk with her about it at dinner before they left for the ball, or in the carriage on the way.

But she had looked so pretty dressed in a gold-colored gown, which had arrived just that day, and with her bouncing curls, and she had been so absurdly excited at the prospect of dancing again that he had not found the right moment to speak.

And now she was tired and happy. She was humming again. He smiled, realizing that her claim to be unmusical was no false modesty. He could not think of the words to begin what he wanted to say.

"Everyone was kind, Miles, don't you think?" she said.

"I think they have all recovered from the shock of knowing that you once earned your own living, yes," he said with a smile. "And I don't believe that any gentlemen ever were displeased with your candid way of speaking, Abby."

"I ought not to have said what I did to Mr. Shelton at supper, ought I?" she said doubtfully. "I should have kept my mouth shut."

"But he was the one who mentioned the embarrassment of being almost as bald as an egg before the age of thirty," he said.

"I merely wanted him to feel better," she said. "But when I told him that I would prefer to see him bald than to see him wear a wig and watch it sail away in the middle of a country dance, I did not realize that Lord Cardigan was wearing a wig. I should have done so.

When one looks closely, or even not so closely for that matter, it is quite obvious that it is not his own hair. It is too perfect and shows no part. But I did not realize until Miss Quail began to titter. I really should have held my peace then, shouldn't I?"

He laughed.

"Cardigan took it as a joke," he said. "He has a good sense of humor."

"I meant it as a joke," she said. "But Miss Quail looked so shocked. How could she have thought I was serious when I asked him if he ties it beneath his chin in a stiff breeze?"

The earl laughed more loudly.

Abigail giggled too. "I really meant it as a joke," she said, "to relieve the discomfort of the moment. But I ought to have buttoned my lips together, oughtn't I?"

He continued to laugh.

13

$\mathcal{H}$E WOULD TALK WITH HER AS SOON
as she came through from her dressing room,
the Earl of Severn decided. He would do it before they
went to bed. There would be no need to make a grand
issue of it—merely a mention that someone had commented on seeing her go into Mrs. Harper's house.

Perhaps she did not know that Mrs. Harper was not
considered quite respectable, he would suggest to her.
Or perhaps she had gone there to try to help her
brother? But of course now that she had thought of a
definite plan of how to release him from the burden of
their father's debts, she would see that there was no
need to return to Mrs. Harper's or any other gambling
hell—ever. That was what he would say to her.

If she claimed that she had been there on her own
account, then he would have to think on the spur of
the moment.

Her plan for her brother would not work, of course.

There were too many factors that made it a quite impracticable scheme. But he had not told her that. She had been so very pleased with her idea. There was, in fact, only one plan that might work, and he was not at all sure of that.

He turned resolutely when he heard the door of her dressing room open, and waited for her to cross his and appear in the open doorway.

But when she did so, he knew that the moment was not right even then. She had the sides of her nightgown grasped in her hands so that her bare feet and ankles showed beneath, and she was waltzing and humming again.

He smiled at her.

"Waltz with me," she said. "The night is young. There is not even a glimmering of dawn yet. But you had better provide the music."

"Abby," he said, laughing, "I thought you would have worn your feet down to the bone already tonight. You did not sit out one set, did you?"

"This is called second wind," she said, coming into his arms and resting one hand on his shoulder. "Dance with me, sir, or you are no gentleman."

He danced and hummed the first waltz tune that came to his mind.

"Are you always this mad?" he asked after a while.

"Am I likely to find myself waltzing at dawn for the rest of my life?"

"At dawn, yes," she said. "Are there some lovely vistas at Severn Park, Miles? Are there hilltops or lakesides where we can dance at sunrise?"

"If not," he said, "I shall have the hills built and the lakes dug."

"And we can leave the sunrise to God," she said. "Why have we stopped?"

"Because I cannot dance without music," he said, "and I cannot hum and talk at the same time."

"Then stop talking," she said.

She was light on her bare feet and soft and warm through the cotton fabric of her nightgown. She was smiling, her face lifted to his, though her eyes were closed.

"Are you happy?" he asked her softly, the music coming to an abrupt halt again.

"Happy?" She opened her eyes and looked up at him, a little dazed. "Yes, I am."

"And so am I," he said, cupping her face with his hands and rubbing his thumbs lightly over her cheeks. "Happy anniversary, Abby."

She smiled and her eyes dropped to his chin and lifted to his again.

He felt a surging of desire for her and knew that the moment for talking had gone for that night. It would have to wait until the morning. He lowered his head and kissed her, coaxing her lips apart with his own and with his tongue, waiting for her to relax and open her mouth before sliding his tongue deep inside and stroking the warm, wet flesh there.

"Is that a common way of kissing?" she asked when he moved his mouth down to her throat.

"Yes, I suppose so," he said. "Do you mind?"

"No," she said. "Oh, no. I would have thought it would be repulsive if anyone had described it to me, but it is not."

He undid the buttons of her nightgown while her head was thrown back and her eyes closed. And he lifted it off her shoulders and slid it down her arms and let it fall to the floor.

"Oh," she said, her head jerking up and her eyes snapping open. "Oh."

"Don't be embarrassed," he said, holding her by the shoulders, looking at her. "You are my wife, Abby. And you are beautiful. And don't," he said firmly, drawing her against him and lowering his mouth to hers as she drew breath to speak, "tell me that that is a bouncer. You are beautiful."

She was not voluptuous. But she was slim and youthfully firm and pleasingly proportioned. She was beautiful. And he was on fire for her.

"I am going to leave the candles burning," he told

her as he moved her back to the bed behind her. "Do you mind?"

"It would be foolish to say yes, wouldn't it?" she said. "What happens happens whether it is dark or light, and you have seen just about all of me there is to see. Of course," she said, flushing suddenly, "I have not seen . . ."

"Me," he said, smiling down at her as he removed first his dressing gown and then his nightshirt. "But now you have, and appear to be still alive and not noticeably suffering from a heart seizure."

"I cared for my father for a year," she said as he lay down beside her and slid an arm beneath her neck. "But I did not know a man could be quite so beautiful, Miles. Except in the pictures of Greek gods and heroes, of course."

He kissed her again, and she opened her mouth eagerly to his tongue, circling it with her own, sucking on it, wrapping her arms up about his shoulders. And he felt her temperature soar with his own.

He explored her with his hands and his fingertips and his mouth, using the expertise of years to arouse her further, to have her twisting and moaning on the bed. And her hands moved over him, at first tentatively exploring his chest and the upper part of his back, at last touching him everywhere with seeking fingers, demanding palms.

"Abby," he said, lowering himself onto her and between her thighs when he felt close to madness. "Abby," he said, lifting her with his hands, steadying her, easing into her. "Abby."

She moved with him, rotating her hips against his hands in rhythm with his thrusts and withdrawals, gasping with him, moaning with him.

"Abby," he said, almost beyond madness at last, unfamiliar with her climax, not sure how close it was, holding back his own by sheer determination.

"Yes." Her voice was a whisper, her body still with tension. "Yes. Yes."

He moved in her.

And he slipped his arms about her and held her tightly as she shouted out his name and jerked against him. He held her tightly as she shuddered beneath him and whispered his name. And then he let go of his control and drove inward, releasing his seed deep in her.

"Abby . . ." he said, resting his cheek against a soft cluster of curls above her ear, letting all his weight down on her trembling body as her arms came up about him, relaxing as he had never before relaxed.

And he slept.

EVERYTHING WAS DIFFERENT, and the world was a wonderful, wonderful place. Abigail was surprised to discover when she passed through her own bedchamber on the way down to breakfast from her dressing room that it was raining outside. But the sun was shining just beyond those clouds, she thought, peering upward through the window and smiling.

She ran lightly down the stairs. She was late. She had overslept despite herself.

"There is no point in sleeping now," she had told her husband after their third loving, when it was already light outside. "We should get up and go for a gallop in the park, Miles. We would have it all to ourselves, I think."

"I think so too," he had said, "but I would prefer to leave it to the birds until a later hour. Much later. Go to sleep, Abby."

And he had hitched up the blankets with one foot, grasped them with one hand, and pulled them up over her. She had been lying on top of him, where he had positioned her for the loving, her legs spread comfortably on either side of his.

She had called him a poor sport, burrowed her head to find the cozy hollow between his shoulder and neck that had become her regular resting place, and fallen promptly asleep.

She did not know how he had got out from beneath her and up from the bed later without waking her, since she had always considered herself a light sleeper, but he had. She had woken on her side, her face on one hand, the blankets bunched untidily about her, her person very naked beneath them. She had blushed for the benefit of the empty room.

And the breakfast room was empty too, she discovered when Alistair opened the doors for her, though the food was still on the sideboard.

"His lordship?" she asked.

"In the study, my lady," he said, and strode smartly across the hallway to open the door for her.

He was standing at the desk looking through his mail. And she was suddenly shy, remembering the night before, when he had looked at her unclothed body and called her beautiful, and when she had believed him. When she had given up the remaining secrets of her body to him and explored the secrets of his. When they had loved and slept and loved and slept and loved and slept through what had remained of the night and on into the dawn.

When she had discovered that there was indeed something beyond the aches and excitement that had always led to disappointment and a nameless dissatisfaction during the first week of her marriage. When she had let go of any inhibitions she had clung to during that week.

When she had lost the last remaining corners of her heart to her husband.

She loved him with all the passion she had not expected ever to be able to focus on any man.

And yet, standing at his desk, dressed as immaculately as usual, looking quite as handsome as ever, he seemed again remote, unknown, not the man who had shared hours of naked passion with her in the bed upstairs a few hours before.

She felt shy.

"Did we stun the cuckoo last night?" he asked her, setting down his letters and turning to smile at her. "I was forced to read my newspaper at the breakfast table, having only it for company."

She hurried into the arms he held out for her and lifted her mouth for his kiss.

"How could you have got out from under me without waking me?" she asked, and felt the blood rush to her face.

"Very slowly," he said, "and to the accompaniment of many muttered grumblings—from you. There are enough invitations here to keep us running for forty-eight hours a day all spring, Abby. I will leave you to choose. Pick the ones you would like to accept."

"Oh," she said, "but I would like to attend everything. How do I know that in attending one event we will not be missing something at another?"

He picked a card from the top of the pile. "Do you fancy a literary evening at Mrs. Roedean's?" he asked.

She pulled a face. "No, not particularly."

He tossed it into the basket beside the desk. "That is how it is done," he said, grinning at her. "Abby, I need to talk with you."

She did not trust his expression. She did not want to be talked to. She wanted to be in love. She wanted to be loved. The night before, he had called her beautiful—not plain, but beautiful. And he had made her feel beautiful in what he had done to her and with her in the next several hours. He had made her feel that he had come into her because it gave him pleasure to do so, because he needed to be in her, not just because he was planting his seed in her. And he had made her feel that a marriage, a love commitment, was beginning, not just a pregnancy so that she could be taken to Severn Park in the summer and left there.

She did not want to talk.

"I don't want to talk," she said warily.

"What?" he said, smiling and reaching out one hand to set flat against her forehead. "You do not want to talk? You must be sickening for something."

She said nothing. She knew him well enough to know that despite the lightness of his tone and his teasing manner, he had something serious to say to her. He was going to send her early to Severn Park? Last night had been an ending, a farewell, instead of a beginning? She had misunderstood in her naïveté.

He took both her hands in his and held them warmly. "Abby," he said, "I don't want you to misinterpret what I am going to say. I have no intention of being a tyrant, dictating what you do and where you go and with whom you associate. You are an adult who has known considerable responsibility in your lifetime. But I do feel a duty to protect you from people and dangers you may not know about."

He knew about Rachel, she thought.

"I have heard mention of the fact that you called on Mrs. Harper the day before yesterday," he said.

"Yes," she said. "I did."

"I suggested to you at Lady Trevor's ball that she is perhaps not a suitable associate," he said.

"Yes," she said. "You did."

"Yet you visited her, Abby?"

"Yes, I did."

He searched her eyes with his own. "Are you able to tell me why?" he asked.

It would be easy. In fact, it was unavoidable. She would tell him everything, and he would be able to advise her on how best to see to it that she would have the bringing up of Bea and Clara. It would be a great load off her mind to confide in him. And he would go with her to Rachel's that afternoon.

But he would know. He would know whom he had loved the night before, whom he had called beautiful.

He would know on whom she had spent five of the six thousand pounds he had placed at her disposal.

She wanted him to love her, to admire her, to respect her.

"I just thought it would be the polite thing to do," she said, "having made her acquaintance at Lady Trevor's."

"It was not done in defiance of me?" He frowned.

"No." She shook her head.

"It was not like the cutting of your hair?" he asked, smiling fleetingly.

"No."

"I thought perhaps it had something to do with your brother," he said. "I thought perhaps you had heard that he was gambling there and had gone to beg Mrs. Harper not to let him play too deep."

"Yes," she said, brightening. "That was exactly it, Miles. I did not like to tell you. But you guessed it for yourself. She was very kind and understanding. She said that she will not allow Boris to play cards there again. She had suspected, of course, because he is so young, that he is not a hardened gambler, and she has no wish to see him go to his ruin or end up in debtor's prison. We had tea together and we were in quite amicable accord by the time I left. She is not near as bad as you think, Miles. She . . ."

He was looking keenly at her. He still held her

hands. And he knew, of course, that she was lying. She wished she could recall her words. She wished she had told the truth or at least simply told him that she could not say why she had been at Rachel's. But it was too late now.

"She was kind," she said lamely.

"I am glad," he said, squeezing her hands again. "I shall see about setting your plan in motion as soon as possible, Abby, and your brother will have no more need to go to Mrs. Harper's or anyone else's. You will not be going there again yourself, then?"

She swallowed. "No," she said. And she felt wretched saying it. It was one thing to lie about a past event. It felt infinitely worse to lie about the future, to assure him that she would not go to Rachel's again when she knew very well that she would be calling there that very afternoon.

"Abby," he said, "you are not in any trouble, are you?"

"Trouble?" she said. "What sort of trouble would I be in?"

"I don't know," he said. "You have not incurred any rash debts and find that you cannot meet them?"

"No, of course not," she said.

"You would tell me if it were so?" he said. "You would not be afraid of me?"

"How silly you are," she said. "Is it because I asked

for all that money in advance? It was just that I want to buy some pretty things for the girls before we go into the country. And I want to buy Christmas gifts this year. There have been no gifts for three years, except what I could make myself. And I am not skilled with my fingers."

"Christmas in April, Abby?" he said.

She smiled lamely at him.

He raised one of her hands to his lips and kissed it. "Don't ever be afraid of me, will you?" he said. "I want a marriage with you, you know, not a master-servant relationship."

"How foolishly you speak," she said. But she gazed into his eyes and had to swallow against a lump in her throat. She wished she could go back—even ten minutes back—so that she could give different replies to his questions.

But to tell the truth? To admit to him who Mrs. Harper was? And who the two children were that he had agreed to allow her to bring up in his own home? And what her father had been?

And who she was? But no, she need never tell that. No living soul knew of that except her.

"I have promised to visit Prudence this morning," she said. "She was kind enough to invite me, even though your mother and Constance are still a little cross with me. Though Constance has been a little mollified by my having my hair cut, since she believes I did it on her advice, and I did not like to disabuse her mind."

"And I agreed to be Thornton's sparring partner at Jackson's this morning," he said. "Will I see you at luncheon?"

"Yes," she said, "but if we don't hurry, we can just walk in to luncheon from here, Miles. I must go."

"Go, then," he said, bending forward to kiss her on the lips and releasing her hands at last. "Shall I dispose of these invitations, or will you see to them later?"

"I shall," she said, turning to the door.

"Shall we spend the afternoon together?" he asked. "The Tower, perhaps?"

"Oh," she said. "I have agreed to go walking with Lady Beauchamp."

She bit her lip as she anticipated his reply.

"Again?" he said, eyebrows raised. "Did you not walk with her the day before yesterday?"

Yes, she had, and had forgotten until the words were on their way out of her mouth. Besides, it was raining and not suitable for walking at all. She hated lying. She would not see Rachel after today, she vowed to herself, and she would never ever lie to Miles again.

"She is becoming a particular friend," she said, hurrying through the door before he could make any further comment.

• • •

"I DID NOT ANTICIPATE that I would have so much trouble with the house," Mrs. Harper said. "It is not easy to go away for a year or longer, Abigail, and make suitable arrangements for one's absence."

Abigail walked to the window of the small cluttered office where she had been entertained on her previous visit to her stepmother. She said nothing.

"The house is rented, of course," Mrs. Harper explained. "Now, you might think that it would be best for me to let it go, but then there is all the problem of what to do with my possessions. Besides, I like the house and the location and would like to know that it will be here on my return. But the owner is demanding a whole year's rent in advance. And of course there are staff to be paid, and I would like to leave the tradition of entertainment I have been at some pains to build in the hands of a manager. Sadly, Abigail, I do not see how I am to go to the Continent after all." She sighed. "But perhaps it is as well. Doubtless the summer spent with my daughters will be more rewarding."

Abigail watched a pair of pedestrians moving slowly down the street, though she did not see them at all.

"How much?" she asked.

Her stepmother laughed. "You have been kind enough already, Abigail," she said. "I could not possibly ask any more of your kindness. It could not be done on less than two thousand pounds, and I would not ask that of you."

Abigail turned from the window. "You are asking," she said. "But the answer is no, Rachel. I was foolish to give in to you the first time. I might have known that the demands would never end, that the girls' future would never be securely established this way. I suppose I did know, but I hoped. I used to like you and feel sorry for you. I thought you were decent, that only Papa's drunkenness and cruelty had driven you to do what you did. Maybe it was so, but no longer. You have become a heartless woman who will use two helpless children—your own daughters—to gain the money and luxury you have craved."

"Abigail!" Her stepmother clasped her hands to her bosom. "How can you possibly say such things? Did I ask for the money you gave me? Have I not just said that I will not ask for more? Am I the heartless one? I think your sudden good fortune has destroyed your ability to feel compassion. You used to be a kind-hearted girl. I was always fond of you."

"I shall speak with Miles," Abigail said. "I am sure he will know what to do to ensure that Beatrice and Clara can grow up with a secure future. I will fight you for them, Rachel. But there will be no more money."

"You have not told him about me?" Mrs. Harper

smiled. "Why, Abigail? Were you ashamed of me and of your connection to me? I suppose you have good reason to be, haven't you? A bridegroom of one week might be somewhat shocked to learn such a thing about his wife's connections. Does he know about your papa?"

Abigail crossed the room to the door. She set her hand on the handle.

"It will not work, Rachel," she said. "I am going to tell him everything. You will have no more power over me. And I don't believe you will find that the girls are a powerful weapon. You abandoned them six years ago, remember?" She turned the handle.

"Does your husband know about you?" Mrs. Harper said.

Abigail froze. "About me?" she said.

Her stepmother laughed. "It would make a quite delicious scandal, would it not?" she said. "Of course, I would imagine that you and I are the only two people in the world who know. And your secret can be safe with me, Abigail."

"What secret?" Abigail had released the handle again. She felt as if she had walked into the middle of a nightmare.

Mrs. Harper laughed again. "Your father told me," she said, "soon after we were married, when he was foxed one night and feeling sorry for himself. I really wondered what I had done, Abigail, marrying into such a family."

"I don't know what you are talking about," Abigail said, but the words sounded lame and foolish even to her ears. And there was a dull buzzing in those ears.

"The *beau monde* would be delighted with the story, I am sure," Mrs. Harper said. "It would keep everyone abuzz for all of a week, I swear. And wouldn't your husband love to find himself at the center of it all!"

Abigail could think of nothing to say.

"Perhaps Severn has two thousand pounds to spare," her stepmother said. "I am sure he would not miss such a trifling sum, and it would be money well spent, would it not, to preserve his good name and that of his new countess?"

Abigail turned to look at her.

"Or perhaps you are fond of him," Mrs. Harper said. "Are you? I could scarcely blame you, I must admit. He could spend a night in my bedchamber anytime he chose. Yes, after a whole week I am sure you must be very fond of him. It would be a shame to lose his favor so soon, would it not? Two thousand pounds, Abigail, in order to keep his caresses for a little while longer? Is it too great a fortune?"

"You are an evil woman," Abigail said. "And after the two thousand pounds are paid, how much will you ask for next?"

"Ah, Abigail," the other said, "I am not greedy. Two thousand and there will be an end of the matter. I have not said anything all these years, have I? And I will not say anything in the future either."

Abigail turned away again and opened the door.

"One week," Mrs. Harper said. "If I have not had the pleasure of your company again in that time, Abigail, you may inform Severn, if you wish, that I shall be calling on him."

Abigail left without a word and without looking back.

14

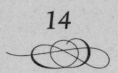

"WELL, GER." THE EARL OF SEVERN WAS grinning at his friend. "Is the red nose a product of your cold or of the punching you were just entertained to? I could not quite believe the evidence of my own eyes when I saw you sparring this morning."

"If Dibbs would not prance around so much, just like a damned dancing master," Sir Gerald Stapleton said, touching his nose gingerly, "one might be able to concentrate on discovering where the next fist is going to land. Deuced unsporting, I call it."

The earl laughed. "You expect him to advertise his strategy?" he said. "Left hook to the jaw on the way? Watch for the right uppercut coming—now?"

"You choose to make fun of me," his friend said as they left Jackson's together and turned in the direction of White's. "We are not all veritable Corinthians like you, Miles."

Lord Severn looked up at the sky. "The sunshine is holding," he said. "I was afraid that after yesterday's rain, today would not be suitable for Abby's picnic. But it should be perfect. You haven't forgotten about it, Ger?"

"No," the other said. "How could I forget, with either you or your wife reminding me about it each day—just like a Greek chorus?"

The earl grinned at him. "Abby has been reminding you too?" he asked. "Have you seen her?"

"Yesterday," Sir Gerald said. "She was walking in the park despite all the puddles and gloom."

"Ah, yes," the earl said. "She was with Lady Beauchamp. They seem to have become fast friends. I can't say I'm sorry. I like the lady. She certainly seems to have tamed old Roger."

"She was alone when I saw her," Sir Gerald said. "Lady Severn, I mean. Had her head down and was wandering along as if her mind were a million miles away."

"Ah," Lord Severn said. "She was not feeling well last evening, though she insisted on going with me to Sefton's concert. She was out of sorts this morning too, though she swore she would be in the best of health and spirits for the picnic. She is planning a de-termined siege on your heart, Ger. I imagine Miss

Seymour's auburn hair will show to advantage in the sunshine, don't you?"

But his bait was not taken, as he had expected it would be. His friend was walking at his side, a frown on his face, looking quite as far away as he had said Abigail was the day before.

"Look, Miles," he said abruptly at last. "It's none of my business. You have told me that before, and I can see it for myself. I think you are fond of her, and I have been determined to get to like her."

"She cannot force you to the altar," the earl said, slapping him on the back. "I won't let her, Ger. I shall help preserve your freedom with my life. Are you reassured?"

"Eh?" Sir Gerald looked at him blankly. "Oh, that. Listen, Miles, I don't know if I should tell you this or not. I might wreck your marriage if I do, or I might wreck it if I don't. And I have to tell you that I resent being put in this position. I didn't get a wink of sleep last night thinking about it. And there was no Priss to go to."

Lord Severn stopped walking. He looked keenly at his friend. "What has happened?" he asked.

"I went walking with her," Sir Gerald said. "It seemed the proper thing to do since for some reason she did not have even a maid with her. And it seemed the civil thing to do, my being your friend and all. And besides, I had decided that I must come to know her better and to like her. Lord." He lifted his hat in order to run his fingers through his curls. "I don't know, Miles. Why are we standing here?"

"Because we are almost at White's," the earl said, "and this sounds like private talk. We had better walk in a different direction, Ger. What happened? You did not try anything with her, did you?" His voice was tight and clipped.

"Eh?" Sir Gerald frowned at him. "You mean did I try to flirt with her? What do you take me for, Miles? She is your wife. Besides, I have Priss. No, actually I don't, do I? Devil take it, I could kill that swain of hers with my bare hands. He had better treat her right, that is all I can say. He had better not once—even once— throw in her face the fact that she was a whore. I'll kill him and carve him into little pieces."

"Good Lord," the earl said impatiently, "when are you going to admit that you are in love with the girl, Ger? But haven't you gone off the point?"

"Devil take it," Sir Gerald said, striding along the pavement in the direction set by the earl. "Lady Severn prattled on for all the world as if someone had told her that she had to do all her talking in the next half-hour and remain silent forever after. And then she put me in the deuce of a dilemma. I shouldn't have even started saying this to you."

"But you did," the earl said dryly. "You had better finish now."

"Look," Sir Gerald said, "I may be far wide of the mark, Miles. There may be a perfectly decent explanation. Perhaps she wants to buy you a special gift without your suspecting, in which case I am spoiling things for her. Or maybe you are closefisted with her and she wants something for herself. I don't know. I never thought of you as miserly, but one never knows what goes on between a man and his wife. You bought her all those clothes and jewels, of course."

"Gerald." The earl stopped walking again. "You are beginning to sound remarkably like Abby. Would you care to get to the point sometime this morning, since there is a picnic to attend this afternoon?"

"I think she must have lost a pile at Mrs. Harper's," Sir Gerald said. "I think she must have, Miles, and is too afraid to come to you. She asked me if she could borrow fifteen hundred pounds. She told me she could not pay it back for a year but would pay me faithfully and in full one year from now. She asked me not to say anything to you. I don't know if she noticed that I avoided promising."

"Fifteen hundred pounds." Lord Severn stared at his friend without moving. "Just like that she asked for that much money? Did she give any reason?"

"I believe she gave about six," Sir Gerald said, "but

by that time her jabbering had become somewhat incomprehensible. There was even something about Christmas presents, if I am not mistaken. I'm not sure if she was referring to last Christmas or next. She has been gambling, Miles, take my word on it. And I don't say that out of spite. It is the only explanation that fits."

"Or her brother has been gambling and losing," the earl said. "To the tune of seven and a half thousand pounds—or more like seven, I suppose. She bought me that pin."

Sir Gerald took off his hat and ran his fingers through his hair again. "She has already had money from you?" he said. "Devil take it, Miles, why did I have to get caught in the middle of this? I feel like a villain telling you, but I can't stand by and let my friend's wife get in deep like this without trying to warn him. She needs taking in hand—and keep your fists at your sides, please. I am in earnest."

"Ger." The earl rubbed at his jaw with one hand. "I need to be alone. I have to think this out. Her brother will be at the picnic this afternoon. Maybe I will talk to him first before tackling Abby. I'll see you later."

"Lord," Sir Gerald said, "I don't know if I have done the right thing. Priss would have known. But she isn't here."

"One thing," Lord Severn said. "Did you agree to give her the money, Ger?"

"I would have," Sir Gerald said, "but she went rushing away before I had given her my answer. There was no apparent reason—there was no one coming, nobody much in sight. But she just turned without a word and went hurrying away, right through the middle of a puddle. I think maybe it was that, Miles. I mean, I think she wants help. Not only needs, but wants, but doesn't quite know where to turn. You haven't been harsh with her, have you?"

"Nothing beyond beating her every morning," the earl said irritably. "I'll see you later, Ger."

And he strode away while his friend watched him out of sight with troubled eyes.

It was the brother. Boris. It had to be, the earl decided. But seven thousand pounds to pay off his gambling debts just so that he could keep playing in the hope of winning enough to pay off their father's debts? They were insane, the pair of them.

But why had she not come to him? He had begged her just the morning before never to be afraid of him. He had told her that it was a marriage he wanted with her. He had not told her that he loved her. It seemed an absurd thing to say after only a week of marriage and such a very short acquaintance. But she must have known that his feelings were involved in their relationship. There had been the night before that with its magical lovemakings.

But she had not come to him. She had gone to Gerald instead. The thought made him angry. If he had her there with him at that moment, he would probably have stopped in the middle of the street to shake her until her head flopped on her neck.

Was that what had made her ill—the need for more money? She had been pale and listless and absent-minded the evening before, and when questioned, had explained that it was the end of her month and she was always ill and out of sorts for a day or two. She had even chosen to sleep in her own room the night before and had given him a restless night as a result. He had kept waking and reaching out to the empty bed for her. He had missed her head butting and burrowing its way into the hollow between his shoulder and neck.

One of his former mistresses had always suffered cramps and headaches during that particular week of her month. Perhaps Abigail was the same, though doubtless a worry over money and an inability to confide in him had made it worse. She had not joined him for breakfast that morning, but had been sitting quietly in her sitting room—doing nothing—when he had gone up to her before leaving the house.

Damnation! he thought. He did not need this. He had married her because he wanted a peaceful life, because he had wanted to preserve his freedom and independence while enjoying all the advantages of being a married man. He did not want to be involved with a woman who had quickly become addicted to gambling or one who had the foolish notion that she could save a brother from ruin by paying off his enormous gambling debts.

If he were wise, he would go home, give her a sound beating, and pack her off to the country—preferably not to Severn Park.

Except that the notion was foolish. For one thing, he had never been able to see the logic of beating one's wife—or one's children, for that matter—merely because one was of superior strength physically. For another, he would not be able to pack Abigail off to the country without going with her. He had been mad enough to fall in love with her.

Besides, marriage was not as he had expected it to be. There was no way of preserving one's freedom and independence once one was married. It was a contradiction in terms. Like it or not, his life was now bound up inextricably with Abigail's, and hers with his. A beating and banishment might momentarily soothe his anger, but it would solve nothing in their marriage.

If Gerald was to be believed, she had not glibly asked for money. Her behavior had suggested that she was quite distraught.

Poor Abby!

His steps hastened in the direction of home.

• • •

ABIGAIL WAS SITTING in an open barouche, twirling a sunshine-yellow parasol above her straw bonnet, smiling brightly at the gentlemen of the party, who rode alongside, and chattering with great animation to Laura, Constance, and Miss Lestock, Constance's friend.

No one looking at her would have guessed quite how wretched she was feeling. Or how embarrassed.

She had walked home from the park the day before, having sent the carriage home earlier, eager to find her husband, bursting to tell him the whole sordid story. Everything. He must take it as he would. Perhaps there would be grounds for divorce in what she told him. Perhaps it was possible for a man to obtain a divorce if a lady—a female—married him under false pretenses. Perhaps she was heading for the worst scandal the decade had known.

But whatever the results were to be, she was going to tell him.

If only he had been there when she had arrived home. If only! The nightmare would now be over. Instead, he had been from home, but his mother and Prudence had been upstairs in the drawing room, awaiting her return.

They had been most gracious. Prudence had hugged her and told her how happy Abigail's visit had made her—and her children—that morning, and Lady Ripley had told her that she and Miles must join her party at Lord Sefton's concert that evening.

"You have conducted yourself with a good deal of spirit in the past week, dear," she had said. "And if it is true that you were forced to work for a living, it is true also that you have done nothing to hide your past, but have held your head high and been quite frank about yourself. And Miles is fond of you. That is clear to see. I am proud of you."

Abigail would have been delighted by the new state of amity with her mother-in-law had it not happened at quite such in inopportune moment.

By the time Miles had arrived home she had been feeling quite literally ill and suffering from verbal paralysis. Instead of rushing into his arms and telling all, as she had planned to do, she had said nothing at all except to make up a whole depressing arsenal of lies about her afternoon with Lady Beauchamp.

She had told him she was ill. And she had used that excuse to spend the night in her own bed, unable to face his lovemaking with such a burden on her conscience. But she had tossed and turned and cried a little all night long.

"I would change places with you in a trice, sir," she said now with a laugh to Lord Darlington, who had been teasing the ladies about the comfort in which they were traveling, "except that I would not look quite the thing on your man's saddle and I would not know quite what to do with my parasol."

"But I could shade my complexion with it, ma'am," he said, laughing back at her.

"Its purpose is not to shade me from the sun," Abigail said, "but to make me look lovely and alluring." She gave the parasol an energetic twirl.

"This is the moment at which you are to bow from the saddle, Darlington, and assure the lady that she needs no parasol to achieve that effect," Sir Gerald Stapleton said.

They all laughed, and Lord Darlington leaned forward to address a remark to Constance.

She could die of embarrassment, Abigail thought, looking at Sir Gerald and feeling her eyes slide away again. She had always had an alarming habit of speaking first and thinking after, but the afternoon before had taken the prize. How could she have asked him for a loan? It was unthinkable that she had done so. He was a virtual stranger to her even if he was Miles's friend. She was going to have to find a moment during the afternoon to explain the episode satisfactorily to him, though she had still not decided exactly what she would say.

She turned her head to look at her husband. It was difficult not to keep staring at him when he looked so splendid on horseback. She smiled when she caught his eye, and dipped the parasol.

Another major embarrassment! How was she going to explain to him in a week or so's time that she was bleeding again? Would he believe that a recent marriage and unaccustomed sexual activity—but would she find the courage to say just that to him?—had sent her system awry? Why, oh, why had she not simply told him that she had the headache the day before?

It was a relief to arrive finally in Richmond Park and to be able to busy herself organizing everyone for a walk along the rolling lawns and among the ancient oaks. She soon had everything arranged to her satisfaction, and Sir Gerald was strolling with Laura, Boris with Miss Lestock, and Lord Darlington with Constance. Abigail slipped her hand through her husband's arm.

"You must be feeling very proud of yourself, Abby," he said. "Everyone is behaving like a puppet on a string—so far."

"Don't laugh at me," she said gaily. "I will take no credit for Constance and Lord Darlington, but I will claim all the glory for Laura and Sir Gerald—you see how compatible they are in height and how easily they converse together? And I shall be observing Miss Lestock and Boris to see if a match can be promoted there. Of course, Boris will have to be more eligible first. Have you found a suitable cheat yet?"

He had been very quiet all through luncheon and had not smiled or conversed a great deal during the journey to Richmond. But he smiled now, and she felt a twinge of relief. She had been wondering if he resented having to attend her picnic.

"I have been interviewing them all morning," he said. "There are a dozen men eager for the job, not to mention the women."

"Are there?" she said, smiling at his teasing. "And have you chosen one?"

"I think so," he said, touching her hand. "I hope that in a couple of days' time, everything will have been settled. And then you will be able to relax and enjoy your new life."

She smiled a little but said nothing.

"Are you feeling better?" he asked.

"Oh, yes," she said brightly. "That indisposition does not last long, you know. One day and I am myself again."

"Shall I call in a physician?" he asked. "Perhaps he could prescribe something that will help you."

"No, thank you," she said, feeling wretched. "I am not always unwell." She hated the lie. She had never ever felt ill as a result of her monthly cycle.

"Well," he said, moving his fingers lightly over hers,

"perhaps we can arrange it by the time the next one is due, Abby, that we will give you nine months free of even the possibility. Would you like that as much as I would?"

"Oh," she said. "Do you mean . . . ?"

But of course he meant. She flushed. And remembered his reasons for marrying her. And thought of what he would hear from Rachel long before that month was over unless she could suddenly produce two thousand pounds within the next six days. And she wound up her resolution to tell him the truth even then.

Except that then was a quite inopportune time.

"Yes, I do," he said, smiling. "There is a very cozy nursery at Severn Park, Abby, just crying out to be occupied."

At Severn Park. Yes, of course.

"Boris." The Earl of Severn got up from the blanket on the grass and the remains of a banquet spread on it and patted his stomach. "Would you care for a stroll to work off some of this feast?"

Boris Gardiner looked up from his conversation with Laura and scrambled to his feet. "A good idea," he said. "My horse may sag in the middle if I mount it as I am now. Your cook is to be commended, Abby."

"I shall be sure to give her your message," Abigail said. "She will be pleased."

The earl clasped his hands behind his back and made remarks about the weather as he strolled away from the group with his brother-in-law.

"It would not be fair to the ladies if we were away for long," he said as soon as they were firmly beyond earshot. "Do you mind if we dispense with small talk and get straight to the point?"

Boris looked at him in some surprise. "Not at all," he said. "But the point of what, pray?"

"Are your debts heavy ones?" the earl asked, looking straight ahead across the wide lawn.

His brother-in-law stiffened. "They are my concern," he said. "They were my father's, my only inheritance, as it happens. They are not Abby's and they are not yours, Severn."

"Those are not the debts I referred to," the earl said. "My question related to your gaming debts."

Boris sounded annoyed. "I have none," he said. "Do you think I would gamble beyond my means when I am already burdened with another man's obligations? I don't know what Abby has told you of our family, but we are not all totally without principle. As it is, I am well aware that I am head of the family yet quite incapable of supporting my sisters."

"I did not mean to touch on a raw nerve," the earl

said. "I had better approach this matter from another angle, it seems. Why would Abby be visiting Mrs. Harper? And why would she have a sudden need of approximately seven thousand pounds? Do you have any idea? Does she have a weakness at the tables?"

"Abby?" Boris sounded incredulous. "Abby has an even greater abhorrence of gaming than I do. How could it be otherwise when she kept our family together almost single-handed while our father gambled everything away and even more than everything? And is it not obvious why she is visiting Rachel? Oh, Lord, she hasn't told you, has she?"

"No, she has not," Lord Severn said quietly. "For some reason, I think Abby is a little afraid of me. You had better tell me, Boris."

"In awe more than afraid, I would guess," Boris said. "It always bothered Abby that we are not quite respectable, that our father frequently made an ass of himself in public and made us all suffer disapproval and even some ostracism as a result. She showed it by loving us all quite fiercely and managing us and caring for us all like a mother. And by raising her chin in public and saying frequently outrageous things so that people would think she did not care. But she did— does. More than any of us. I think she cared for our father more than the rest of us did."

"Your father drank?" the earl asked.

"Like the proverbial fish," the other said. "He drank himself to death. Abby had to feed it to him like medicine at the end. She was as gentle with him as if he were a baby, despite everything."

"Despite everything?" the earl asked.

"He was not a pleasant man," Boris said. "And that is a polite way of saying that he was selfish and brutal. Abby and I were fortunate that he was not quite so bad when we were young children. When he did fly into rages, it was our poor mother who bore the bruises. But in later years Abby had to work hard to protect the little ones. He was usually crafty enough to go for them when I was not around. And I am afraid I played irresponsible brother for many years and kept myself from home as often as I could. Abby did it all even before Rachel left. She held everything together afterward."

"Rachel?" the earl said.

"Abby should have told you before she married you," Boris said. "I scolded her for not doing so, and I think I gave her the notion that she had played a dastardly trick on you. She has obviously been afraid to tell you. Maybe she has good reason. Who knows? But you are going to find out anyway, aren't you?"

"Yes," the earl said.

"Rachel is our stepmother," Boris said, "mother of Clara and Beatrice. She married our father in defiance of her own and lived to regret it almost from the first moment. He gave her several severe beatings. She finally ran off with someone else and surfaced here as Mrs. Harper."

"I see," Lord Severn said. "I thought the lady was dead."

"Well, she is not," Boris said, "and Abby should stay away from her. She is not like she used to be. She used to be a poor abject creature. Bitterness has changed all that. Rachel has learned how to look after herself at everyone else's expense."

"You know nothing of seven thousand pounds?" the earl asked.

Boris shook his head. "It went to Rachel?" he said. "Blackmail, maybe? Would Abby be foolish enough to pay the woman to keep all this from you? Is it that important to her that you have a good opinion of her?" He looked candidly at his brother-in-law for a moment. "Yes, I suppose it could be. Abby never did expect much out of life for herself. When everything came apart after our father's death, I was afraid for her. She looked as if she had been turned to marble. I thought perhaps everything had died in her. Don't hold this against her, Severn. She cannot help anything that has happened. Indeed, for as long as she could, she gave all of herself for the sake of the rest of us. Even for my father, damn him."

"I love her," the earl said quietly. "You don't have to plead her cause with me, Boris. I love your sister."

"Well, then," Boris said, "perhaps there is some justice in this world, after all."

"The question is," Lord Severn said, "how much do you love her?"

His brother-in-law looked at him sharply.

"We have been too long away already," the earl said. "I will make this brief. Abby has concocted a masterly plan whereby I am to hire a card cheat, pay him to see to it that you win a fortune, and then watch you pay off your father's debts with part of it and live happily ever after with the rest, quite unaware that you do not owe your happiness to Lady Luck."

Boris's jaw hardened. "You know what my opinion of that ridiculous idea is likely to be," he said.

"We would never have got away with it," the earl said. "But Abby does not know that. She thinks it a quite splendid scheme."

"She would," Boris said. "Have you discovered yet that she is somewhat lacking in common sense?"

"Sometimes her heart rules her head," Lord Severn said. "It is the quality in her that I love above all else, I believe. Her scheme is going to work, Boris, down to the last detail."

His brother-in-law laughed. "I would have known

even without the warning," he said. "Clearly it is out of the question now, Severn."

"Do you still wish to buy a commission in the army?" the earl asked. "It was your ambition, was it not? I think you are not too old. If it is what you still wish, then you will win precisely enough to pay off your father's debts and to buy a pair of colors. You will be astounded and ecstatic at your good fortune. And afterward you will make your own way in the world."

Boris's manner had stiffened again. "This is my concern," he said. "I will not brook interference, Severn, well-meant as I know it is. I am not your concern."

"But Abby is," Lord Severn said. "I am going to do this for her happiness, not for yours. And if you love her, if you wish to repay some of the love she lavished on you and your family, then you will let me do it. I know this will mean sacrificing some of your pride. But remember some of the sacrifices Abby has made in her lifetime."

Boris clenched his teeth. "The devil!" he said.

"Remember that your father was hers too," Lord Severn said, "and my father-in-law."

"You have me backed quite firmly into a corner, don't you?" Boris said, his voice revealing his frustration.

"I'm afraid so," the earl said. "I will play quite unfairly, you see, when Abby's happiness is at stake."

"I don't understand," Boris said. "You have known her for less than two weeks."

The earl smiled. "One does not have to know Abby very long to know that she is a very precious gem," he said. "Good fortune was smiling on me when she decided to pay me a call to remind me of a very remote kinship. We have an agreement?"

"It seems so," Boris said, "though I wish there were some other way."

"There is not," the earl said. "Give me your direction and I shall call on you tomorrow. I shall tell Abby that everything is set up for tomorrow evening. You will call on her the morning after to delight her with your good fortune and the grand success of her plan. Shall we rejoin the ladies?"

"I suppose so." Boris scratched the back of his neck. "Why is it that so often one could hug Abby and shake her all at the same time?"

The earl grinned. "I am becoming familiar with the feeling," he said.

15

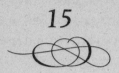

"I WAS VERY VEXED WITH BORIS," ABIGAIL said. "But I think the picnic went well, don't you, Miles?"

The Earl of Severn sat back in his chair and twirled the stem of his empty wineglass between his fingers. "If the amount of food consumed was an indicator," he said, "I would have to say it was a roaring success, Abby. What did Boris do to incur your wrath?"

"Oh," she said, "he monopolized Laura's attention during tea, and then afterward, when you came back from walking with him, he took her off for a stroll. It was most provoking."

"While the ardent lover panted in the background?" he said. "But why did Gerald not bear her off while I was talking with your brother?"

"Because Lord Darlington was discussing horses with him," Abigail said, "at great length. I could have screamed. However, I must not be impatient. They will have the whole of the summer in which to become better acquainted. And there was a definite spark there this afternoon, was there not?"

"Abby." The earl smiled at her. "You see Gerald womanless and at the age of thirty and you feel that you must add a woman and happiness to his life. You see Miss Seymour, pretty and alone and making a dull living as a governess, and you want to add brightness and marriage to her life. Your feelings are admirable. But you cannot live other people's lives for them, you know."

"I don't intend to," she said. "I just wish to give them a chance to get to know each other and to realize how very compatible they are."

"Gerald is in love with someone else," he said. "And I believe that Miss Seymour is soon to be in that happy state too, if she is not already."

Abigail stared at him blankly. "Sir Gerald?" she said. "In love? And not with Laura? With whom, then?"

"With someone he has known and been fond of for more than a year," he said. "He is only now realizing, I believe, that he cannot live without her."

She looked searchingly into his eyes. "A mistress?" she asked.

He nodded. "A sweet girl," he said. "Of course, he would not expect to fall in love with his mistress, and has been quite blind to his feelings. He thinks he is opposed to marriage and to women in general. He is not—only to any marriage that does not involve his Prissy."

"Oh," she said, "and what about Laura? Where are we to find a husband for her?"

"I would imagine that we have no responsibility to find one at all," he said. "But I think you have done just that already, Abby."

She frowned. "I?" she said. Her eyes blazed. "And don't go mentioning Humphrey Gill, Miles. You have not seen him. Besides, he is years younger than Laura."

He laughed. "Abby," he said, "is that a nose on your face? Can you see beyond the end of it?"

She looked at him in mute indignation.

"Your brother and your best friend had eyes for no one but each other this afternoon," he said. "A blind man would have been affected by it. Indeed, they disappeared from sight for ten whole minutes after tea, and when they reappeared, her face was looking remarkably rosy—remarkably as if it had been thoroughly kissed, in fact."

"Boris?" she said blankly. "And Laura?"

"I plan to put my disreputable cheat into action tomorrow night," he said. "He comes highly recommended, Abby. He has never been caught in his life even by the sharpest of card sharpers. After tomorrow night your brother should be in a position to offer some sort of future to a young lady who cannot have very high expectations of a great fortune."

Abigail folded her napkin very carefully and set it beside her empty dessert dish. "Laura," she said. "And Boris. She would be my sister-in-law. My sister-in-law." She smiled. "Are you quite sure."

"That she will become your sister?" he said, smiling back at her. "No. That they are starry-eyed over each other? Definitely."

"Well," she said. "Well."

"Abby speechless?" he said, getting up from his place and coming around the table to hold back her chair for her. "I must have given you startling news indeed. Are you sure you do not wish to go to the Vendrys' tonight?"

"I liked your suggestion," she said, "that we spend the evening in the library again, just the two of us. You do not find my company dull, Miles?"

"Dull?" he said, taking her hand on his arm. "If I think back on all the evenings we have spent together, Abby, the one that stands out most in my mind is the one we spent at home together. I think I enjoy being a staid old married man."

She smiled. "Laura and Boris," she said. "I have been remarkably foolish, haven't I?"

"Now, how can I agree with that," he said, "without appearing quite ungallant? 'Eager,' I think, would be a better word. Eager to see to the happiness of your friend and mine."

"Will Sir Gerald marry his mistress?" she asked. "Is it done?"

"It is not done," he said, "though there is no law against it, as far as I know. Anyway, it may already be too late. She left him a week ago to go and marry someone else. Or perhaps the truth has still not punched him on the nose. I don't know, Abby."

"Perhaps," she said, "you should tell him, Miles, that—"

"No," he said firmly.

She sighed. "I have to go upstairs for my embroidery," she said.

"Do you?" he said. "I shall see you in the library in a few minutes' time, then."

HE WAS BEING COWARDLY, the Earl of Severn thought as he drew the book he was currently reading from a shelf and sat with it in his favorite chair beside the fireplace. There was a great deal of talking to be done, and he had intended to do it as soon as they came home. But Abigail had been happy and had disappeared into her room, humming tunelessly.

He had intended to talk to her at the dinner table, but had realized as soon as they were there together that he could not talk about such private and personal matters in the presence of servants.

He had suggested to her that they miss the evening's entertainment, intending to bring her into the library and have his talk with her. And yet he was being seduced by the memory of that one evening they had spent there together, and he was settling down to a hoped-for repetition of it. She would come in with her embroidery and seat herself opposite him, and he would relax with his book, concentrating on it, but feeling even so the contentment of knowing that she was there with him.

He set the book down impatiently and got to his feet. He stood with his back to the fireplace, his hands clasped behind him, and watched her when she came in a few moments later, her workbag in one hand.

"Everyone at home would have been amazed to see how dedicated a needlewoman I would become one day," she said. "Embroidery was never one of my accomplishments."

"I suppose," he said, "you were too busy drying tears and soothing headaches and bandaging cuts and telling stories. And nursing your father."

She smiled at him a little uncertainly and sat down on the chair she had occupied a few evenings before. "Life was never dull at home," she said.

"And compensating two little girls for their mother's

desertion," he said. "And protecting them from the violent rages of a drunken father, standing in for the half-brother who might have been there to protect them himself but was away much of the time."

"What did Boris tell you?" she said, releasing her hold on her bag, which fell with a plop to the floor.

"And taking all the burdens of the world on your own shoulders," he said. "And looking to everyone's happiness but your own, Abby."

"What has Boris told you?" She stared up at him from her large gray eyes.

"Enough," he said. "Enough that I think I understand everything, Abby. Except your opinion of me. Did you really think it would make a difference to me?"

"You know about Rachel?" Her voice was a whisper.

"About Mrs. Harper?" he said. "Yes."

"I said I was your cousin," she said. "You married me, knowing nothing else about me. You would not have done so if you had known what a ramshackle lot we are. A drunken, violent father who shamed us in public and abused us in private and gambled away all of his son's inheritance and all of his daughters' security. A stepmother who ran away with another man and who now operates a gaming hell and a brothel in London. Even what you knew was bad enough. I had been dismissed from my job for flirting with my employer's son. Yes, Miles, I thought it would make a difference. In fact, I know it would have."

"Abby," he said, his head to one side.

She looked up at him, her jaw set, her face pale. "Can you tell me honestly," she said, "that it would not have done? Had I told you everything on that first morning, what would you have done? Given me a letter of recommendation? I think not. Sent me on my way with a few coins? Probably. Married me? Never. And do you think I have not had that fact on my conscience?"

"And is that what the six thousand pounds was for?" he asked. "And the fifteen hundred more that you tried to borrow?"

She looked down sharply at her hands. "I thought he was a gentleman," she said.

"He is," he said. "He was concerned about you, Abby. First asking for the money and then rushing away without waiting for an answer. He thought I was the best person to help you. Is your stepmother blackmailing you, threatening to come to me with all these facts?"

He watched her hands twisting tightly in her lap. "She threatened to take Bea and Clara," she said. "She said she would go away to the Continent if she had five thousand pounds. I love them, Miles. They are just little children and have already been forced to live through disturbing upheavals. It killed me—I know you will think I am dramatizing, but it is true that it killed something inside me—when I lost them the first time. But there was no possible way I could keep them with me. Then, after two whole years, hope was rekindled and she tried to dash it again in the most cruel of ways. She would have taken those little girls into that house."

"No, she would not have." He stooped down on his haunches and took her cold hands in his. They were rigid with tension. "She would have to spend time and money on them if she had them here with her, Abby. But she knew that you love them. She knew that you were a mother to them between the time of her leaving and your father's death. And she knew that you do not always think with your head but with your heart. She saw a sure way to a never-ending supply of money. How much have you given her?"

"Five thousand," she said, her eyes on their clasped hands.

"And she wants fifteen hundred more?"

"Two thousand," she said. "That will be all, Miles. She will leave as soon as she has that."

"You do not believe that any more than I do," he said.

There was a blank look in her eyes, and one of her fingernails dug painfully into his palm.

"But let me give it to her anyway," she said. "Just this once, Miles, to avoid unpleasantness. I shall tell her that it will be the last. I shall tell her that you know everything and that you will see to it that Bea and Clara come to me. She will understand that there cannot possibly be more. I know it is a dreadful lot of money to ask of you, but you can take it off my allowance for next year. And indeed six thousand pounds is far too much to give me. I would not have dreamed of asking for so much if I had not needed it so desperately. I'll go tomorrow—"

"Abby," he said, easing the cut on his palm away from her nail. "Hush, dear. You don't have to be so agitated. I shall call on Mrs. Harper myself and tell her—"

"No!" she said sharply. "No, Miles. It will be better if I go. We know each other and understand each other."

"We will go together if you insist," he said. "But you are not to go alone, Abby. I expressly forbid it."

"Oh," she said. "But, Miles, we will give her the money? Please? I promised, you see, and I cannot feel good about going back on a promise."

There was a look of something in her eyes—terror, desperation, he was not quite sure what. He rubbed his thumbs over the backs of her hands.

"There is really no need to do so," he said. "Indeed, we should not do so, Abby. No one should be allowed to get away with blackmail or extortion." He watched her face closely. "But if it will make you feel better, then perhaps we will make an exception in this case. There will be not one penny more, though."

"Thank you," she whispered. "I am costing you a prodigious amount of money, am I not, what with my own debts and Boris's?"

He got to his feet and drew her up with him and into his arms. "I think you are probably worth ten times more, Abby," he said. "In fact, I think perhaps you are priceless."

"Not plain and dull and likely to fade into the background?" she asked. "Not someone to be got with child and taken to Severn Park and left there forever after?"

He searched her eyes, a mere few inches from his own.

"I heard it from the gentlemen in the box next to ours at the theater," she said.

He closed his eyes briefly. "Abby," he said.

"It's all right," she said quickly. "I know I am not lovely. You did not make any false claims when you offered for me."

"You have felt guilt over withholding information from me?" he said. "I have felt no less guilt over choosing you so glibly to fit a cynical ideal that I thought was desirable. Shall we just forgive each other and get on with our lives?"

He saw and heard her swallow. "Yes," she said.

"You are nothing whatsoever like the woman I thought you were that morning," he said. "It would serve me right if you were. As it is, I could not have chosen better if I had spent a whole year searching with my heart."

She looked at him warily.

He smiled into her eyes. "Is it all over now?" he asked. "Is everything out in the open at last? All the sordid details that we did not really wish to share with each other?"

She nodded, her eyes on his neckcloth.

"And we have survived," he said, "and are still together. And, gracious me, yes—we are actually in each other's arms. Do you think there is hope for us and our marriage, Abby?"

She nodded and leaned her forehead against his neckcloth.

"But how foolish you were," he said, "to believe that I would think the worse of you if I had known all the truth about you. What I have heard has only deepened my affection for you. Will you lavish as much love and loyalty on me and our children as you did on your own family, I wonder."

"Yes," she said.

"Will you, Abby?" He tightened his arms about her.

She pushed away from him after a few moments. "Do you mind if I don't embroider tonight after all?" she asked. "The day has been a busy and an emotional one. I feel ill again."

He looked at her in immediate concern. "The headache?" he said. "Cramps? Do you feel bilious?"

"Yes," she said. "Don't let me disturb you, though. I see you have your book ready to read. I shall go to bed."

"Your own?" he asked. "I hoped to have you in mine again tonight, Abby. Let me come with you now, shall I, and hold you until you sleep. The book can wait. I would rather be with you."

She shook her head. "I will be more comfortable alone," she said.

He drew her back into his arms and kissed her warmly on the lips. "Go on, then," he said. "I shall have a warm drink and some laudanum sent up to you."

"Thank you," she said. "Good night, Miles."

"Good night," he said. "I am glad we have had this talk, Abby, and cleared the air between us. I am just sorry that the tension of it all has made you ill again."

She smiled and turned away from him. He watched her leave the room, and stood for a long time where he was, thinking, his hands clasped behind his back.

He frowned.

• • •

ABIGAIL HAD NOT LIED about feeling ill. She vomited after reaching her room, until she felt that she must surely die, and felt quite shaky with weakness afterward.

She lay two hours later on top of the covers of her bed, diagonally across them, her face buried against a blanket. The cup of chocolate that Ellen, her new maid, had brought her had grown cold on a side table with the laudanum. She had rejected Ellen's offer to undress her and put her to bed.

She was not going to sleep that night. That much was clear to her. She was cold, yet felt too listless to get up long enough to change into a warm nightgown and climb beneath the blankets.

She was not going to tell him. She had thought she could. Downstairs, when it had become clear that Boris and Sir Gerald between them had told him everything else, she had thought that she would tell him that one last detail.

But she had not. He had talked of how they had brought everything into the open and of how they had survived and of how there was still hope for their marriage, and she had made the mistake of thinking before she spoke. Usually she was guilty of the opposite, but each was equally unwise in its own way.

What if that one last detail made all the difference? she had thought. What if he could overlook everything but that, forgive her silence on everything else, but not on that? What if, after all, she should lose him?

She would die, that was what.

She could remember how it had felt to kiss Bea and Clara good-bye and to watch the stagecoach take them on their way to Bath and out of her life. It had felt like death, only worse, because there had been intense pain.

She could not go through that again. She could not bear to lose him now. Not when hope had been kindled. He had spoken to her earlier as if he really cared, as if she were precious to him. All that nonsense about his having married her because she was plain and uninteresting was just that—nonsense. It had been true but was so no longer.

She had it within her grasp—the dream that warmed every growing girl's heart, the dream that she had never dared dream for herself. But it was there now, hers for the taking. She could live happily ever after with a man she loved more than all the dreams of love combined.

But what if that one remaining secret made the difference and shattered the dream?

What if Rachel said something when they visited her? Abigail's fists closed on the blankets and her stomach contorted.

She must just stop Rachel from saying it. She must

steer the conversation away from that particular detail. She must persuade Rachel that Miles knew all without arousing her suspicions—or his.

And then she must put it all behind her. There was so much to be happy about. So very much.

Abigail surged over onto her back suddenly and stared up at the canopy over her head, dimly seen in the darkness. Her candle had burned itself out long since.

She was cold. And so very alone. Her aloneness frightened her. She must get up, change into her nightclothes, get properly into bed. She must try to sleep. She would look perfectly haggard by the next morning.

For half an hour after she had undressed and curled up beneath the bedclothes, she tossed and turned and tried to put all the teeming thoughts from her mind so that she could sleep. Finally she flung back the blankets.

He was asleep. She could tell that as soon as she stepped into his room and closed his dressing-room door softly behind her. He was breathing deeply and evenly. She climbed slowly into the bed, careful not to bounce the mattress. And she inched closer to his warmth, to the comfort of him, the smell of him.

"Mm," he said, as her cheek finally found a resting place against his shoulder. "Abby?"

She moved hurriedly against him when he turned onto his side and slid one arm beneath her head. She felt that she would have moved right into him if she could.

"But you are so cold," he said, his arm closing about her. He lifted one of her hands and set it between them, against his chest. "Put your feet against my legs. They are like blocks of ice. What is it?"

"I couldn't sleep," she said, and clamped her teeth together again. They were chattering.

He drew the blankets right about her. "I'll have you warm in just a minute," he said. "And you will be asleep before you know it. Are the cramps gone? Women are very unfortunate to have to live with this so frequently."

"Yes," she said, clinging to him, feeling the warmth seeping into her body from his. "Thank you."

"Go to sleep, then," he said, finding her mouth with his own and kissing her warmly. "Ah, yes, that is better. Now your head is where it belongs."

She was warm and safe and comfortable. And sleepy. Almost.

"Miles?" she whispered.

"Mm?"

"I lied to you," she said. "I have never had cramps in my life. Not at that time of the month, anyway. And it is not that time of the month—not for at least another week. I just needed to be alone."

"Mm," he said. "What are you saying, Abby? Do you want me to make love to you?"

"Yes," she said. "Yes, please."

She searched for and found his mouth again, wrapped her arms about him, turned onto her back, pulling him on top of her.

"Easy," he said soothingly, moving to her side again, sliding her nightgown up her body. He kissed her. "Let's take it slowly, my love."

"Don't call me that." She grabbed at her nightgown, which he had lifted over her head, and threw it over the side of the bed. "Miles." She reached blindly for him.

"Why not?" He came onto her and into her and brushed his lips across her own. "You are, you know. My love. My lover."

"Don't talk," she said. "Don't talk. Just make love to me."

She moved against him, urging him on, repeating his name over and over, sighing out her satisfaction when he came to her finally, relaxing beneath his weight.

"Better?" he said, moving to her side, bringing her with him, tucking the blankets close about her. "Have I banished the devils?"

"Mm," she said. "Better. Thank you."

"Sleep, then," he said against the side of her face. "There's nothing else to worry about, Abby. I love you."

She closed her eyes tightly and burrowed her head deeper into his shoulder.

16

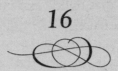

$\mathcal{T}$HE EARL OF SEVERN WOULD HAVE liked to take his wife to Mrs. Harper's the very next morning. He would have liked the whole wretched episode out of the way and behind them. He wanted to get on with his life and his marriage. He wanted to be away from London, at Severn Park, becoming familiar with his principal country seat, getting to know his wife better, reuniting her with her half-sisters without further delay.

But it was not to be. His steward had arrived very early that morning from Severn Park, and there was enough business to be attended to to occupy him for at least the whole morning. And somehow too, of course, he had to find time to pay a private call on his brother-in-law. When he suggested the afternoon to Abigail, it was to discover that she had promised to call on Prudence after luncheon and to proceed from there with his mother on another round of visits.

"We will go tomorrow morning without delay, then, Abby," he said to her, standing behind her at the breakfast table before leaving the room. He squeezed her shoulders.

"Yes," she said. "That will be good, Miles. Thank you."

He noticed, though he did not comment on the fact, that she had scarcely touched the food on her plate, even though she had been at the table all of ten minutes.

Perhaps, he thought, he should have delayed his business with his steward. His wife was, after all, more important than any property of his. But she had said that she would join Lady Beauchamp and her sister on a shopping trip now that she had no other plans.

He could not quite understand why she was still so tense and unhappy. He had thought their talk of the evening before quite satisfactory. Everything had been brought into the open—even, he had been horrified to find, his description to Gerald of the type of woman he would marry if only he could find such a one before Frances came to town. Nothing they had spoken of had seemed to pose any barrier to their present or future happiness.

Perhaps it was just that she dreaded the visit to her stepmother, that she could not relax and smile again until that was all in the past. He wished that he had insisted on going alone. And he certainly wished he could have persuaded her to make a stand against the woman, to refuse to pay even one more penny.

But for some reason it was important to Abigail both to see Mrs. Harper once more and to pay her the additional two thousand pounds. Perhaps it was difficult for him to understand. The woman was, after all, Abigail's stepmother. They had lived together in the same house for a number of years. The two children Abigail loved were Mrs. Harper's. Perhaps there was a fondness there, beyond all reason.

Certainly there was something. He could not shake from his mind the memory of her coming to him the night before, cold and forlorn and desperate to be loved. No, not to be loved—she had sounded almost panic-stricken when he had called her his love, and she had made no response at all to his final words before she fell asleep. She had been desperate for love in its purely physical form, desperate for the forgetfulness that an energetic coupling could bring for a few brief moments.

After holding her close until she had finally fallen asleep, he had been a long time getting back to sleep himself.

There was something.

He was interrupted late in the morning when his butler appeared at the study door to inform him that

Sir Gerald Stapleton was in the yellow salon, asking for a few minutes of his time.

Lord Severn rubbed his eyes and stretched his arms. "It is time for a break anyway," he said to his steward. "I think we can finish this in an hour after luncheon."

"Yes, my lord," the man said, getting to his feet.

Sir Gerald was standing looking out through the window. He turned when his friend came through the door.

"Ah," he said, "you aren't dead after all, Miles. I missed you at Jackson's this morning."

"Business," the earl explained. "Don't tell me you were sparring again, Ger."

"Not quite," his friend said. "Merely cheering and jeering those who were. Are you coming to White's?"

The earl pulled a face. "I have to get back to the books," he said. "My steward is here from Severn Park. Perhaps tomorrow."

"That's why I am here," Sir Gerald said. "I asked for Lady Severn, actually, Miles, but Watson said she was from home. I wanted to apologize to her, try to set things right with her. Did you tell her that I told you?"

The earl nodded. "All is well," he said.

"Ah, good." Sir Gerald looked relieved. "I asked her for a set at Warchester's ball tomorrow night, Miles, but I shall have to excuse myself, I'm afraid. I'll be out of town. I'm leaving this afternoon, as a matter of fact."

The earl raised his eyebrows.

"She has probably been to the altar and back already and settled down to cozy domestic bliss," Sir Gerald said, "but I am going down there to see anyway. Perhaps if I offer her a raise in salary and buy her a few more jewels she will come back. Do you think?"

"Is that what you want?" the earl asked. "I thought you were feeling a little tied down, being with the same woman for more than a year."

His friend shrugged. "I was comfortable with her," he said. "She suited me. She knows how to please me. The damned woman I had at Kit's last night wanted to tell me what I wanted, but it was not it at all."

"Are you sure you want to destroy Prissy's chance of marrying?" the earl asked. "You are fond of her, are you not? And you can't be thinking of marrying her yourself, surely?"

"Eh?" Sir Gerald looked at him in surprise. "Marry Priss? My mistress? Good Lord, Miles, she was one of Kit's girls for a few months before I set her up. She was a whore."

"Why do I get the impression," the earl said, looking keenly at his friend, "that you would flatten the nose of anyone else who used that word to describe her, Ger? You are on your way, then?"

"Yes." Sir Gerald ran one hand through his fair curls. "I'm on my way."

"You had better have some luncheon here with Abby and me," Lord Severn said. "She should be home any minute. And then you can make an early afternoon start."

"Yes," his friend said, "that's what I'll do, Miles. You had better not go mentioning Priss in Lady Severn's hearing, though. She would have forty fits. I am on my way to visit my aunts, if she asks."

The earl chuckled.

ABIGAIL SPENT ONLY AN HOUR with her friends. Lady Chartleigh wished to be home early because her husband was taking her and their son to Astley's amphitheater in the afternoon.

"I am quite sure Jonathan is far too young to appreciate the performances of the horses," she said, "but Ralph and I will enjoy it all, and having a child gives us an excuse to go." She laughed gaily. "We will be returning to the country soon. Ralph would be happy to live there his whole life, but he forces himself up to town for a few weeks each year for my sake, though he has no need to do so. I am happy wherever Ralph happens to be."

"Georgie!" her sister said. "You know you would waste away if you could not view the newest fashions at least once a year and dance the night away a few times."

Lady Chartleigh laughed again.

Abigail did not want to go home so early. The less time she had to herself to think, the better pleased she would be. She would call on Laura, she decided. Perhaps Mrs. Gill was impressed enough by her new title and consequence to allow her to spend a little time in the schoolroom.

Good fortune was smiling on her, she found a little later. Mrs. Gill was from home with the children, and Laura had just returned from running an errand. Edna, the thin and nervous little maid, took Abigail all the way up to Laura's room, though Abigail assured her that she did not need to exert herself.

"How fine you look, Miss Gardiner, mum," she said. "I mean, my lady, mum."

"Thank you, Edna," Abigail said. "Did you fall and hurt yourself?"

The girl touched the bruise on her cheek. "Bumped into the door, I did, my lady, mum," she said. "Wasn't looking where I was going. Lucky I didn't take my eye out, I was."

Laura was sitting at the small desk in her room. She jumped to her feet when she saw who was at the door.

"Abby," she said. "Have you come to visit me? How

good of you. Did I thank you yesterday for inviting me to your picnic? It was such a wonderful afternoon."

"You thanked me at least a dozen times," Abigail said. "But I have been hearing strange things, Laura."

"Oh?" Laura gestured her friend to a chair.

"I have been trying to promote a match between you and Sir Gerald Stapleton," Abigail said. "I was determined to have the two of you married before the end of the summer."

"I suspected as much," Laura said. "But it will not do, Abby. There is no spark of attraction between us."

"Miles told me last evening that Sir Gerald is pining away for a mistress who left him recently, poor man," Abigail said. "Is that not deliciously scandalous?" She chuckled.

"Oh, dear." Laura blushed.

"More to the point," Abigail said, "he told me that perhaps I will be acquiring a new sister-in-law soon."

Laura flushed rosily. "Oh?" she said politely.

"And he said that Boris had been kissing you among the trees," Abigail said. "Now, is not that deliciously scandalous?"

"Oh." Laura got abruptly to her feet. "It was just the beauty of the afternoon, Abby, and the romance of the setting. I forgot myself for a few moments. I am just a governess, a younger daughter of a poor parson. I would not so forget myself as to aspire to your brother. I am sorry."

"To aspire to Boris?" Abigail said. "He has not a feather to fly with, Laura. And you know what our father was and who our stepmother is."

"You are not angry?" Laura asked.

"Angry!" Abigail laughed merrily. "I am ecstatic. I schemed to have you the wife of Miles's friend. And yet now there is a chance that you will be my sister."

Laura turned away. "There can be no question of marriage," she said, "or not, at least, for a long time. And don't—" She held up a staying hand. "Don't say that you will get Lord Severn to do something for us. Boris would not allow it and I would not, Abby."

Abigail smiled. "*Boris?*" she said. "And you have talked of marriage? I did not realize my brother was such a fast worker."

Laura bit her lip. "We have been out walking twice since you introduced us at the theater, Abby," she said.

Abigail's smile broadened. "I have a premonition," she said, "that very soon now Boris is going to be lucky at the tables and win a fortune. He can pay off our father's debts and bear you off to live happily ever after with him."

Her friend's face clouded. "Don't, Abby," she said. "I try not to dream too much. And I would never rest my hopes on the fortunes of a gaming table. I tell myself that five years from now I will still be here. I am fortunate. At least I have employment."

Abigail made an impatient gesture. "Has Mr. Gill been behaving himself?" she asked. "And has Humphrey? If they have not, you must come to live with us even before we go down into the country. Miles has said ve must certainly take you away if you are being molested."

"That is kind of him," Laura said, "but there is no need. I have been able to hold them both at bay. But oh, Abby. Poor Edna."

Abigail looked into her friend's troubled face. "She did not run into a door?" she asked.

"Is that what she told you?" Laura frowned. "I think Humphrey ravished her, Abby. She would not admit as much even though she was crying belowstairs fit to break my heart. She merely said that he had held her roughly and kissed her. But I think he ravished her."

Abigail jerked to her feet and strode to the door. "Edna!" she yelled down the stairs. "Come up here immediately."

"Yes, my lady, mum," a voice said from below, and Edna herself came running up a moment later.

"Edna." Abigail took her by the arm and marched her into Laura's room. She closed the door behind her. "What did Humphrey Gill do to you? Tell me the truth now."

Edna darted a frightened look at Laura. "He kissed me, mum," she said, "and cuffed me when I told 'im no. I didn't ask for it, mum. I don't care what Cook says, I didn't give 'im the eye. And 'e didn't give me no money neither, mum, though Cook says 'e must 'ave."

"I am not doubting you," Abigail said. "I want to know what he did to you, Edna. Did he ravish you?"

"He kissed me and cuffed me, mum," the girl said.

"Edna," Abigail said, "if that is the truth, I shall put my nose in the air and look coldly along it like this and use all the consequence of my new position when I go and talk to Mrs. Gill. I shall see to it that it never happens again. If he ravished you, I shall take you away from here and give you a position in my own home. And I shall have the earl advise me on what can be done to punish Humphrey. Tell me the truth, now. Did he only kiss you, or did he put himself inside you?"

Laura turned sharply away and Edna's eyes widened.

"That, mum," she said after a silence. "What you said last, mum. But I never asked for it, I never. I've always been a good girl, mum. And now I won't never 'ave no 'usband."

"I would not lose hope," Abigail said. "Do you want to come with me?"

"Now?" Edna said. "With you, mum? To 'is grace's 'ouse?"

"He is 'my lord,'" Abigail said. "He is an earl, not a duke, Edna. Do you want to come?"

"Yes, Miss Gardiner," the girl said, wide-eyed. "I mean, my lady."

"Then go and pack up your things," Abigail said. "Do you have much?"

"No more than a small bundle, mum," the girl said. And she whisked herself from the room.

"If Humphrey can swing for this," Abigail said viciously, "I want to go and watch."

"Abby," Laura said. "How wonderful you are. You have been very fortunate yourself, but you have not forgotten everyone else who has been less so. What will Lord Severn say?"

"Oh, dear," Abigail said. "He will be afraid to allow me out alone. I have already added Ellen to his staff in the past few days—she was the poor seamstress I told you about. And now Edna. I should have thought first before speaking, shouldn't I? Oh, dear."

"Well, I am very happy for Edna," Laura said. "And I have great faith in Lord Severn's understanding."

"That is the whole trouble," Abigail said. "He is by far too understanding and too kind. And, oh, Laura, I have just thought of something he said last night after we . . . When we were in b . . . I have just remembered. I think I should go to see if Edna needs any help. Don't worry about Boris. I just know everything is going to work out splendidly and you are going to be my sister. I can think of nothing I would like better."

She hurried from the room and up the narrow stairs to the lesser servants' attic. She tried not to remember his voice murmuring quietly into her ear that he loved her. She did not want it to be true.

She would be his wife, perhaps even his lover. But she did not want to be his love. She did not want him to love her. She would not be able to live with herself or her guilt if he loved her.

THE EARL OF SEVERN had warned his brother-in-law to come early with his news the following morning, since he was to accompany his wife to Mrs. Harper's. But he had not really expected the man to walk in on them when they had scarcely sat down to breakfast. Abigail had been looking pale and distracted. She had tossed and turned and muttered in his arms through much of the night.

"Ah, breakfast," Boris said, smiling broadly at them and rubbing his hands together. "I have come to join you."

Abigail looked closely at him. "What is it?" she asked. "Oh, what is it?"

"Does it have to be anything?" he asked, laughing at

her. "Can I not just join my sister and brother-in-law for breakfast?"

Abigail scrambled to her feet. "Tell me," she said. "Tell me or I shall beat a tattoo on your chest."

Boris laughed again. "Can you not control her, Miles?" he asked.

"No," the earl said. "But then, I have felt no great urge to try to do so yet. Sit down, Boris. What will you have?"

Abigail had her hands clasped to her bosom. "It has happened, hasn't it?" she said. "I can see by your face, Boris. It has happened, hasn't it?"

He walked all around the table without saying a word and suddenly caught her up by the waist and swung her in a full circle.

"I could do no wrong," he said. "It was one of those charmed nights. I was afraid that I was going to be accused of cheating, everything was going so well. It seemed too good to be real. A fortune, Abby. A veritable fortune."

Abigail shrieked and the earl nodded to his butler to leave the room.

"Enough to pay Papa's debts?" she asked. "Or some of the worst of them at least?"

"Better than that," he said. "I can spend the rest of today going from creditor to creditor, Abby, paying them all off. And even then there will be some left."

She gasped and linked her hands behind his neck.

"I have been thinking all night," he said, "about what I will do with it. And I am quite certain in my mind now, though it was the first idea I had. I am going to buy my commission in the Guards, Abby, at the grand old age of two-and-twenty. It is something I have always dreamed of doing, and I am going to do it."

"Boris." Her voice was a high squeak and she bumped her head hard against his chest and hid her face there. "Ohh!"

The two gentlemen were entertained to the sound of noisy gulps and sobs. Boris winked at the earl over her head.

"May I offer my congratulations?" the earl said. "I did not think it could be done, Boris, and have been disapproving of your methods, as I told you at the picnic. You have proved me wrong, and I am glad of it. I hope, though, that you will not press your luck and return to the tables."

Abigail's head came up and she glared into her brother's face. "I'll kill you," she said. "If I ever hear of your playing even for pennies, Boris, I'll kill you."

He took her face in his hands and smiled down at her. "Never again, Abby," he said. "Not even for ha'pennies. Or farthings. I swear to you."

She swung away from him suddenly, her face alight.

"You see?" she said to her husband, wrapping her arms about his neck. "I told you so, did I not? But you would not have any faith in luck. I told you Boris would win a fortune soon."

"And so you did, love," he said, laughing down at her as she favored him with an exaggerated and happy wink. "I will not be a doubting Thomas any longer."

"Thank you," she whispered in his ear as she hugged him. "You are wonderful."

"We had better all sit down and have some breakfast," the earl said. "Help yourself from the sideboard, Boris. So it is to be an officer's life for you, is it?"

"At long last," Boris said, heaping eggs and kidneys and toast onto a plate and setting it on the table. "Abby?"

She smiled brightly across at him.

"You aren't still pushing Laura Seymour at Stapleton, are you?" he asked.

"They make a handsome couple, don't you think?" she said.

"Perhaps," he said. "Don't you think she and I would be as handsome together?"

"You and Laura?" she said, her eyes widening. "She would never have you, Boris. She would never follow the drum."

"I think she would," he said. "I think she will. It can be no worse than being a governess in a house with those dreadful Gills, and she happens to have an affection for me. I'll be asking her later today, anyway. Will you mind?"

"Mind?" she said. "Will I mind? I'll show you how much I mind."

The Earl of Severn set his coffee cup clattering back into its saucer and passed one hand across his eyes as his wife threw back her head and shrieked.

"Lord," Boris said, popping a kidney into his mouth, whole. "I haven't heard that for years. I take it you are pleased, Abby."

"Pleased?" she said. "Am I pleased? I'll show you—"

The earl's hand covered hers on the table. "Suffice it to say, Boris," he said, "that we are both bursting with pleasure. Aren't we, Abby? A simple yes or no will suffice."

"Yes," she said. "We are."

17

THEY WERE SITTING SIDE BY SIDE IN the earl's town carriage, her hand firmly clasped in his.

"It will soon be over, Abby, all of it," he said. "Do you want me to do the talking?"

"No," she said. "I must do it. I would rather do it alone, Miles. Will you stay in the carriage?"

"I have forbidden you to go there alone," he said. "I have not relented on that. Were you fond of her?"

"Always a little sorry for her," she said. "She was headstrong and very beautiful when she first married Papa. She had done it to defy the world, her father in particular. I think she thought she could change my father and prove everyone wrong. But it could not be done, of course, and her father would not have her back when she wanted to go the first time she was badly beaten. She was expecting Beatrice at that time. Yes, I suppose I was fond of her. I tried to protect her."

He raised her hand to his lips. "But she has chosen her own course now," he said. "And you cannot reform the world. I will be plain with you, Abby. I do not like what she has done to you. I can understand that circumstances may have forced her into this way of life, but I do not like her ingratitude to you. I am not going to give her soft words merely because she was your stepmother and you were fond of her."

She said nothing.

"And talking of protecting and reforming," he asked, "did you mind my sending your little waif back to Severn Park with Parton?"

"With your steward?" she said. "No, Miles. Edna was very excited to know that she would be going into the country to work at a great house. She has never been out of London. You were not angry with me?"

"For bringing her home with you?" he said, squeezing her hand. "I would expect no less of you, Abby. Poor girl. Servants are so helpless when they find themselves in such a situation, aren't they? I shall see to it that Humphrey Gill is properly dealt with, have no fear."

"What if she is with child?" she asked.

He looked down at her. "Then she will have the child in the relative privacy and comfort of Severn Park," he said. "And if she wishes it, I shall see if I can find someone willing to marry her. Shall I?"

She smiled at him. "Almost the first thing she said to me after admitting the truth," she said, "was that she can no longer expect to find a husband. I think she would like that, Miles."

"I shall see what I can do," he said. "I'll include it in my next letter to Parton. Perhaps he can recommend someone. Or perhaps Edna will prove to be a girl of spirit and find someone for herself by the time we arrive in the country. Are you looking forward to going?"

"Yes," she said.

"Our marriage has had a strange and somewhat strained beginning, hasn't it?" he said. "But in one hour's time or less, the last barrier will be down and we can proceed to live happily ever after. Can we?"

"Yes," she said.

"You are not sorry, Abby?" He squeezed her hand again. "Not sorry that you acted so impulsively and married me?"

She shook her head, watching her free hand, which she spread in her lap.

"I acted just as impulsively," he said, "and I am not sorry at all. And that is such an understatement that it is laughable."

She brushed an imaginary speck of lint from her lap.

"I told you something both last night and the night

before after making love to you," he said. "You did not respond on either occasion. Do you not feel the same way, Abby? Is there any chance that you will in time?"

She pulled her hand away from his and turned to look out through the window. "That is nonsense talk," she said. "That is not why people marry. Marriage is for companionship and for comfort. And for children. The rest is nonsense. Imagination. You were being silly. There is the house. Oh, your coachman knows where to stop."

"Yes," he said quietly. "Are you ready?"

She sat back in her seat. "Yes," she said.

She sat still while a footman put down the steps and while her husband vaulted out and turned to reach up a hand for hers.

"Are you ready, Abby?" he said.

"Yes."

"Abby?" he said when she did not move.

Her hands were twisting in her lap.

"Abby?" He leaned into the carriage and touched her on the knee. "Shall I go in alone, love? I would prefer it anyway."

She turned to look into his eyes, those blue eyes that had always turned her weak at the knees but that now she found it hard to look into for a different reason.

"Miles," she whispered to him, "take me away from

here. Please? Let's go home." She bit down hard on her upper lip.

He turned to give an order to his coachman and was back inside the carriage with her a moment later, her hand firmly clasped in his again.

She closed her eyes. Not a word was spoken on the homeward journey.

SHE HAD ENTERED the house on his arm without speaking a word, and when Watson had stopped him in the hallway with a note that had been delivered half an hour before, she had drawn her arm free and run up the stairs.

The note was from Miles's mother, inviting them to dinner before the Warchester ball. He went to his study to pen a quick reply and sent the note on its way with one of the servants.

She would probably have ordered tea already, he thought as he climbed the stairs. They were going to have to talk again. There was something she had not told him, and until she did so, there could be no happiness for her and no real chance for their marriage.

But she was not in her sitting room. Or in her dressing room.

He found her in her bedchamber. She was lying facedown on the bed. He did not know if she had heard him come in. She did not move. He crossed the room slowly and laid a hand against the back of her head.

"Abby," he said softly.

When she did not reply, he drew up a chair beside the bed and straddled it, his arms draped over the back of it.

He waited.

"I am a bastard," she said at last in a dull voice, without moving.

He repressed the quite inappropriate urge to laugh. He decided that she meant her words literally.

"Tell me about it," he said.

"I am a bastard," she said, her voice a little firmer. "I am not my father's daughter. I am no relative of yours at all. I appealed for your help under entirely false pretenses."

"You are a relative of mine," he said. "You are my wife."

She muttered something into the bedcovers.

"Abby," he said, "will you turn over? Your voice is muffled."

She turned her head to reveal a flushed, bright-eyed face framed by short curls that were considerably disheveled.

"I would not be," she said, "if I had told you the truth. You must be wishing and wishing that it was not so. And perhaps there is a way out for you. Perhaps you will be granted a divorce when you tell them how I have deceived you and how I am nothing but a bastard."

"It's an ugly word, Abby," he said. "Your mother had you with another man?"

"I don't even know who," she said. "She never told me, and I don't think Papa ever knew. But it was the reason she married Papa. She told me that she would never have lowered herself so if she had not been in such a predicament. But my gallant father—my real one—had abandoned her, it seems, and Papa had been pestering her for a long time. She married him without telling him, when I was already almost four months on the way."

He lowered his forehead to rest on his arms.

"The family she married into has turned out to be a ramshackle one, hasn't it?" she said, her voice bright. "Though it has struck me that perhaps—just perhaps—Papa would have turned out differently if Mama had not done that to him. My mother would have to take the family prize, though, no matter what. She was always so proper, always so much the lady. She always despised Papa even after she had Boris with him. And she always favored me over Boris. I suppose she must have loved my real father. I don't know. But those are the facts. I am a bastard. You have married a bastard, Miles."

"Your father accepted you," he said. "He gave you his name. He allowed you to grow up in his home with his own children even after your mother's death. He legitimated you, Abby. That is why you loved him despite everything, I suppose."

She pushed herself off the bed with undignified haste and crossed the room to straighten some ornaments on a dresser.

"Bad blood was drawn to bad blood," she said. "Like found like. I don't think I really loved him. He needed me, that is all. He was ill. I know people despise drunkards and think they can straighten out their own lives whenever they want. But they cannot. My father was ill just as surely as if he had had consumption or a cancer. He was ill and he needed me and I tended him. That is all. It was as simple as that."

"You loved him, Abby," he said.

"He left us all in a terrible case," she said. "We had always been together despite everything. Yet suddenly he was gone, the children were with a great-aunt who dislikes them intensely, and Boris was burdened with debts he had done nothing to incur, and with no possible prospects for himself. And I was all alone. So very alone." She wrapped her arms about herself.

"Come here," he said, getting to his feet and moving the chair to one side. "You are not alone any longer."

She looked over her shoulder at him. "I thought no

one else in the world knew about me," she said, "with Mama and Papa both gone. But he had told Rachel. And she is going to come to you for the two thousand pounds after the week is over, Miles. If she does not receive the payment, then the whole world will know."

"Abby . . ." he said, walking across the room to her.

"Don't touch me," she said, hugging herself more tightly. "Please don't. I shall go away somewhere. I don't know where. But I will think of somewhere soon. I have some money left of the six thousand. Indeed, just two weeks ago I would have thought it a fortune. I should be able to—"

"Abby," he said harshly, and he took her none too gently by the arm and pulled her into his arms. "What nonsense are you talking? Stop it this instant."

"I ought not to have done it," she said. "I would not have done it if I had not been so tempted. But I was overwhelmed by temptation, Miles. You cannot imagine what it was like, coming here knowing I was quite destitute, afraid to hope too strongly for any help at all, and suddenly finding that I could be a countess and married to a man as rich as Croesus. But I didn't know that anyone else knew about me, Miles. I swear it. I didn't even know that Rachel was still alive. I would have fought the temptation if I had known that there was a chance of dragging you down into such a dreadful scandal. I would have. You must believe me. I know that I have done terrible things, and I am a bastard and all that, but—"

He stopped her mouth with his own.

"I may have to take drastic measures if I hear that word on your lips again," he said. "You are in no way responsible for the circumstances of your birth, Abby, and you are not that ugly thing you keep calling yourself."

"But I am," she said. Her eyes were enormous with unshed tears.

"By an accident of birth," he said, "you are not a product of the marriage of your parents, Abby. But from what I have heard, you have proved yourself your father's daughter and your brother's sister and your half-sisters' sister over and over and over again. Abby—my love—forgive yourself."

"For deceiving you?" she said.

"For that too if you like," he said. "But I meant for being an embarrassment to your mother and a shock and a disappointment to your father—if you were. You were the only one he did not mistreat a great deal? The only one who had any influence over him? I think perhaps he realized what a gem had been brought so strangely and unexpectedly into his life, Abby. Forgive yourself."

Two tears spilled over and ran down her cheeks. "I

cannot forgive myself for what I have done to you," she said.

"Can't you?" he said. "For bringing sunshine into my life and a little craziness and a whole world of love? I do love you, you know."

She sobbed quite indelicately and lifted a hand to her mouth. "You can't," she said, lowering her hand. "Miles, you can't. I am a bas—"

He kissed her hard.

"I meant it," he said, "about the drastic measures. If you think I did not, test me. I would hate to have to prove it to you, you know."

"If you were to beat me, I would hit you right back," she said, and this time her sob got all mixed up with a laugh and a hiccup.

"I am sure you would," he said. "Abby, if you can get over this dreadful guilt of yours and this terrible feeling of inadequacy, do you think you can love me, even just a little bit? Enough to build on in the future, maybe?"

"I fell in love with you as soon as I saw your eyes," she said. "What woman could help doing so?"

"Who indeed?" he said. "So you love my eyes. That is a start, at least. Is there a chance that the feeling may spread to other parts of me?"

"Oh, yes," she said. "Long ago. But, Miles, this is just foolish talk. There is still Rachel and the ruin she can bring on you through me. You must take her the money. Will you? Today, before she becomes impatient? There will be unbearable scandal for you if she tells anyone else what she knows."

"For me?" he said. "Shall I tell you how much it would worry me, Abby? That much." He snapped two fingers next to her ear. "How about you? Would it upset you?"

"Yes," she said. "Because I would have dragged you into it."

"Leaving me aside for the moment," he said, "would you be upset?"

She thought for a moment. "No," she said. "Because I realize that despite everything, if my mother and father—my real father—had not been indiscreet, I would not be here at all, would I? And I think I would hate that."

"Would you?" he said, smiling. "And in what corner of the universe would you be sitting at this moment, Abby, hating the fact that you had never been born?"

She smiled slowly at him, and he touched his forehead to hers.

"Does it really and truly make no difference to you?" she asked wistfully.

"It really and truly does not," he said. "And more important than anything else, I shall be able to save myself two thousand pounds and have the pleasure of telling Mrs. Rachel Harper to go hang into the bargain. This is a wonderful day for me, Abby."

"The money is the most important thing to you?" she asked, looking at him a little uncertainly.

He circled her waist with his hands and smiled down at her. "I refuse to answer such a nonsensical question," he said. "Abby, tell me something."

She looked inquiringly up at him.

"Is everything out now?" he asked. "All the murky secrets of your past?"

She thought carefully. "Yes," she said.

"Good," he said. "In a moment I am going to undress you and make love to you—as soon as you have told me if you would prefer to have it done in your bed or mine. And after it is over, I am going to tell you the same thing I have told you for the last two nights. I shall await your response. Will there be one today?"

Her face was flaming when she looked up at him. "Yes," she said. "In your bed, if you please, Miles."

He laced his fingers with hers and led her through the two adjoining dressing rooms to their bedchamber. And he took her by the shoulders to turn her so that he could tackle the long row of buttons at the back of her dress. He bent his head to kiss the back of her neck as his hands worked.

And he lifted her to the bed at last, unclothed himself while their eyes roamed over each other, lay down beside her on the bed, and proceeded to make long and slow and finally frenzied love to her.

When he came to himself, he moved to her side and settled her head on his shoulder and drew the blankets up about them.

"Mm," he said, rubbing his cheek over her curls. "Some things definitely improve with practice, don't they? Can you imagine what it might be like for us in ten years' time? The stars may be exploding around us." He bent his head to kiss her lingeringly on the mouth. "I love you, Abby."

She burrowed her head farther into the warmth of his neck. "I love you too," she said. "Every inch of you and everything that you are." She sighed with contentment.

"And so they lived happily ever after," he said, "and retired to their country estate and domestic bliss the very next day."

She drew patterns on his chest with one forefinger. "There is one little thing I should probably have told you," she said.

He groaned.

"When I once told you something I had said to discourage Mr. Gill," she said, "you said I could not possibly be unladylike enough to have said any such thing. And so I did not tell you what I told him when I caught him trying to pinch Laura. I was afraid that you would be quite disgusted with me."

He groaned again.

"It was really quite dreadful," she said. "It makes me blush even to remember." She chuckled nervously.

He set the back of his free hand over his eyes and sighed. "Abby," he said, "do you think you could possibly confess all without taking ten minutes to do so? Get it off your conscience if you must, my love, and then let me sleep. I have just earned a good rest, haven't I?"

She was giggling. "I can't," she said. "Oh, I can't." She held her nose. "It was most dreadfully vulgar, Miles. It would have you blushing."

"Lord," he said, addressing the canopy over their heads, "am I to be subjected to fifty years or so of this? What have I ever done to draw such punishment on myself?"

"You should have seen his f-f-face, Miles!" And she exploded with mirth.

The Earl of Severn chuckled, though he had no idea yet what exactly it was he was laughing at.

"I have married a madwoman," he said. "This is to be the next secret you will feel impelled to confess, isn't it, Abby? You have escaped from Bedlam and I have married you, Lord help me."

"I am sure if he had leaned forward, his eyes would

have p-popped right out of their sockets and bounced on the f-floor," she said.

They clung to each other, helpless with laughter.

"You had better tell me what I am laughing at," he said when he was able.

"I can't," she wailed. "Oh, I c-can't."

"Abby," he said, hugging her to him, "I have done more laughing in the past two weeks than in all the thirty years previous to them. But I do feel something of an imbecile when I do not even know why I am doing so. Little idiot! I do love you, you know."

"I told him I would pinch his bottom if he ever did so to Laura again," she said quite soberly.

There was a moment of incredulous silence.

And then the Earl of Severn threw his head back against the pillow and bellowed with laughter.

About the Author

*M*ARY BALOGH is the *New York Times* bestselling author of the acclaimed Slightly novels: *Slightly Married*, *Slightly Wicked*, *Slightly Scandalous*, *Slightly Tempted*, *Slightly Sinful*, and *Slightly Dangerous*, as well as the romances *No Man's Mistress*, *More Than a Mistress*, and *One Night for Love*. She is also the author of *Simply Unforgettable*, *Simply Love*, and *Simply Magic*, the first three books in her dazzling quartet of novels set at Miss Martin's School for Girls. *Simply Perfect*, the fourth book in the quartet, is available in hardcover from Delacorte Press. A former teacher herself, Balogh grew up in Wales and now lives in Canada.

Read on for a sneak peek
at the next enchanting novel
in Mary Balogh's series
featuring the teachers at
Miss Martin's School for Girls.

Simply Perfect

CLAUDIA MARTIN'S STORY

On sale now
from Delacorte Press

MARY BALOGH

SIMPLY PERFECT

Simply Perfect
on sale now

CLAUDIA MARTIN HAD ALREADY HAD A HARD day at school.

First Mademoiselle Pierre, one of the nonresident teachers, had sent a messenger just before breakfast with the news that she was indisposed with a migraine headache and would be unable to come to school, and Claudia, as both owner and headmistress, had been obliged to conduct most of the French and music classes in addition to her own subjects. French was no great problem; music was more of a challenge. Worse, the account books, which she had intended to bring up-to-date during her spare classes today, remained undone, with days fast running out in which to get accomplished all the myriad tasks that needed doing.

Then just before the noonday meal, when classes were over for the morning and discipline was at its slackest, Paula Hern had decided that she objected to the way Molly Wiggins *looked* at her and voiced her displeasure publicly and eloquently. And since Paula's father was a successful businessman and as rich as Croesus and she put on airs accordingly while Molly was the youngest—and most timid—of the charity girls and did not even know who her father was, then *of course* Agnes Ryde had felt obliged to jump into the fray in vigorous defense of the downtrodden, her Cockney accent returning with ear-jarring clarity. Claudia had been forced to deal with the matter and extract more-or-less sincere apologies from all sides and mete out suitable punishments to all except the more-or-less innocent Molly.

Then, an hour later, just when Miss Walton had been about to step outdoors with the junior class en route to Bath Abbey, where she had intended to give an informal lesson in art and architecture, the heavens had opened in a downpour to end downpours and there had been all the fuss of finding the girls somewhere else to go within the school and something else to do. Not that that had been Claudia's problem, but she *had* been made annoyingly aware of the girls' loud disappointment beyond her classroom door as she struggled to teach French irregular verbs. She had finally gone out there to inform them that if they had any complaint about the untimely arrival of the rain, then they must take it up privately with God during their evening prayers, but in the meantime they would be *silent* until Miss Walton had closed a classroom door behind them.

Then, just after classes were finished for the afternoon and the girls had gone upstairs to comb their hair and wash their hands for tea, something had gone wrong with the doorknob on one of the dormitories and eight of the girls, trapped inside until Mr. Keeble, the elderly school porter, had creaked his way up there to release them before mending the knob, had screeched and giggled and rattled the door. Miss Thompson had dealt with the crisis by reading them a lecture on patience and decorum, though circumstances had forced her to speak in a voice that could be heard from within—and therefore through much of the rest of the school too, including Claudia's office.

It had *not* been the best of days, as Claudia had just been remarking—without contradiction—to Eleanor Thompson and Lila Walton over tea in her private sitting room a short while after the prisoners had been freed. She could do with far fewer such days.

And yet now!

Now, to cap everything off and make an already trying day more so, there was a marquess awaiting her pleasure in the visitors' parlor downstairs.

A *marquess,* for the love of all that was wonderful!

That was what the silver-edged visiting card she held between two fingers said—the *Marquess of Attingsborough.* The porter had just delivered it into her hands, looking sour and disapproving as he did so—a not unusual expression for him, especially when any male who was not a teacher invaded his domain.

"A *marquess,*" she said, looking up from the card to frown at her fellow teachers. "Whatever can he want? Did he say, Mr. Keeble?"

"He did not say and I did not ask, miss," the porter replied. "But if you was to ask me, he is up to no good. He *smiled* at me."

"Ha! A cardinal sin indeed," Claudia said dryly while Eleanor laughed.

"Perhaps," Lila suggested, "he has a daughter he wishes to place at the school."

"A *marquess?*" Claudia raised her eyebrows and Lila looked suitably quelled.

"Perhaps, Claudia," Eleanor said, a twinkle in her eye, "he has *two* daughters."

Claudia snorted and then sighed, took one more sip of her tea, and got reluctantly to her feet.

"I suppose I had better go and see what he wants," she said. "It will be more productive than sitting here guessing. But of all things to happen today of all days. A *marquess*."

Eleanor laughed again. "Poor man," she said. "I pity him."

Claudia had never had much use for the aristocracy—idle, arrogant, coldhearted, nasty lot—though the marriage of two of her teachers and closest friends to titled gentlemen had forced her to admit during the past few years that perhaps *some* of them might be agreeable and even worthy individuals. But it did not amuse her to have one of their number, a stranger, intrude into her own world without a by-your-leave, especially at the end of a difficult day.

She did not believe for a single moment that this marquess wished to place any daughter of his at her school.

She preceded Mr. Keeble down the stairs since she did not wish to move at his slow pace. She ought, she supposed, to have gone into her bedchamber first to see that she was looking respectable, which she was quite possibly not doing after a hard day at school. She usually made sure that she presented a neat appearance to visitors. But she scorned to make such an effort for a *marquess* and risk appearing obsequious in her own eyes.

By the time she opened the door into the visitors' parlor, she was bristling with a quite unjustified indignation. How dared he come here to disturb her on her own property, whatever his business might be.

She looked down at the visiting card still in her hand.

"The Marquess of Attingsborough?" she said in a voice

not unlike the one she had used on Paula Hern earlier in the day—the one that said she was not going to be at all impressed by any pretension of grandeur.

"At your service, ma'am. Miss Martin, I presume?" He was standing across the room, close to the window. He bowed elegantly.

Claudia's indignation soared. One steady glance at him was not sufficient upon which to make any informed judgment of his character, of course, but *really*, if the man had any imperfection of form or feature or taste in apparel, it was by no means apparent. He was tall and broad of shoulder and chest and slim of waist and hips. His legs were long and well-shaped. His hair was dark and thick and shining, his face handsome, his eyes and mouth good-humored. He was dressed with impeccable elegance but without a trace of ostentation. His Hessian boots alone were probably worth a fortune, and Claudia guessed that if she were to stand directly over them and look down, she would see her own face reflected in them—and probably her flat, untidy hair and limp dress collar as well.

She clasped her hands at her waist lest she test her theory by touching the collar points. She held his card pinched between one thumb and forefinger.

"What may I do for you, sir?" she asked, deliberately avoiding calling him *my lord*—a ridiculous affectation, in her opinion.

He smiled at her, and if perfection could be improved upon, it had just happened—he had good teeth. Claudia steeled herself to resist the charm she was sure he possessed in aces.

"I come as a messenger, ma'am," he said, "from Lady Whitleaf."

He reached into an inner pocket of his coat and withdrew a sealed paper.

"From Susanna?" Claudia took one step farther into the room.

Susanna Osbourne had been a teacher at the school until her marriage last year to Viscount Whitleaf. Claudia had always rejoiced at Susanna's good fortune in making both an eligible marriage and a love match and yet she still mourned her own loss of a dear friend and colleague *and* a good teacher. She had lost three such friends—all in the same cause—over the course of four years. Sometimes it was hard not to be selfishly depressed by it all.

"When she knew I was coming to Bath to spend a few days with my mother and my father, who is taking the waters," the marquess said, "she asked me to call here and pay my respects to you. And she gave me this letter, perhaps to convince you that I am no impostor."

His eyes smiled again as he came across the room and placed the letter in her hand. And as if at least his eyes could not have been mud-colored or something equally nondescript, she could see that they were a clear blue, almost like a summer sky.

Susanna had asked him to come and pay his respects? *Why?*

"Whitleaf is the cousin of a cousin of mine," the marquess explained. "Or an *almost* cousin of mine, anyway. It is complicated, as family relationships often are. Lauren Butler, Viscountess Ravensberg, is a cousin by virtue of the fact that her mother married my aunt's brother-in-law. We have been close since childhood. And Whitleaf is Lauren's first cousin. And so in a sense both he and his lady have a strong familial claim on me."

If he was a marquess, Claudia thought with sudden suspicion, and his father was still alive, *what did that make his father?* But he was here at Susanna's behest and it behooved her to be a little better than just icily polite.

"Thank you," she said, "for coming in person to deliver the letter. I am much obliged to you, sir. May I offer you a cup of tea?" She willed him to say no.

"I will not put you to that trouble, ma'am," he said, smiling again. "I understand you are to leave for London in two days' time?"

Ah. Susanna must have told him that. Mr. Hatchard, her man of business in London, had found employment for two of her senior girls, both charity pupils, but he had been unusually evasive about the identity of the prospective employers, even when she had asked quite specifically in her last letter to him. The paying girls at the school had families to look after their interests, of course. Claudia had appointed herself family to the rest and never released any girl who had no employment to which to go or any about whose expected employment she felt any strong misgiving.

At Eleanor's suggestion, Claudia was going to go to London with Flora Bains and Edna Wood so that she could find out exactly where they were to be placed as governesses and to withdraw her consent if she was not satisfied. There were still a few weeks of the school year left, but Eleanor had assured her that she was perfectly willing and able to take charge of affairs during Claudia's absence, which would surely be no longer than a week or ten days. Claudia had agreed to go, partly because there was another matter too upon which she wished to speak with Mr. Hatchard in person.

"I am," she told the marquess.

"Whitleaf intended to send a carriage for your convenience," the marquess told her, "but I was able to inform him that it would be quite unnecessary to put himself to the trouble."

"Of course it would," Claudia agreed. "I have already hired a carriage."

"I will see about *unhiring* it for you, if I may be permitted, ma'am," he said. "I plan to return to town on the same day and will be pleased to offer you the comfort of my own carriage and my protection for the journey."

Oh, goodness, heaven forbid!

"That will be quite unnecessary, sir," she said firmly. "I have already made the arrangements."

"Hired carriages are notorious for their lack of springs and all other comforts," he said. "I beg you will reconsider."

"Perhaps you do not fully understand, sir," she said. "I am to be accompanied by two schoolgirls on the journey."

"Yes," he said, "so Lady Whitleaf informed me. Do they prattle? Or, worse, do they giggle? Very young ladies have an atrocious tendency to do both."

"My girls are taught how to behave appropriately in company, Lord Attingsborough," she said stiffly. Too late she saw the twinkle in his eyes and understood that he had been joking.

"I do not doubt it, ma'am," he said, "and feel quite confident in trusting your word. Allow me, if you will, to escort all three of you ladies to Lady Whitleaf's door. She will be vastly impressed with my gallantry and will be bound to spread the word among my family and friends."

Now he was talking utter nonsense. But how could she decently refuse? She desperately searched around in her head for some irrefutable argument that would dissuade him. Nothing came to mind, however, that did not seem ungracious, even downright rude. But she would rather travel a thousand miles in a springless carriage than to London in his company.

Why?

Was she overawed by his title and magnificence? She bristled at the very idea.

At his . . . *maleness,* then? She was uncomfortably aware that he possessed that in abundance.

But how ridiculous that would be. He was simply a gentleman offering a courtesy to an aging spinster, who happened to be a friend of his almost-cousin's cousin's wife—goodness, it *was* a tenuous connection. But she held a letter from Susanna in her hand. Susanna obviously trusted him.

An *aging spinster?* When it came to any consideration of age, she thought, there was probably not much difference between the two of them. Now *there* was a thought. Here was this man, obviously at the very pinnacle of his masculine appeal in his middle thirties, and then there was she.

He was looking at her with raised eyebrows and smiling eyes.

"Oh, very well," she said briskly. "But you may live to regret your offer."

His smile broadened and it seemed to an indignant Claudia that there was no end to this man's appeal. As she had suspected, he had charm oozing from every pore and was therefore *not* to be trusted one inch farther than she could see him. She would keep a *very* careful eye upon her two girls during the journey to London.

"I do hope not, ma'am," he said. "Shall we make an early start?"

"It is what I intended," she told him. She added grudgingly, "Thank you, Lord Attingsborough. You are most kind."

"It will be my pleasure, Miss Martin." He bowed deeply again. "May I ask a small favor in return? May I be given a tour of the school? I must confess that the idea of an institution that actually provides an *education* to girls fascinates me. Lady Whitleaf has spoken with enthusiasm about your establishment. She taught here, I understand."

Claudia drew a slow, deep breath through flared nostrils. Whatever reason could this man have for touring a girls' school except idle curiosity—or worse? Her instinct was to say a very firm no. But she had just accepted a favor from him, and it was admittedly a large one—she did not doubt that his carriage would be far more comfortable than the one she had hired or that they would be treated with greater respect at every toll gate they passed and at every inn where they stopped for a change of horses. And he was a friend of Susanna's.

But really!

She had not thought her day could possibly get any worse. She had been wrong.

"Certainly. I will show you around myself," she said curtly, turning to the door. She would have opened it herself, but he reached around her, engulfing her for a startled moment in the scent of some enticing and doubtless indecently expensive male cologne, opened the door, and indicated with a smile that she should precede him into the hall.

At least, she thought, classes were over for the day and all the girls would be safely in the dining hall, having tea.

She was wrong about that, of course, she remembered as soon as she opened the door into the art room. The final assembly of the school year was not far off and all sorts of preparations and rehearsals were in progress, as they had been every day for the past week or so.

A few of the girls were working with Mr. Upton on the stage backdrop. They all turned to see who had come in and then proceeded to gawk at the grand visitor. Claudia was obliged to introduce the two men. They shook hands, and the marquess strolled closer to inspect the artwork and ask a few intelligent questions. Mr. Upton beamed at him when he left the room with her a few minutes later, and all the girls gazed worshipfully after him.

And then in the music room they came upon the madrigal choir, which was practicing in the absence of Mademoiselle Pierre under the supervision of Miss Wilding. They hit an ear-shattering discord at full volume just as Claudia opened the door, and then they dissolved into self-conscious giggles while Miss Wilding blushed and looked dismayed.

Claudia, raising her eyebrows, introduced the teacher to the marquess and explained that the regular choirmistress was indisposed today. Though even as she spoke she was annoyed with herself for feeling that any explanation was necessary.

"Madrigal singing," he said, smiling at the girls, "can be the most satisfying but the most frustrating thing, can it not? There is perhaps one other person out of the group singing the same part as oneself and six or eight others all bellowing out something quite different. If one's lone ally falters one is lost without hope of recovery. I never mastered the art when I was at school, I must confess. During my very first practice someone suggested to me that I try out for the cricket team—which just happened to practice at the same time."

The girls laughed, and all of them visibly relaxed.

"I will wager," he said, "that there is something in your repertoire that you can sing to perfection. May I be honored to hear it?" He turned his smile upon Miss Wilding.

" 'The Cuckoo,' miss," Sylvia Hetheridge suggested to a murmur of approval from the rest of the group.

And they sang in five parts without once faltering or hitting a sour note, a glorious shower of "cuckoos" echoing about the room every time they reached the chorus of the song.

When they were finished, they all turned as one to the Marquess of Attingsborough, just as if he were visiting royalty, and he applauded and smiled.

"Bravo!" he said. "Your skill overwhelms me, not to mention the loveliness of your voices. I am more than ever convinced that I was wise to stick to cricket."

The girls were all laughing and gazing worshipfully after him when he left with Claudia.

Mr. Huckerby was in the dancing hall, putting a group of girls through their paces in a particularly intricate dance that they would perform during the assembly. The marquess shook his hand and smiled at the girls and admired their performance and charmed them until they were all smiling and—of course—*gazing worshipfully at him.*

He asked intelligent and perceptive questions of Claudia as she showed him some of the empty classrooms and the library. He was in no hurry as he looked about each room and read the titles on the spines of many of the books.

"There was a pianoforte in the music room," he said as they made their way to the sewing room, "and other instruments too. I noticed a violin and a flute in particular. Do you offer individual music lessons here, Miss Martin?"

"Indeed we do," she said. "We offer everything necessary to make accomplished young ladies of our pupils, as well as persons with a sound academic education."

He looked around the sewing room from just inside the door but did not walk farther into it.

"And do you teach other skills here in addition to sewing and embroidery?" he asked. "Knitting, perhaps? Tatting? Crochet?"

"All three," she said as he closed the door and she led the way to the assembly hall. It had been a ballroom once when the building was a private home.

"It is a pleasingly designed room," he said, standing in the middle of the gleaming wood floor and turning all about before looking up at the high, coved ceiling. "Indeed, I like the whole school, Miss Martin. There are windows and light everywhere and a pleasant atmosphere. Thank you for giving me a guided tour."

He turned his most charming smile on her, and Claudia, still holding both his visiting card and Susanna's letter, clasped her free hand about her wrist and looked back with deliberate severity.

"I am delighted you approve," she said.

His smile was arrested for a moment until he chuckled softly.

"I do beg your pardon," he said. "I have taken enough of your time."

He indicated the door with one arm, and Claudia led the way back to the entrance hall, feeling—and resenting the feeling—that she had somehow been unmannerly, for those last words she had spoken had been meant ironically and he had known it.

But before they reached the hall they were forced to

pause for a few moments while the junior class filed out of the dining hall in good order, on their way from tea to study hall, where they would catch up on any work not completed during the day or else read or write letters or stitch at some needlework.

They all turned their heads to gaze at the grand visitor, and the Marquess of Attingsborough smiled genially back at them, setting them all to giggling and preening as they hurried along.

All of which went to prove, Claudia thought, that even eleven- and twelve-year-olds could not resist the charms of a handsome man. It boded ill—or *continued* to bode ill—for the future of the female half of the human race.

Mr. Keeble, frowning ferociously, bless his heart, was holding the marquess's hat and cane and was standing close to the front door as if to dare the visitor to try prolonging his visit further.

"I will see you early two mornings from now, then, Miss Martin?" the marquess said, taking his hat and cane and turning to her as Mr. Keeble opened the door and stood to one side, ready to close it behind him at the earliest opportunity.

"We will be ready," she said, inclining her head to him.